EDGAR

Companion to "Want To Go West Lady?"

Ben Steinlage

ARPress
ILLUMINATING IDEAS.
EMPOWERING VOICES

ARPress LLC
45 Dan Road Suite 5
Canton MA 02021
Hotline: 1(888) 821-0229
Fax: 1(508) 545-7580

Ordering Information:
Quantity sales. Special discounts are available on quantity purchases by corporations, associations, and others. For details, contact the publisher at the address above.

Printed in the United States of America.

ISBN-13: Softcover   979-8-89330-732-0
          eBook   979-8-89330-733-7

Library of Congress Control Number: 2024902541

Other books, by the Ben Steinlage

You can find these books online, CreateSpace, Barnes and Noble as well as through your local bookstore can order them for you, or go to;

amazon.com/author/bensteinlage

Books that stand alone:

A Fundraiser's Dilemma

A Tusk for Two

For you Mom

In His Footsteps

In the Evening Hours

Nrevac (Cavern)

Sally's Wishes

The Canning Jar

The Legacy

The Tapestry

White Water

Why the Chief

A night time read

Collections of short stories:

Ant-Hology

A Honeycomb of Smiles

A Sunset Full of Mysteries

Books one – three

Christmas Ramblings

Shared: Short Stories

Books one - ten

Western Shorts

Different series (that stand alone):

Bird Boy Series:

Bird Boy

Stand Up to Them

Want to Go West Lady series:

A Deputy and a Cornfield

Edgar

Suspenders

Want to Go West Lady

Writing my shorts series:

Writing my Shorts

More Shorts within a Mystery

Contents

Dedication i

Introduction iii

My formative years 1

What's a station? 28

I Don't Care Anymore 58

It Doesn't Get Any Better 81

Messenger and Spy 103

The End Was Near 129

The Start of the Reconstruction 157

A New Start for Us 186

Everything is coming together 210

It Was Getting To Be Too Much 216

Kearny Is Now Behind Us 240

Dedication

I want to dedicate this novel to a good friend of mine in Estancia named Barbara. Visiting with her one day, she asked me "Who is Edgar? You didn't say much about him in your book *Want to Go West, Lady?* Something tells me he might be interesting." I didn't want to disappoint a favorite reader, so I wrote this story.

I would also like to thank my wife for her input.

Introduction

As I said in *"Want to Go West, Lady?"* in the late eighteen-nineties and the early the twentieth century, my great-great-grandfather was a runner for a San Francisco newspaper. As a runner, he had dreams of being a reporter. Then in 1906, he found his subject. With the interest in the westward movement still being high, he decided to write about it, and it seemed that the best place to start was to find a couple who had made the move across the country and learn about their experience. His search led him to Matt and Ida Duncan, whom he interviewed.

I found the notes of his interview with the Duncan's, labeled "Notes on a couple coming west," in an old piece of luggage. It turned out that he never wrote his article. By chance, he had left the project to me to finish. The trouble was that the interview contained too much information for an article. I saw right away that the story of the Duncan's needed to be written as a book, and I felt that I was the one to write it. The story this couple told my great-great-grandfather intrigued me, but it didn't have an ending.

After some searching I found a relative of the couple, a woman named Clara Anderson (her maiden name was Clara Duncan) and she had had Ida Duncan's diary. When she gave me the diary, I learned the ending to the Duncan's' story.

Neither my great-great grandfather's Duncan interview, nor the diary told me much about Ida's first husband, Edgar. The little I did know piqued my interest, so I went to Clara for some answers. I was to find more than I could have expected

Clara told me, "I think I have something you might want to look at. As you know, the first diary I found in a box of books in my attic that belonged to my great-great-grandmother Ida."

Once again I thanked her for giving me the original diary. At the time she had gave it to me, she told me she hadn't known much about her great-great-grandmother and that finding it answered many questions. With the notes of the interview and the diary I went on to write the first book in this series.

When I went back to see her I hoped she had found something besides the diary, so I asked, "Have you have found anything else?"

"Yes, I have. Going through the trunks again, sorting out the stuff not worth keeping, I found a Civil War uniform wrapped up in a piece of canvas. It had a few small holes and a little dirt, but other than that it was in good shape. I figured it had to be the oiled canvas that had kept the moths from chewing it up. I wasn't sure where I would display it but I knew I'd find a place for it...," she began to answer.

Just the thought of seeing the uniform excited me. I had no idea whether the uniform belonged to Matt Duncan or Edgar Buchanan, but in any case it was exciting. Then her expression told me there was more.

"I knew it had to be my great-great-grandfather's," she continued, "but it surprised me that no one had taken it out to show and talk about it. I took it downstairs to show my husband. I knew his attitude would probably be like my parents' and theirs before them. I could hear him ask, 'Why do we need that old rag cluttering up the house?'

"Once I got the uniform downstairs, I laid it on the kitchen table. My plan was to take it to the museum first and then to the cleaners. I wanted to get it cleaned, but I decided to go to the museum to see what they might suggest. I gave it a gentle pat and as I brought my hand down, I felt something, like maybe a little book. Going through the pockets, I found a diary. To my great surprise, I realized I was looking at entries written by my great-great-grandfather, Edgar Buchanan," she said as she handed the diary to me.

"Thank you so much. This is wonderful, and I'll return it as soon as I'm through with it," I assured her. When I had first gone to see her I didn't expect to get anything that would tell me more about Edgar. How wrong I was! Full of excitement and anticipation, I went straight home to read the diary.

At my desk I removed the old rags from around the diary that had kept it together all these years. As I opened it I expected the binding to crack but it didn't. The yellowish water stained paper had a feel to it that said it was old. As I ran my fingers across the first page I felt a tear run done my cheek. I knew what I held in my hands were the dreams and sorrows of a man not that much different than myself.

The diary began:

"You can't go in right now," my mother shouted to me from the yard.

> *These words are from memories that I find myself smiling about, when I think back to my childhood. As the war rages on, my memories keep me going. After a while, I decided to write down some of the things I remember, so now I sit and write down these recollections in front of a campfire, while I wonder what the war will bring.*
>
> *Hearing someone tell me I couldn't go into our house was a common event for the first few years of my life. It wasn't that I heard it every time I wanted to go inside, but I did hear it frequently. I never gave_it much thought because I had too many interests outside to worry about going inside. My father owned the largest plantation for miles around. The only plantation that came close in size to ours was the Marsh place. At times we spent as much time there as at our own place.*

Knowing what I knew about Edgar, I was surprised to see he signed the last page. I also found where pages had been torn out. I realized these pages were the ones I had gotten with Ida's. I found it interesting that they would have been removed as they had been.

I think you'll find his diary as interesting as I did. His viewpoint comes to us as that of a soldier in the field.

Footnote – Unlike Ida and Matt notes, Edgar did date some pages. I couldn't read all of the dates because of age and wear. All I can tell you for sure is that the story begins in 1860 and ends somewhere around 1873. Rather than worry about the dates I have concentrated on the story.

As you might guess, I have also filled in the blanks with what might have happened. For as secretive as Edgar was, his notes alone wouldn't tell the whole story. I wrote the first story from Great-Great-Grandfather's notes on his interview of the couple. Those who have read my first book know the interview was with Ida and Matt Duncan with no input from Edgar. This one is from Edgar's diary, so the details of the two books may not always agree.

Note from the real Author:

Some parts of the first book *"Want to Go West, Lady?"* were based on actual events, but most of it was fiction. This book, including the introduction, is also fiction. The purpose of the introduction is to set the tone for the novel. What you are about to read comes from many years of research.

My formative years

Today my teacher asked me to keep a diary. She said it would be a good experience for me to keep one. She also said it would be fun to read when I get older. With that, these are my first entries:

This is a scene that was repeated time after time:

"You can't go in right now," my mother shouted to me from the yard.

"I want to get a…," I would shout back to her. I knew from her stern look what her answer would be without hearing it. As she watched me, she was sitting in her favorite position on a swing that hung from the tree in front of our house.

"Not right now…, Elsie can get you a drink."

With that, she stopped swinging to say something to Elsie. Elsie would then head for the house to get me a drink.

"Yes, Mother," I said. Then as I sat down I saw a colored man go into our house. This pattern repeated over and over, beginning when I was about ten years old. I began to think that if I needed a drink of water, all I had to do was threaten to go into the house.

I was born on June 3, 1847, on my father's plantation eighteen miles northwest of Richmond, Virginia. Unlike most people, we didn't live in the city or have a little town of any size nearby. I remember hearing people refer to our area as Buchanan, but it didn't have an official name. With the village of sorts only having a church, a one-room schoolhouse, Marsh Manufacturing and a few homes for the workers, there wasn't enough there to justify giving a name to the place. It didn't even have a general store or blacksmith shop that was worth mentioning.

We grew most of our food and made most of our clothing. Everything else we needed, we went to Richmond to get. A mile or two from their manufacturing place was the Marsh plantation.

Our house was on the road to Richmond so we could see everyone travel to and from the city. As people passed by and stopped to talk, we got the news faster than most.

What used to be the Slave Village was some distance behind the main house. Closer to the house was something most people didn't have, a kitchen behind the main building. In the South, baking was a problem during the summer because of the heat. The best place for the main oven was outside, about twenty feet from the main house. Our cook, Elsie, spent most of her time cooking and baking in this outside kitchen.

Starting when I was about nine or ten years old and continuing for the next four years, each time an unfamiliar colored man or couple would go into the house I was told not to go in. That must have happened twenty or thirty times. With our family having slaves, seeing colored people come and go from the place was common, although I never remembered seeing these particular men or women before. I would always ask the same question, "Who is that?"

"One of the workers from the field," whoever was with me would answer. They would follow it with a suggestion that I find something to do. It was obvious that they didn't want me asking questions. I always had more than enough to keep me busy. Even if I didn't find anything to do, something would come up that would keep me occupied. I would forget about my question about the colored people. Being young, I would let it go and go about whatever I was doing.

I followed my father and other workers around, interested in observing what they did and learning from them, and at other times I played with the children of our workers. When I was about eight years old I learned to ride horseback, and that became my favorite pastime. I also learned how to handle a team of horses, though my father thought I was too young for that.

"Joe sent me a letter saying he is coming for a visit," Father told Mother one afternoon.

Joe was my uncle who lived in Ohio.

"But he was just here," Mother said as she shook her head.

"You have something against him coming? I thought you enjoyed visiting with Edith."

"I do," she answered. "And I think Edgar enjoys having Joe Junior to play with. But I'm not sure I like how our conversations always turn to politics or the abuse the Quakers are getting."

"In his letter he mentioned they are thinking about moving, because of problems with neighbors they are having," Father told her.

"It doesn't surprise me, since most of your other relatives have already gone north…I'm surprised they didn't move with your cousin Henry and his family," she said.

"That surprised me, too. I miss having them around here. I have always had family that I could turn to," Father admitted to her.

I asked when they both stopped talking "Where are they going?"

Joe Junior was one of my best friends, other than Ida Marsh. For a girl, she wasn't bad looking and everyone noticed her. Like me, she had blonde hair and blue eyes. She wasn't a large girl. Thinking of her hair, I knew her mother liked to put her hair up in curls, but Ida didn't like it any way but natural. But most of my other friends were children that belonged to our workers.

"I don't know yet," Father said.

"Will they be staying here long?" Mother asked. As we walked, her attention seemed to drift to the weeping willow. At the top of the weeping willow in the yard a bird was singing. She paused a moment and listened to the bird. I had planted the willow a year or so earlier, and she called it "Edgar's tree."

When I was growing up in western Virginia, my grandmother (born 1802) and her mother before her would not allow a weeping willow to be planted. They believed the superstition that wherever a weeping willow grows will become a place of sorrow. In view of what happened to the Buchanan place, a weeping willow might be the proper tree to have there.

Turning back to Father, she said, "There's plenty of room. I don't know of anyone else coming this way for a while."

"He didn't say," Father told her.

"It might be a good idea to invite a few people over," Mother said as she got up.

"It wouldn't hurt…, I would rather he talked to someone other than me," Father said. "Contact the Marshes, of course. If Robert or Jefferson are around, we should invite them."

Once a month my parents held a garden party and invited their friends. Noted men like Jefferson Davis and Robert E. Lee came by, but we also entertained the Marshes, our relatives, and other neighbors. Now my parents wanted to include them in a meeting with my Uncle Joe.

"Would you like me to invite Ida?" Mother asked me. "I'll have to get the invitations out."

"She's just a girl," I answered.

If it hadn't been for the fussing Mother and Father did, I'd have told them I was looking forward to seeing Ida. She was the only person my age I knew who listened to me. She had a way of looking at life differently from anyone else I knew.

"That's right, son, she's just a girl," Father replied with a smile and a wink.

At this, Mother told him, "William, that's no way to raise your son."

As he put his arm around her, he asked, "What do you mean, Janet?"

As Mother and Father left I wondered as I had before, what it was like being a Quaker. I didn't know what a Quaker was except that they were a religious group. All I knew was that my Uncle Joe and his wife were good people. I didn't see what anyone would have against them. It might be true they didn't believe in God like some religions, but they were Christians. They had formed several relief programs that helped many people in need. From what Father had told me, they didn't approve of slavery, so they moved north.

A few days later, Uncle Joe and his family arrived. Right away Joe Junior and I headed to the stable to look at the horses. I didn't see anything different about Joe Junior, even though he was a Quaker. He seemed just like the rest of my friends. We laughed and enjoyed each other's company.

The next day I was sitting on the porch in my white shirt, tie, and hat. I was waiting for Ida's parents to show up and I wanted to look my best. With me on the porch were the men, talking about the change in the politics of the country.

"You know my feelings about slavery…," Dad was telling Mr. Jefferson and Mr. Lee. "I can't afford slaves, and it's been that way for many years now. These people are free to go north any time they want… In fact, some of them have already left. The rest of them have stayed here out of loyalty to my family. Then others are staying here to work their land. If there are any slaves around here, they're me and my family."

"It might not be a major issue, but it is becoming one," my Uncle Joe replied.

"It's not our real issue with those northerners…my issue as with most of us, is more financial. If we don't band together, we will never get the money we need to eke out a living," Mr. Davis told the men.

"I have to say I support many of the ideas of the northerners, but I don't support the way they are pushing their ideas on everyone. I'm proud to say I have many friends in the North. However, if it comes to it, I'll fight for our right to do what we want with our land," Mr. Lee assured them.

Father asked him, "But what about your position in the Army?"

"I don't care because my countrymen come first," Mr. Lee said as he brought his fist down on a railing.

I saw a buggy coming up the drive and shouted out, "The Marshes are here…, they're here, Father."

"I appreciate your support," Mr. Davis told Mr. Lee.

Father always referred to Mr. Davis as the politician who looked out for the people. I wondered how he could do that if Father was right about the war. How could he direct a war and look after the people at the same time?

Uncle Joe asked Father, "What's got Edgar so excited?"

"I think it's because his little friend Ida is here. He says he's not interested in her, but if he isn't, there's something wrong with my thinking," Father replied.

"I remember being…," I heard my uncle start to say.

I was more eager to meet Ida than to listen to their discussion. I ran to meet the buggy, and when it stopped, I reached my hand out to Ida to help her down. With the best smile, I could muster, I offered, "I'm glad you came. You look beautiful today."

"I always worry when you are so polite. I don't know if you are planning to hit me with a bucket of water…, or mud," Ida said. She took my hand and looked around.

I looked back towards Father and saw him nod his approval as I was helping Ida down. He had a grin running from ear to ear and so did the rest of the men on the porch.

"He's a gentleman's gentleman," Mr. Lee said as he gave me a salute.

My father greeted Ida's parents, "Good to see you." He turned to Ida's mother. "Janet's on the back porch driving Elsie crazy."

"Thank you. I know how your wife is," Mrs. Marsh said as she shook hands with Father.

"We can walk around and talk if you like," Ida suggested.

"Sounds good to me," I answered.

Some of the men were wearing tan suits, but most of them wore white suits and hats and carried a walking stick with a gold head. The women were wearing billowy dresses and hats of different shapes. Everyone was standing almost at attention, and it made my back hurt to watch them. The magnolia trees were in bloom and were the prettiest part of the scene, except for Ida.

Looking around at all the people, I saw that my parents were the most striking couple there. Father's red hair and goatee were his most striking features, in contrast to his coarse facial features. He stood half a head taller than most of the men and he was in good shape for being a plantation owner. The fact that he had lost an arm from the elbow down didn't detract from his appearance. He had lost it fighting in the Mexican-American War, and Mr. Tyler, who lived nearby, had made him an artificial hand and arm. Mother, on the other hand, had fine features with blond wavy hair and blue eyes. She wasn't short but she still had a dainty figure. Most of the men gave her a long look when they came to our place.

Mrs. Marsh didn't have features as fine as Mother's, but she was still a beautiful woman. If Ida turned out like her, any man would be proud to call her a wife, my father always said. Mr. Marsh was a little taller than his wife and dark-haired.

In spite my excitement at being with Ida, my thoughts turned to Father and his friends. None of them said it outright, but I knew they were afraid war was about to break out between the North and the South. Mother and Father had told me the Southern States had voted to secede back in '31, but one vote had defeated the idea. Father was afraid that if the measure were to come up for a vote again, it would pass. Father feared that if the South were to secede, our lives would be in for a drastic change. I didn't fully understand what he was talking about, but it didn't sound good.

In my conversations with a few friends, that I did see occasionally, we talked about whether we would have to fight. My colored friend Raymond and I swore we would look after each other no matter what happened. Raymond lived with his mother, Elsie, in the main house, where we had grown up together. Most people laughed every time they saw us together, me with my light complexion compared with his dark skin. I was shorter than most boys my age, but he was even shorter. The only way he could match my height was by not cutting his hair.

Ida asked, "What are you thinking about?"

Her smile instantly made all of my fears disappear. I was honest and told her, "Dad thinks we might go to war with the North."

"My father has the same fear," she told me as her smile vanished. Looking down at her feet, she added, "I'm scared."

As we came around to the back porch, we saw the men were already there, getting ready to eat the dishes that Elsie had prepared. I heard Mr. Lee tell mother, "My wife Anne loves whatever your cook does to the chicken."

As the words came out of his mouth, Elsie was bringing out more food. Her tall, lean figure moved with determination. I had often wondered what her hair looked like, for I had never seen her without a scarf around her head.

"Thank you. I've been trying to get the recipe for years, but Elsie won't give it to me," Mother said.

"It looks like mud," Aunt Edith said with a smile. That got everyone's attention. Then she added, "It tastes good, whatever is in the mixture."

The party went on in the same way that our parties usually did. After everyone ate, the men went in one direction and the women in the other. The women talked about fashions and the men discussed war and cigars, while the young people played games and talked.

Even though Ida lived only a few miles away, I didn't see her very often. Our families seldom left our place just to visit. Though I certainly did enjoy seeing Ida again, I would never reveal that to my parents.

A few days later, one of our field workers, Jimmy (or "Pan Face," as we called him) and I were walking along the front fence by the main road. We called him Pan Face because he looked as if his mother had hit him with a frying pan at birth. His face was black, flat (hardly any nose), and round. He was about the same height as Raymond and I, but he looked as if he outweighed us by a lot. Pan Face told me he had found a family of rabbits and we went to look for them.

Just in case we found any rabbits, I had brought one of Father's older rifles with me. I hadn't asked him for permission to bring the gun, but I didn't think he would mind. Pan Face and I had been hunting rabbits together two or three times, so I knew how to handle the rifle, but I was afraid that Father might think otherwise. I was in hopes of getting a rabbit and returning the gun to its place before he found out it was gone.

"Where did you find these rabbits?" I asked Pan Face.

He answered, "Between those bushes and rocks, as he pointed to bushes on our left.

As we got closer to the bushes, I could hear the sound of horses coming our way. We both stopped to see who might be coming. From our left, down the road that went along our fence, a team of four horses was pulling an open coach full of people. The driver and passengers waved as they went by.

"I wonder where they're going," Pan Face said as his eyes followed the coach.

"It might be fun to find out," I told him. I turned my attention back to where I often saw rabbits. "Let's find those rabbits. I promised your grandfather I'd bring him one." We called Pan Face's grandfather Old Raspberry, and sometimes joshed him about how he liked to eat rabbit for dinner.

As he watched the coach and walking towards me he said, "All right."

Then from behind another bush, I heard, "Psst."

I turned around to see who it might be. "What was that?"

"Psst...Over here," an unfamiliar voice said.

I asked, "What do you want?"

A colored man came around the bush. "Is this the station? They told me there was a station here," he said.

I knew there wasn't a railroad station for miles. I began to tell him, "Not here...It's..."

"Go behind the main house," Pan Face told him.

"Thank you, sir," the man said. He looked hesitant, uncertain. Then he asked, "Are the people here friendly?"

"Yeah," Pan Face assured him. The man walked towards the house.

I asked Pan Face "What was that all about?"

"I don't know. My father told me that if anyone was to ask about a station, I was to send him to our place," he explained.

"Strange," I said as I watched the man walk away from us.

Our house was larger than most. It was a two-story with six bedrooms upstairs. Above that was an attic where Elsie and her family lived. In front of the house were two rows of trees that blocked the wind. The windows to my room were over the center of the porch.

The grounds were a brilliant field of grass that stretched from the fence to the drive in front of the house. Sometimes when I saw my father walking or riding a horse across the grass, I thought he looked like one of the paintings that hung on his smoking-room wall.

I liked the windows we have in our house, compared to what my friend's places have. When we opened our windows, the opening went from the floor almost to the ceiling. Father said he had them designed that way to let the breeze through in the summer. I liked them, because I could run through the house and out the long windows without having to worry about opening a door.

As I looked around the land Father owned, I could see changes. The fields used to be full of cotton as far as the eye could see. Now, the summer I was thirteen, we still grew some cotton, but we didn't get nearly as big a crop as we had when I was younger. Our sharecroppers were growing corn, peas, and beans instead. Once they sold the crop, Father took a portion of the profits. Quite often he would remind us that if it weren't for the money they made, we would not be able to live here.

"I don't see the rabbits," Pan Face announced, interrupting my train of thought.

Pulling the bush back, I could see tracks that looked like they had been made by rabbits. "I guess you frightened them away."

"I didn't even get close to them," he said.

"You must have done something. They're not there." I threw my hands in the air. "We might as well go back. It doesn't look like we're getting any rabbits today."

"You're worried your father might catch you with the rifle," Pan Face said. He gave me an understanding smile.

"A little," I confessed. I didn't care if he caught me with the rifle that much. I realized that with the threat of war his attitude towards me had changed. It seemed to be secretive and he didn't answer questions. The change in him and everything else that was going on, was creating a bad attitude in me. I felt as if no one trusted me or talked to me. I couldn't get straight answers from anyone.

As I thought about the changes that were happening, my mind kept going back to the colored man who asked if our place was the station. Most of the ones asking about the station asked one of our workers, not me, and like Father, they would quit talking when they saw me. The few times this had happened, I hadn't thought much about it, but with this man asking about a station, I was getting very curious. I wanted to find Father and ask him about it.

I heard Father shout from behind us "What are you boys doing out here?"

As I turned around, I set the rifle down barrel first, onto the ground. I didn't answer at first. Then I heard him ask, "What have I told you about handling a rifle?"

I looked down and saw the barrel was in the dirt. Looking up at him, I swallowed hard, knowing what was coming next. Lifting the rifle up, I answered sheepishly, "Never put the barrel into the dirt."

He asked, "Why?"

"Because it will damage the barrel, and it might plug it so that it wouldn't work right the next time I shoot it," I answered. I turned the rifle over and blew out the dust from the barrel.

"By the time I get into the house I want that rifle cleaned and put back where it belongs. Then I want you in your room for the rest of the afternoon," he told me sternly. As he turned his horse, around he added, "Then I'll decide whether I'll whip your backside or not for taking the rifle."

"Yes, Father."

He headed back towards the stables.

"I wouldn't want to be you right now," Pan Face said as we walked back toward the house.

I knew I would regret doing what I did.

"Yes, I'd rather be someone else right now," I said, as I picked up my pace. I didn't get into trouble with my father very often, but when he was mad, he became very stern and you knew, some punishment was coming. Pan Face went to the barn, as I went inside.

As Mother came into the house, she saw me and asked. "Why are you running?"

"Father is mad at me," I told her, as I went into the smoking room.

As she leaned against the doorframe, she asked, "What did you do this time?"

"I borrowed the rifle," I confessed.

"And you didn't ask him," she replied with a smile.

"No," I admitted.

"I guess you know what you can expect," she warned me.

"I know, Mother. I should have asked him first." I told her as I began to clean the rifle.

When Father came into the house, I had cleaned and put the rifle away. I was in my room, waiting to get my backside warmed. I had just sat on my bed when I heard his footsteps coming up the stairs and I stood up.

Father came into the room and said just one word. "Well?"

"I'm sorry. Old Raspberry says he would like a rabbit for dinner. Pan Face thought he knew where we might find some rabbits, so I thought I would get him one," I explained. I didn't think that explanation would do any good, but I thought I might as well tell him.

"You're referring to Mr. Tyler I suppose…No, I guess it wouldn't do any harm to get a rabbit for him. Still, you know the rules: You don't use my rifles without permission."

"Yes, sir," I said.

"I'm getting tired and I guess I won't give you a whipping. Just remember the rules." He gave me a pat on the shoulder. He seemed to be thinking about other things, not about the rifle. As he got up he added, "I think we will be at war in a year or two…three at the most."

"Why? The northerners are no better than we are." I couldn't understand why we would have to go to war.

"Part of it is that up north there are more people in one city than there are in the entire area around here. All of them are crowded into an area no bigger than our place," he explained. He wiped his brow. "They're jealous because they think we have everything… if they only knew. When that man Whitney invented the cotton gin, it took our life away from us."

"That's not fair," I said.

"No it isn't. Men are never fair when it comes to money and war. When man has a problem, he doesn't correct it, but blames someone else for whatever is wrong." He looked sad, and defeated. Then walking over to one of my windows, he added, "All that you can see from here will be a battlefield. With that in mind, I think tomorrow I'll be teaching you how to use a rifle and pistol. Those two weapons might be all that you'll have to keep you alive."

"That sounds good to me." I was so happy that I wasn't getting a whipping that I couldn't worry about war. I looked out the window and I saw a beautiful blue sky.

"We're not going out there for fun. I plan to work you, until you can defend yourself," he warned me. Then looking back out the window he added, "Enjoy it as long as you can, for it'll be changing."

Hoping he would also teach them, I asked, "What about Raymond and Pan Face?"

"I don't see why not. They may be your only backup," he said as he left my room. Then sticking his head back into my room he added, "We might even see what a dirty barrel does for you, and the rest of the day you can lie there and think about what you did."

I was so happy to get out of the whipping, and so excited about his plans to teach us to shoot, that I forgot to ask Father what "station" meant. Looking out the window, I saw Raymond walking up to the house. When I heard his footsteps coming down the hall I called to him. "Hey, Raymond, guess what?"

"What, Master Edgar?"

"Father wants to teach you, Pan Face and me how to shoot tomorrow."

He didn't seem too impressed at my announcement, "I know how to shoot rabbits already."

"He has more in mind than rabbits," I told him.

"Like what?"

"You'll find out in the morning," I said.

"Then I'll see you in the morning. I understand you're in trouble," he said with a grin.

"I borrowed Father's rifle without asking him first," I admitted.

"I know. Mammy told me all about it," he said as he turned, still wearing the silly grin.

"You can lose that grin any time," I told him.

"Not when it concerns you, I can't," he said as he went up the stairs.

The next morning I got up looking forward to a day of shooting lessons. As I walked past a window in my room, I saw Pan Face in the field not far away. I shouted out to him, "Hey, Pan Face."

He waved at me and began to run towards the house. The two of us had talked in the past about going hunting, though yesterday was the closest he had ever come to hunting in his life. Knowing how he felt, I knew he would be happy to hear what Father wanted to teach us, and I couldn't wait to tell him the news.

When he got under the window, I called down to him, "Have anything planned for today?"

"I know we'll be doing some shooting," he answered.

"So he told you already." I had wanted to be the one to tell him, but Father had beaten me to it.

"That's what happens when you sleep in."

"Right," I called back to him. As I headed downstairs, I muttered, "Thanks, Father."

"You slept in, too," Raymond called to me as he started coming down the stairs.

"It appears that I did. Father has already told Pan Face what we're doing today."

"Oh well.., what can I say," he returned as we headed for the kitchen where Elsie had breakfast waiting for us.

"If you don't eat now, you won't get anything for a while," Elsie warned us.

"She's mean this morning." I said as I gave Raymond a punch on the shoulder.

"I don't want Master Buchanan mad at me," she said.

"I doubt there is anything you could do that would make him mad at you. With your father being as big as he is, Father wouldn't have a chance," I said.

After breakfast, the three of us met in the smoking room to wait for Father. We were too excited to talk, so we sat in silence for a while. I could hear birds singing and I blurted out, "There are enough birds out there. It'll take all day to shoot them."

"I think you're right," Pan Face replied.

Then the birds quit singing and I knew why. The blacksmith down in the stables was pounding on some horseshoes. I knew that if I could hear them, so could the birds.

"No, we won't be shooting birds," Father announced as he walked in and opened the gun cabinets. He turned back to us and said, "Grab one."

He gave Raymond a Pennsylvania percussion long rifle, and Pan Face the Basler and Denk percussion rifle. He gave me his new Remington "Sniper" rifle. With them, he gave us powder flasks, a pouch of shots, wads, and percussion caps plus everything else we needed for a day of shooting. He gave us some basic safety instructions and finished with, "And may I stress, we do not put a rifle down barrel first."

Once we had everything we needed, we were all as excited as we could be. The idea of doing some shooting with Father was especially exciting for me. Adding to the excitement was having two of the best friends at my side.

As we walked out to the field, Father explained his reason for wanting to make marksmen out of us. He told us again that war could break out at any time, and it was his duty to give us the training we would need to protect ourselves. He added that it didn't matter what the women folks thought, the war was coming.

Once he had finished his speech, he began to show us the basics of handling a rifle. We paid close attention as he showed us how to take apart all three rifles and clean them. During the first two hours we never had a shell in our rifles. He was so intent with his lesson we paid close attention to him. At the time, I wondered if it was worth it but as time went by, I realized it was. Thinking about his sermons, I knew they had saved my life a couple of times. I was impatient to get to the best part, the actual shooting.

"I wish my hands were a little smaller. I have trouble holding those little percussion caps and getting them onto the nipple," Pan Face said.

"At the rate you're going, the enemy will have you tarred and feathered before you get it loaded," Raymond warned him. With a laugh, he added, "But I'm having the same problem myself."

"And then who'll protect my backside. Thanks, Pan Face," I added to the conversation. I had used one of the newer rifles before, so I wasn't having as much trouble as the others were.

"Now this is serious business, I want you three boys to relax and breathe as I showed you," father shouted at us. Then looking around he called out, "Raymond… You try to hit the knothole."

He finally let us shoot at rocks and at knots in trees to get the feel of the rifles. We did that for four or five days and Pan Face was the best at that of the three of us. Even Pan Face could only hit the target about forty percent of the time, and that wasn't good enough for Father.

The noise of the guns had made our ears ring and made it harder for us to hear, but after giving us a few days off to get our hearing back, Father had us at it again. After another couple of weeks we were hitting the targets about ninety percent of the time.

After we had been shooting one entire day, Father told us, "Once you get the basics of shooting down, we'll try moving targets."

Apparently Pan Face was in hopes of getting his grandfather a rabbit for dinner when he asked, "What, deer or rabbits?"

"If any are available, you can. I know how your grandfather likes rabbit for supper," Father said.

One day I said, "Mother hasn't had anyone over for a while. Are we going to have a party soon?"

"Your mother and I have talked it over, and we both feel this is more important," Father answered. With a hand on my shoulder, he added, "Miss seeing Ida?"

"I don't know about that," I lied. I wanted to tell her what we had been doing. I also wanted to see the other boys who came over so that I could tell them, too. They would probably like to learn how to shoot."

"Once you get good at hitting moving targets, I have something else in mind," Father told us.

"What's that?"

"You'll find out. When I get through with you, you will all be the best marksmen in the country," he answered with a grin. "Even after years of practice, most are not as good as you three are."

"We're just special," Raymond replied, sticking out his chest.

"Yeah... Especially dumb" as I gave him a playful shove.

"But I can shoot," he said. He shoved me back.

"That's not the way you act when you are carrying a rifle," Father reminded us.

"Sorry, Father."

"At least the weather has been good to us, Master Buchanan," Pan Face observed

"That it has," Father agreed.

Mother was on the porch waiting for us. She asked "How did it go today?"

"About the same," Father answered. Turning back to us, he said, "I want all three of you in there cleaning and putting away those rifles."

"I hope you boys are getting better. For all the shooting that you've been doing, it would be a waste of bullets if you're not," Mother said with a smile.

"They're improving," Father assured her. He turned and reminded us, "Cleaning."

"Yes, sir," we answered as we went into the smoking room.

"And what have you been doing…?" Father began to ask Mother, but we were soon out of earshot and didn't hear the rest of their conversation.

As we were cleaning our rifles, Raymond asked, "Do you think the Master is right that we'll be in a war soon?"

"From what I've overheard from Mr. Davis and Mr. Lee, I think so. If anyone would know, they would." I answered as I wiped oil off the barrel of my rifle.

Pan Face asked, "Does the Master think we'll be fighting in the war?"

"I doubt it. We're too young to join an army. I don't see why people want to fight anyway," Raymond said.

"Father said the war might be right out the front door," I said. "If that happens, we might have to defend ourselves. I agree with Mother. I don't see any reason for everyone to fight. What would we be doing, fighting our friends and relatives?"

"I think it would be fun. I can think of a couple of people I wouldn't mind fighting," Raymond stated with a mischievous smile.

"It does sound like fun," I said. But I wasn't sure that I really agreed with him. The way Father talked, I got the idea that there wasn't any fun fighting a war. I remembered him telling me he had fought in the Mexican-American war, and I figured he should know whether it was fun or not.

"I can't fight in any war," Pan Face replied with a sad look on his face. "Who would take care of my grandfather?"

At supper Father told me he was suspending our shooting lessons. He had to make a run up north, but when he got back, we would take up shooting again. I found it disappointing but I had plenty of chores to keep me busy while he was gone.

Father went on his trip, bring secretive, he did not tell us where and came back as he promised a couple of days later. The next day all of us went out and shot at the rocks and trees again. I began to wonder if the trees might fall over from all the lead in them. Everybody laughed at the idea when I mentioned it.

"I don't know. That tree over there might need another bullet in so it can fall over," Raymond suggested as he fired a shot. His shot took off a branch and all of us laughed.

"The bullet has to go into the tree to make it heavier," I told him.

"I was trying to take the weight off the one side," he explained.

"Sounds good," Pan Face replied.

"Let's get serious," Father told us. He began picking out the targets.

With the targets agreed on, we began taking turns shooting at them. We were improving, but not enough for us to brag about. We called it quits when we saw dark clouds building up in the sky.

After supper that night, we finished shooting at rocks and trees. We came back to the house, after we cleaned the guns, Father and I sat down on the front porch. I thought about the man looking for the station. I asked, "When people refer to a station, what are they talking about?"

Father took a puff on his cigar. "Well, there's a railroad station twenty miles north of here."

"I don't think that's what they are referring to," I told him. From the way he looked, I knew he wasn't being honest with me. He seemed afraid to tell me anything. Seeing his reaction made me more eager to learn what a station was.

"I wonder what your mother is doing," he said, getting up quickly.

He was obviously nervous. He flipped his half-finished cigar into the yard. I didn't see why he found the question so difficult. The fact he didn't give me an answer wasn't my problem. It was as if he just didn't want to confide in me. In the past, I had never had any problem getting him to answer my questions. I let him go inside and decided to ask Mother in the morning.

As I went to bed that night, my thoughts turned to what I wanted to tell Ida. I decided I would wait until I went hunting and then brag. I started wishing she had been part of the training with the rest of us. I wondered whether she might know what "station" meant. Not knowing was really beginning to bother me.

In the middle of the night something woke me, and I sat up and tried to figure out what it was. I went to the window by my bed and looked out. I saw an unfamiliar colored man coming towards the house from a wagon in the drive. I watched Father go out to the wagon and talk to the driver, but I couldn't hear what they said. I went back to bed, thinking I would hear about it in the morning. Whenever Father woke up in the middle of the night, he always complained about it the following morning.

The next morning I got up with the crowing of the roosters. I was sleepy, but I wanted to find out about the colored man in the middle of the night. It made me feel good when I heard Father's voice talking and laughing with Elsie in the kitchen. It sounded as if he was in a good mood.

"All I know is that son of mine is mighty proud that you are showing them how to shoot a rifle," I heard Elsie tell Father.

"He's a good lad. You may have to depend on his ability to hit something with a rifle before all of this is over," Father told her.

I didn't mean to listen in on their conversation, but they were speaking so loudly I couldn't help it. It appeared that Father wasn't upset about the man coming in last night, and something told me I wouldn't learn anything from him.

"Good morning, Master Edgar," Elsie greeted me.

"Good morning," I said, looking at Father. His back was to me and it appeared he was enjoying a morning cup of coffee.

"Good morning, Edgar." He turned around to look at me.

"Good morning, sir," I answered as I sat down at the table. My question was uppermost in my mind, so I didn't wait for him to say anything else. I asked, "Who was that man last night?"

"What man?"

"The man in the wagon last night, you went out and talked to the driver after the man came inside," I reminded him.

"You must have been dreaming." He put his cup down. Looking over at Elsie, he added, "I don't remember any man coming in last night. Do you remember a man coming here last night, Elsie?"

"No, Master," she answered, turning her head away.

"I had better go down to the stables. The stable boys have been having problems with a mare." Turning back to me he added, "I'll be back shortly."

"Yes, Father," I replied. Why had he denied that a man had come in the middle of the night? I just could not understand what was going on.

Elsie turned to me. "You ready for something to eat?"

"I guess so. I just wish I knew what a station meant," I muttered under my breath. At that, her eyes got wide like saucers. I knew she understood what I had said. I then asked, "What does station mean?"

She acted as if she hadn't heard.

"I wish that boy of mine would get up," she said.

"Elsie, tell me what it means," I begged her.

"I don't know what you are talking about," she answered as she stirred some mush. Before I could say anything else, she asked, "Some mush?"

"Yes, please. But I can see it in your eyes. You know what it means," I told her. From her reactions, I would have thought she had ants crawling all over her. I knew as well as what my name was she knew the answer to my question.

"It's not for me to say anything," she answered as she brought me a bowl of mush. "I know my place."

"I understand. If you can't tell me, you can't," I said.

Seeing I wouldn't get any information out of her, I turned to my mush.

Instead of continuing to wonder why Father wouldn't answer my question, I started thinking about the fact that he had only one arm, and how well he handled himself in spite of that. I wondered whether he would be as powerful in action if it wasn't for the arm and hand old man Tyler made for him.

"Morning," Raymond's voice came from the hallway. Before his mother or I could say anything, he added, "Are we ready for another day of shooting?"

"Unless you have something better in mind," I told him as I took my last bite of mush.

As he came back into the kitchen, Father asked, "Are the two of you ready?"

"I told you to get up early. You know the Master doesn't wait till noon," Elsie told Raymond.

"A shooter can't shoot well on an empty stomach. Grab yourself a bite. We can wait," Father said to Raymond.

"Thank you" Raymond grabbed a bowl and dished up some mush for himself.

We went out for the day and shot for another eight hours. During that time, Pan Face got his grandfather his rabbit. I had seen him with a smile on his face before but not as large as the one he had as he picked the rabbit up. His white teeth blended in with his eyes. If I hadn't known better, I would have thought he was as white as I was. We gave him a bad time about it and he thought it was funnier than we did.

Off and on, this routine went on for months and all the shooting finally got boring. If it weren't for the rocks, trees or the bottles thrown into the air it would have been worse. Father had us shooting at everything.

When Father saw us getting bored, he would tell us, "The life of a loved one and your own life may depend on your ability to shoot. The way it's going, it won't be long before we will be at war."

During this time, I saw two more colored men going into our house. Once again I asked Father about them, and once again he told me nothing. One night I could have sworn that Samuel and Rachel from the Marsh Plantation came into our house, though it didn't make any sense that they would be coming over here. When I didn't hear any commotion downstairs, I figured there wasn't any problem at the Marsh place. It still bothered me to think that they had come to our place; why would they do that, and risk being captured as runaway slaves? I looked out my window again and realized the man and woman might not have been who I thought they were. Still, I was pretty sure it had been Samuel and Rachel. Even if they weren't from the Marsh place, a colored man and woman had come into the house. I decided to ask Ida if they were missing. If anyone would know if there were missing slaves, it would be her.

When I thought of Ida, I smiled when I remembered her parents told me how every time she had a disagreement with them, she would tell them she was going to run away and marry me. She had been saying that for as long as I could remember. Even thinking about that part of her, I found myself smiling.

The next morning, I went to look for Samuel and Rachel. I went around looking in all the places where they should be, but I couldn't find them. When I asked about them, everyone looked at me as if I were crazy. By this time, I no longer found it surprising that no one was telling me anything.

A few days later I got my opportunity to ask about Samuel and Rachel, when we went to a party the Marshes were giving.

Once everyone had said their hellos, Ida gave me a wink as she turned to her parents and asked, "Can Edgar and I take a walk down to the pond and talk? "

That's enough of that idea, Miss Ida," Mr. Marsh told her in a sharp tone of voice.

"Why not, Father? We can discuss the number of children we'll have, and where we'll live."

"Ida!" her father said sternly.

"I was only kidding," Ida said.

As they were talking, I was looking at the steps going up to their porch. I counted thirteen steps. Father had told me that our steps would have been thirteen also if it hadn't been for his father. He wouldn't have thirteen steps or thirteen of anything because of his superstition that thirteen was an unlucky number, so he had each step made an inch higher than it should be.

"Now, now, that's enough of that. I think the two of us should let the children go and we should join the rest of the party. The music has started. I bet everyone is dancing," Mrs. Marsh said.

Ida asked her father "You're not going to make me dance or any of that stuff, are you?"

I stepped away to let Ida and her family have their discussion, as did my parents. Both sets of parents seemed to take us seriously. These little talks were one reason I enjoyed our trips to the Marshes' place. My parents always had something to say about the two of us as we went home.

It wasn't long before Ida came over to me.

She asked, "It might be wise for us to join the rest of the young people. I think they're playing that game called baseball."

"Let's go and see what's happening. I don't feel like playing, but I'm willing to watch," I told her as I took her hand. We walked slowly around the house, bypassing the rest of the guests. I glanced back at the adults and I knew they were talking about the coming war with the North. For the past six months, it seemed they had talked about nothing else. Ida and I had listened to enough conversations about war and didn't want to hear any more.

"Edgar, you ought to be in on this conversation," Mr. Lee shouted to me.

"Ida needs someone to keep her company," I answered.

"I understand," he said.

"I find you more interesting than that group," I told her.

"Thank you…I think." she replied.

"You're welcome… I've had enough of their talk," I told her.

Once we got to the knoll overlooking the meadow we sat down. Neither of us talked while we watched the people playing this new game of baseball. I told her, "Some guy named Doubleday supposedly invented the game."

With a bored look she asked, "Oh, really?"

"Just thought I would start a conversation," I answered.

"I'm sorry, but I've listened too much to Mother and Father's conversations lately. I'm tired of thinking about the war. I'm enjoying sitting here with you not worrying about what I should say," she said.

"I understand." I reached over and stroked her hand. As soon as I touched it, she pulled it away, but she gave me a smile.

We finally began talking about what we had been doing lately. I told her about my father's growing fear of a war coming and his insistence that I learn how to shoot. When I was through, she had a sick look on her face. I wished I hadn't told her.

"I'm afraid Father might join in the fight," she said.

We continued to talk until it was finally time to eat.

It wasn't until I was halfway home that I realized I had forgotten to ask about Samuel and Rachel. I was absorbed in thinking about that and wasn't listening to Mother and Father. Then

Mother poked me in the ribs, and asked "Did you and Ida have a fight?"

"No." I answered.

"You're so quiet I thought the two of you might have had words," she said, but she didn't ask any more questions.

"Sometimes a man has to think," Father said.

"So the rest of the time you can do nothing but talk," she said with a twinkle in her eyes.

"We learn from our women folk," Father told her.

A few days later Father had us in the field shooting again. This time he was throwing twigs in the air and having us shoot at them. We had done this before, but he added a twist to the game; he had us blindfold ourselves before shooting at the twigs. He said he wanted us to be able to hit a target by what we could hear and not see.

Midmorning I had my blindfold off and was looking around the meadow. From the corner of my eye, I saw movement in some woods to my left. Looking closer, I saw a colored man. I wasn't sure, but I didn't think I had seen him before. As I watched him move through the woods, I prayed he wouldn't get in our line of fire. I heard the sound of gunfire, before I could say anything, I saw him fall. As I turned to my father, I saw smoke from a firearm rise in the air from behind a bush. I saw that Father had seen what I had, and he had a look of concern on his face.

"Give me your rifle," Father said in a hushed voice.

He took my rifle and stepped behind me. I could feel his breath on the back of my neck and wondered what he was doing.

"Don't breathe or move," he said in the same hushed voice.

I felt him rest the rifle on my shoulder. From the movement it was making, I knew he was having trouble getting it into position with just one hand. As I watched the area around the bush where the shot had come from, I didn't see any movement. After what seemed like hours, Father fired the rifle and a white man fell through the bush to the ground.

"Take it," Father said, shoving the rifle into my side.

I was in shock from what I had seen. I asked, "What?"

"Take it." He shoved the rifle at me again.

"Yes, sir," I took it from him.

With the rifle in my hand, I turned to look at Pan Face and Raymond. They were just taking their blindfolds off. Both of them looked over at me with a questioning look as they rubbed their eyes.

Raymond asked, "What happened?"

Then Pan Face asked, "Was that you shooting?"

"It was Father," I answered as I ran to catch up with my father.

Pan Face was doing his best to catch up with me. With a confused look, he asked, "You mean the Master?"

Raymond caught up with the rest of us. The four of us looked around but we didn't see anything moving. Ahead of us lay the white man, face down. Beside him was the rifle he had used to kill the colored man.

I asked, "Who is he?"

With his foot Father rolled the man over. A hole in the man's chest was oozing blood. His eyes were wide open, and I knew he was dead. A look of shock was in his eyes, as if when he felt the pain of the slug hitting him he suddenly knew what a bad mistake he had made. Although I had seen my grandfather dead, it wasn't anything like looking down at this man. I wondered how many members of his family were waiting for him to come home. The thought made me feel a little sick to my stomach. Remembering it was my father who had shot him; I began to get sicker. I looked at his chest and saw a "Slave Police" badge pinned to it.

I pointed to the man's badge and asked, "What are we going to do now?"

Father said "Billy is a trusted worker and would keep his mouth shut." He then said,

"Raymond, I don't want you to talk to anyone about this. I want you to get Billy and tell him to bring a shovel. I want him to bury this man and his victim over there in the woods," Father said as he looked away from the body.

"Yes, Master… I'll go get him for you right now," Raymond handed me his rifle and went to find Billy.

"Take his rifle," Father told Pan Face. He watched Pan Face reach down to pick it up. "We might as well go back to the house…and get cleaned up for supper."

What's a station?

I wonder what Raymond and Pan Face would say if they knew I was keeping a diary. Maybe one day when we are old I'll let them read what I had to say about them. It doesn't matter if they read it or not because I'm writing it for myself:

I remember that afternoon well. As we walked back to the house, I asked my father, "What now?"

"I think we can suspend shooting for a while," he answered.

To my surprise I saw a tear in his eye. Never having seen him cry before, I didn't know what to say or do. I had the feeling he felt as bad for the man he had killed as for the colored man. I remembered him telling us that no matter how bad it got, there was always a better way than fighting. I wondered how he could apply that belief to a situation like we had just been through.

When we reached the house Raymond joined us to clean the guns then Pan Face went back home.

A few weeks later, I said to Father, "I wonder if that colored man was looking for a station."

As he looked around nervously Father asked, "What?"

"That dead colored man in the forest… I wonder if he was looking for a station."

Without answering my question, he gave me a stern look. No matter how much I wanted to know the answer, we never talked about the incident again. Colored strangers, both men and women, still came to our house during the day and night, and when they came in the daytime my parents still wouldn't let me come into the house. I remembered what Pan Face has said—that he had been told to tell strangers asking about a station to go behind the main house. It began to dawn on me that when they were looking for a station, they were looking for our place. There were times a few came into the house when I was there and I was pushed outside or sent to my room. I also realized I had never seen any of these colored people leave our house.

"A beautiful day," Raymond said one morning as he walked up to us.

"Sure is…I was getting tired of nothing but rain," I responded.

"Why don't the two of you go off and find something to do and see if you can stay out of trouble," Father suggested.

I hesitated, "Can we hunt for rabbits or raccoons?"

"I guess so. Just remember to clean the rifles when you're through," Father said as he walked off.

I asked Raymond, "Do you want to ask Pan Face to join us?"

"He's not here," was Raymond's reply.

"What?" Then before he could answer, I asked, "Why, what happened?"

"His grandfather's worried about the war that's about to break out, so they both left," he explained.

"And he didn't say anything?" I told him, feeling hurt that Pan Face hadn't told me about his plans.

"He left you this," Raymond said with a solemn expression.

We didn't think of our slaves as slaves, we thought of them as workers. To some degree, they were part of our family. Feeling about them as we did, I never expected any of them to just move somewhere else. Making it harder to understand, Father had given them their freedom in writing so I expected them all to stay with us. I took the note from Raymond's hand and read it:

Edgar

I wanted to say good-bye but I didn't know how to tell you. I will always be your friend. If you ever need me just let me know. Raymond knows how to get a message to me.

Your colored brother,

Pan Face

As I put the letter into my pocket, I asked Raymond, "Where did he go?"

"Somewhere up north," he answered.

I didn't understand how he might get a message to Pan Face. I asked, "You don't know where?"

"Mama knows how to get a message through to them," he told me. With a grin, he added, "Let's get some rifles and see if we can get ourselves a rabbit."

"All right," I said. I didn't feel like hunting anymore, but I didn't know what else to do.

I thought about how Raymond, Pan Face, and I had spent most of our lives together. I remembered the three of us having smoked our first cigar behind the barn and how we got our backsides whipped for doing it. One of my fondest memories was of us fishing together in the creek. We also played soldiers, as if we were fighting in the Mexican-American war. I would pretend that I was the father who had just lost his arm due to a gunshot. I knew I would miss my Pan Face as if he were a brother.

Before Father gave all of our slaves their freedom, Jimmy, as we called him then, wore a registered brass slave tag that bore the number 835. Seeing him out in the fields, I would call him 835. Once he removed the tag, we began calling him Pan Face.

We grabbed some rifles and walked along without saying much. I looked up at the sky and saw a few puffy clouds floating by. Then some birds flew overhead and chirped as they landed in a tree. What were the birds saying to each other? They reminded me of the three of us lying on the bank of the creek talking about our dreams for the future. I turned to Raymond and said, "I'll miss that crazy character."

"Me, too, he was like a brother to me. I'm afraid more will be going away as the war gets closer. I understand why they are leaving, but I'll miss old Flat Nose." He pointed to a rabbit he had just spotted.

I had planned to fire first, but when I saw him raise his rifle I changed my mind and let him take the first shot. When the shot rang out, the rabbit toppled over dead.

"I got him," Raymond shouted.

"Another three or four and we'll have enough for dinner," I said as I thought of Pan Face's grandfather. He would have enjoyed the rabbit if he were here. I guessed that now Pan Face and his grandfather would have to get their rabbits wherever they found themselves. Stopping to let Raymond get his prize, I asked him, "How many more are going north?"

"Most of the men are saying they'll be leaving soon," he answered.

"What will they do once they get north?"

"Blacksmithing, farming…I don't know. All Mother knows is cooking and taking care of homes," he answered as he picked up the rabbit. Then turning back to me, he added, "Let's see if we can get a couple more.

"Your mother isn't thinking about going north, is she?" I was a little scared of what the answer might be. As I waited for his answer, I watched him load the rifle with another round. I felt a smile coming across my face as I thought of Pan Face. If he had been here loading the rifle, he would've dropped more percussion caps than he would have used.

"No, she wouldn't ever leave your mama," he assured me. He took aim again.

"I know Mother would miss her," I said as he fired another shot. Mother had more than once said Elsie was the second daughter her mother never had. I even wondered at times who the true mistress of the house was.

He asked, "Are you planning on doing any shooting?"

"You're not giving me a chance," I told him. Then as if on cue, I saw a rabbit take off at a run. I watched him take a route along a line of trees. I took careful aim even though the rabbit wasn't that far from me. As I pulled the trigger, I heard a horse and rider race along the front fence towards the house. The rabbit scampered away.

Raymond asked, "How did you miss him?"

"What?" Then realizing what he was talking about, I pointed to the rider. "He distracted me."

As he watched the rider Raymond said, "He went to the house. I wonder what he wants."

"Let's go see what's up," I suggested. I began to run, not waiting for his answer. As we got to the house, the rider was leaving.

I could see Father reading a note, with Mother standing at his side. Putting the note down, he looked towards the rider. He turned to Mother shaking his head and said something to her that I couldn't quite hear.

"Looks like it might be something important," Raymond said.

"I hope it doesn't mean they've declared war." I stopped for a minute to catch my breath. As we reached the steps I asked Mother, "What's wrong?"

"Your father has to meet a representative from France," she answered as she walked back into the house.

I repeated under my breath "A representative from France?"

"I guess we might as well give it up for the day and clean the rifles," Raymond suggested as he set his rabbits down.

"And you might want to give those to Elsie," I told him as I went into the house.

I got halfway down the hall when Father met me. He said, "I want you and Raymond to take a load of hay to the Schmitt's this evening after dark. I'll be back in the morning after I meet with this man from France and Mr. Davis."

"I hope all goes well, Father," I told him. He was carrying his writing slope, so I knew he would be taking notes or writing letters. Looking at the slope, I remembered the time Pan Face asked him where the legs were for his writing desk.

Grinning, Father told him, "Well, I'm using my legs."

Pam Face looked confused. "You're using them?"

Father smiled and said, "To walk with."

He finally explained to Pan Face that you place a writing slope on your lap when writing letters. He opened the wooden box to show him the slope, which had a leather covering that one would write on. Everyone around the room had had a good laugh at Pan Face and his question. I started to laugh when I thought about it.

Father stepped through the door and asked, "What's so funny?"

"Just thinking of Pan Face and the writing slope," I told him.

"That was funny, wasn't it?" Then he added, "I know we'll miss him."

"Yes, we will," Raymond and I said together.

I wondered what Father's meeting with the representative from France was about. Thinking about what he had asked me to do that evening confused me. Why were we taking hay to the Schmitt's, and how would I find their place?

"Raymond knows the way," he said as he went out the front door.

"Yes, Master," Raymond said. He turned to me and gave me a funny look.

"What's that all about? We don't sell hay to people," I said as we approached Father's smoking room. "I wonder what this meeting with Mr. Davis and the man from France is all about."

"From the look on the master's face I would say it was important." Raymond gabbed a rag and began wiping the rifle down.

"What about this load of hay Father was talking about?" I asked, "Do I know this Schmitt family?"

"You'll find out later," he told me as he put his rifle away. Turning around, he added, "Maybe we can get a few more tomorrow?"

"We'll see," I replied. I was getting the feeling I was a stranger in my own home. People were coming by looking for a station, and it seemed we were now supplying other places with hay. The part about the hay that confused me the most was that we had to buy our own hay. We didn't grow any on our place even for our own use, let alone anyone else's.

I didn't see Raymond again until after supper. As the sun went down, he walked into the kitchen and asked, "Are you ready?"

"Yes," I answered as I set my empty glass down.

"Be careful," Elsie said. Looking at me, she added, "The Missus wants to see you in the sewing room before you leave, Master Edgar."

"Thanks, Elsie," I told her as I headed for the sewing room.

"Make it quick," Raymond said.

"That's no way…." I heard Elsie start to tell Raymond something, but soon I was out of earshot.

In the sewing room I found Mother working on a gray jacket. I looked around and saw there were at least a dozen gray jackets hanging around the room. I asked, "What are you doing? What are all these gray jackets for?"

"Preparing for the war your father is sure will happen," she answered. "Many women are making uniforms the men will need. In fact, the Marsh factory is making belt buckles and our saddle man is making holsters and belts for carrying sabers."

"How is it I didn't know about these preparations?" I asked. I would never have guessed. I couldn't believe what she had been doing and what was going on in my own home.

As I waited for an answer, I wondered how much Ida knew about what her father was making. The manufacturing business produced gold-mining pans for the miners in the goldfields out west. Now on the sly they were making belt buckles for an army for a war that might never come about. I couldn't wait until I saw Ida the next time to discuss all of this with her. I knew she would have something to say about it.

"I have learned its best not to talk too much," Mother replied.

I knew what she was talking about. Thinking about Ida, I figured if she didn't know about her father's doings, it wasn't my place to tell her. If she already knew about it, she would have told me. None of that mattered to me. I just wanted to see her. Her smile made me feel better no matter what my problems were. I realized I was praying Mother and Father would have a get-together soon and that Ida would be there.

"Have you made one that will fit me?" I asked. At the time, I hadn't thought about joining an army, but when I saw the jackets I began thinking. I knew it might be time for me to decide whether I would join the army or not.

"You're not joining any army if I have anything to say about it," Mother told me in a very firm tone. "The least I can do is support the army in whatever manner I can, but it's another thing to fight in it." Before I could say anything, she added, "With this run tonight, be careful."

From the doorway Raymond asked, "Are we ready?"

"I want the two of you to be careful," Mother said. "And Raymond, be sure you have your papers with you."

"Yes, Ma'am," he replied.

"I'm ready, I guess," I answered Raymond as I gave Mother a kiss on the cheek. I was saying under my breath, "I'm ready but I don't understand any of it. Delivering hay to someone, I don't know and Mother making uniforms. I just don't understand any of it."

"You will, later," Raymond said.

I wondered how he knew what was going on. He was my age and just part of the help, so if he knew what was going on, why didn't I know about it too? I wished someone would tell me what all the secrecy was about. I also wondered why my aunts and uncles were leaving their homes in Ohio. I had never heard of so many from one family moving all at one time. I didn't understand what was going on at home or anywhere else, and I wondered whether Ida had the same problem.

As we got into the wagon, I asked Raymond "Since you know everything else that I don't, do you know why my aunts and uncles are moving from Ohio?"

"That's simple. To keep from getting killed," he answered calmly.

"Who would want to kill them?" I exclaimed.

"I know, but it doesn't mean I can talk about it," he said as he snapped the reins.

"You're my friend. Friends don't keep secrets from each other," I reminded him a little roughly.

"Some have to know and others are better off not knowing. When the time is right, I'm sure the master will explain."

"I almost feel like an orphan in my own home," I heard myself muttering.

"Yes, your father and mother know what's going on, but they're still trying to keep everything the same as it's always been," he told me.

"You're talking about the war, aren't you?"

"Yes… and everything behind it," he added.

If I hadn't known better, I would have thought Raymond and Father were the same age. The two of us had had many conversations, but none sounding so serious. From the tone of his voice, I got the idea I hadn't been paying attention to what had been going on. I decided I must not be old enough to understand the reasons for us going to war. All I knew was that Father was complaining about financing. When he talked about those problems, I figured they were part of owning your own place. I didn't see why they would start a war over financing.

As we traveled down the road going north, the cloud cover was heavy and I couldn't see much more than the road in front of us. A little moonlight would have helped. I prayed that Raymond knew where we were going. I didn't have any idea where we were and I couldn't see enough to help him. Then suddenly I heard the sound of water running.

I asked Raymond "Is that the same creek that runs through our place?"

"Sure is," he answered. "If you were to follow it, it would take you to the Marsh place."

"I might look for a log to float down and see what color nightgown she's wearing," I replied. He laughed, knowing I was referring to Ida. He knew how I felt about her and he wished he had a sweetheart of his own. As I was looking around to see if I could get my bearings, I heard a sneeze.

I was pretty sure it wasn't Raymond sneezing, but the wagon was noisy and I could have been wrong. I asked, "What was that?"

He asked, "What?"

"I thought I heard a sneeze."

"Not me," he replied.

"I know about the uniforms Mother has been working on. How long has she been making them?"

"Mammy and the Missus have been working on them for better than six months. They've even been working into the night lately," he told me. With a note of pride in his voice he added, "They've made more than a hundred so far."

"Over a hundred..." I began to comment, but then I heard a noise. I listened but didn't hear anything more. Then feeling the only button holding my suspenders I replied, "That explains why she hasn't replaced the button on my pants. She's been too busy working on other projects."

"Halt," a voice from the dark shouted out to us.

"We have more to worry about than your pants. Don't say anything more than you have to," Raymond warned me in a hushed voice. He brought the wagon to a stop.

The voice got closer. "Slave Police... Where are you going?"

Raymond answered, "The master's son and I are taking some hay to a friend."

A man seated on a horse asked, "Who are you, son?"

"Edgar Buchanan," I answered, trying to keep my answer short like Raymond suggested. As he got closer, I saw he had a pistol trained on us. Looking down the barrel was frightening, but it also made me mad. This so-called officer had no reason to stop us. I wondered what he would do if he knew Father had killed one of his friends.

Looking up at him, I decided that his face was scarier than the pistol he was holding. Even in the dim light, he looked rough and mean. His face was pockmarked and he hadn't shaved for days. I wondered if he had taken a bath in the past year or not, because his face, hands and clothes had a coat of mud on them.

The man pointed at Raymond and demanded, "Who's this Darky?"

"Our cook's son, his name is Raymond. They're freed slaves. We are delivering some hay," I answered.

He said, "I don't care if he's free or not. He ain't to be out this late." Then he asked Raymond, "Got your papers, Darky?"

"Yes, sir," Raymond answered him as he held his papers up for the man to examine.

"His name is Raymond," I told the man. "Darky" was a commonly used term but my father never allowed anyone to use it around our place. He said that the term indicated that the colored person was less than human, and he wouldn't stand for it to be used in his presence.

"One Darky is as good as another. It doesn't matter what name you give them," he said.

"I don't...," I began to shout at him but Raymond tugged on my sleeve and whispered "Hush!"

The man took the papers from Raymond and appeared to read them. I had my doubts as to whether he could read, but I didn't say anything. With a disgusted look, he threw the papers back. "Like I said, you shouldn't be out this time of night. You might find someone shooting you."

"Yes sir." I answered. As he rode off, I wondered how much truth there was in his warning.

"That was close," Raymond told me. Then he added, "We may have to spend the night."

Just as he said that, the wagon took a good bounce. Hearing the clatter of wood under the hoofs of the horses, I knew we were going over a bridge. I wondered if I were to jump off the wagon if I could float to Ida's place. It would be so much better to be with Ida than to be sitting where I was.

"Why?" I asked. As I waited for his answer, I looked to see if I could see the slave police ahead of us. Having a member of the slave police stop us worried me quite a bit, for no one had ever questioned my doings until then. Suddenly, I no longer felt as sorry about the one Father had killed. In fact, I wanted to kill this one for threatening us.

"They don't like us blacks on the road…day or night," Raymond explained as he snapped the reins. Then as the horses picked up some speed, he added, "This is the second time they have stopped me so far."

I asked, "You've made runs like this before?"

"A couple of times with the master… Billy normally rode with him," he told me.

"So Father has made this trip more than once?" A picture was forming in my mind and I wasn't sure that I liked what I was seeing. I knew I would be asking Father questions he wasn't going to welcome.

"Yes…and thankfully we're almost to the Schmitt place," he answered.

"I could use a drink of water," I replied as I looked around for a lit window. Then off to our right through some trees I saw a few lights. It was comforting to know we didn't have much farther to go. As we got nearer, I thought I heard movement, but I decided it was just the normal noise from the hitch and the horses.

"I think we can take care of that thirst," he answered as he snapped the reins.

As we got closer, I saw the place was nothing like ours. The main house was only a little bigger than a slave shack. Made of wood, it looked like it had never seen a drop of paint. There was no yard and the outbuildings were small. I couldn't think of any reason Father would even know these people, let alone have anything to do with them. I commented to Raymond, "Not much of a place."

"No, it's nothing like the main house…but it depends on your needs," he replied.

As we pulled into the yard, a man came from the house to greet us. "Good evening, Raymond. This must be the Buchanan boy with you."

Out of the corner of my eye, I saw Raymond hold a finger to his lips. Not understanding why he did that, I greeted the man with, "Yes sir…, Edgar Buchanan."

"Your father has told me a lot about you," he said with a smile.

"Good evening, Master Schmitt," Raymond called down from the wagon. Then with a nod towards me he added, "The master here could use some water."

"Take the wagon to the barn and I'll see that he gets a drink," Mr. Schmitt said.

"Thank you." I got down from the wagon. Even in the semi-darkness I could see that this man was about our height. If it weren't for his skin color and a big red nose, I would have taken him to be Pan Face's father.

"I think it might be wise if we stay the night," Raymond added as he pulled away.

Mr. Schmitt asked, "Riders, I take it?"

"Yes," I answered. As we walked towards the house, I noticed he was shorter than I was and he was about as round as he was tall. He walked with a limp, and from his crusty appearance I judged that he worked the place. As we went into the house, he took his hat off and wiped his brow. He was completely bald. He wore clothes our workers would have thrown out as rags. From all appearances, I wondered where he would get the money to pay for the hay. "That Raymond is a good boy," Mr. Schmitt told me. As he was talking, he took a ladle from a bucket and dipped out some water.

"Yes, he is. We've been friends all of our lives," I told him. Taking the ladle from him I thanked him for the water.

"I know that ride can be a dusty one, my pleasure." Then pointing to a couple of spare beds he added, "You and Raymond can sleep here. Since my Missus and my son died a few years ago, they're never used."

"Thank you," I answered. As I looked around I found it easy to believe there hadn't been a woman in the place for some time.

"I had better get out there and give Raymond a hand with that hay. You might as well lie back and relax." He grabbed his hat and went outside.

"I can help," I offered.

"I think Raymond and I can handle it," he said as he shut the door.

I looked at the two beds he had pointed out. As tired as I was, I still questioned whether the floor wouldn't be better than the beds. The one I examined was a standard rope bed but it didn't have a feather mattress, and it appeared that no one had tightened the ropes for a year or two.

Before Raymond came back, I fell asleep and had a vague, confused dream—something about telling Raymond we could go shooting with revolvers. Then with one eye half open, I saw him in the other bed. Half asleep, I muttered something about the dream and then said, "Remind me in the morning."

"All…right," he said, half asleep himself.

The next morning we barely stayed long enough for a cup of coffee. Raymond explained to Mr. Schmitt that his mama had breakfast ready for us. As we left, I looked around the place and found it looked better at night than in the daylight. The hay was still in the wagon. I figured Mr. Schmitt must have changed his mind about buying hay, and I wondered what had happened that had made him change his mind.

As we pulled up to our place, one of the field workers waved to us. Raymond stopped to see what he wanted.

Raymond asked, "What's the problem?"

The man looked at me questioningly and answered, "I don't know why the master wants this here field picked. In fact, I don't see any reason to pick any of the cotton."

I looked out onto the field and had the same question. I remembered how some years ago a picker could fill a bag with cotton about every three feet, and I thought it would probably take an entire row to fill a bag now.

"It's not my place to ask questions of the master," Raymond told him.

"I doubt that he'll get enough off his crop to feed his family for a week," the worker shook his head.

"I haven't paid much attention to the fields lately, but I'd be asking the same question," I told them. Looking at the field-worker, I knew I would never want to fight with him. He had muscles on his muscles like a workhorse.

"The sharecroppers will make more money off our crops than the master. It's sad he won't get enough from his to make it worthwhile," the worker said as he went back to the field.

As he left, I watched a woman walk to a plant and pick two balls of cotton off it. At another, she got only one ball, and from a third plant she got five. That one plant had more than most of the others. I was glad grandfather wasn't here to see such a bad crop. I remembered hearing Father telling Mr. Marsh that he wished he had the money for seed for a different crop. Mr. Marsh agreed with him, saying he doubted that he would be able to keep his workers much longer.

As Raymond and I were about to board the wagon again, we heard horses coming our way. A company of Blue Coats rode by. They didn't slow down or wave, but rode at a fast trot towards Richmond.

"I wonder where they are off to," I said as I got into the wagon.

"Hard to say," Raymond answered.

Over the next few months, we would see many soldiers going by our place. Every time a company of soldiers went by Father would get mad and go into the house. He never said anything but from his looks, I knew he was mad.

That day we saw the first big company as we finally made it to the house, we could see Elsie run into the house. Halfway there Mother came running out onto the porch as we approached the house.

"I'm so glad to see you are all right," Mother screamed as we rode up. With the words out of her mouth, she came running down the steps to give me a hug and a kiss.

"It was a wasted trip," I told her.

"What do you mean?" She said.

"Mr. Schmitt doesn't have enough money to buy coffee, let alone hay," I explained. I was surprised when she just smiled. That reaction wasn't what I expected from her. I didn't understand why he would ask for hay when he couldn't pay for it. He surely knew how much money he had before he ordered it.

Elsie was standing next to Mother, listening closely. "Just as long, as you made it back …, in one piece. Did you have any trouble?"

"A member of the Slave Police stopped us," I told her.

"I thought it might be better if we stayed the night rather than run into more of them," Raymond said.

"Wise of you, boy," Elsie told him.

"I agree," Mother said.

Raymond excused himself. "I think I had better unhitch the horses."

"You should get something to eat… That coffee we had, didn't have enough grounds to make a meal," I suggested.

"I could use a bite or two," he said as he got back onto the wagon.

"I'll get the two of you some breakfast," Elsie said as she went into the house.

"Clean yourself up before you think about eating" Mother said. "Your father will want to hear about your trip.

"I also want to talk to him," I told her. My list of questions kept getting longer and longer, and I really needed some answers. Then, thinking about the sewing Mother had been doing, I said, "If you get time, this pair of pants needs mending."

"I'll see what I can do," Mother promised. "If I can make uniforms I should be able to mend those for you."

"Thank you, Mother," I said as I followed her into the house. "When is Father coming home?"

As I headed upstairs, she said, "He thought he would be home this evening some time. Why do you ask? Do you have a problem?"

"No, I just want to ask him a couple of questions. I want to find out what's going on around here," I told her. I had the feeling my statement startled her. I knew, I wasn't going to get any answers from her. I had learned as I grew up to ask Father all the important questions.

"Breakfast is ready," Elsie called up the stairs.

"I'm coming," I called down as I put clean pants on. I smiled when I saw that all the buttons were on this pair of pants. As I shut the door to my room, I said, "At least Mother doesn't have to worry about this pair."

As I passed Mothers sewing room she asked, "What was that?"

"Just that this pair of pants doesn't need mending," I said.

"That's good," she said as I started down the stairs.

"Are you down there, Raymond? I'm ready for some food and some shooting," I called down.

"I can't go with you," Raymond called up from the kitchen.

As I sat down at the table, I asked, "Why not?"

"Mammy has some chores for me." He took a bite of pancakes. Then emptying his mouth he told me, "Dig in. These are the best I have ever had."

"Not that they're not good, but you're too hungry to care," I told him as I grabbed a few for me. As I ate, I decided that I would go for a ride or walk rather than go shooting. "I think I'll go for a walk. If you change your mind, give a shout."

Then as the two of us left the house, we heard horses again. Neither of us said anything but we both knew it was more soldiers. It was another company heading toward Richmond.

"You would almost think there is a war on," I said as my eyes followed them.

"I'm glad we weren't shooting. They might have felt the need to check us out," he said as he headed towards the barn.

"You might be right." Not having any direction in mind, I just began walking. I found myself standing next to the creek looking towards the Marsh place. I toyed with the idea of walking over to see

Ida, but I didn't. Instead, I sat down on the bank of the creek and watched the willows sway from side to side. I almost wished I were Raymond. I knew he wasn't lying around doing nothing, like I was. He was probably feeding the big oven. I knew it was hot work but he was doing something worthwhile.

My first recollection of the oven was when I was four or five years old. I followed my mother out back to a big brick structure. It wasn't until we went around to the other side I felt the heat coming from it. Then Elsie opened a steel door and pulled bread out. It wasn't long before I learned the oven was also used for cooking most of our meat.

I looked across the creek and saw an unfamiliar group of three colored people heading towards our place. I almost ran to them to ask if they were looking for a station. Somehow I knew they were, though I wasn't sure what a station was. I felt sure all these strangers coming to our place must mean our place was a station. I watched them disappear in the woods between me and the house; I then decided to go home. I knew no one would admit they had come by. As I stood up, I saw a couple of bubbles rise from the creek. I looked at the bubbles and told the fish or frog, "I have been so dumb. I know what's been going on here."

As I headed to the house, I knew there was no reason to hurry. What I needed right then was for Father to come home. Once he was home, I would get him to tell me the truth. He would have to admit it, once he was aware that I knew what it was.

"I got a letter from your Uncle Joe and Aunt Edith," Mother said as I reached the porch.

"I thought they were moving," I said, as I sat down on the steps.

With a troubled voice she said, "Yes…and I got a note from your father."

I figured there must have been a problem. Otherwise he would have been on his way home by now.

"Is there a problem?" I asked. "I guess he's not coming home tonight,"

"He promises that he'll be home tomorrow. He also said Mr. Schmitt has the money now, so he wants the two of you to take the hay back," she told me.

I didn't want to make the trip again but I knew I would have to. I also knew I needed to pay more attention to what was going on this time. If we went up in broad daylight, I wouldn't miss much. What I didn't count on was Raymond and Mr. Schmitt being smarter than I was.

"From what Raymond tells me, you know a lot about horses," Mr. Schmitt said as I got down from the wagon.

"I've learned a little," I said. While we were talking, I tried to keep an eye on Raymond. To my surprise, he didn't say or do anything.

"Maybe you could come out to the pasture and check out my favorite workhorse," he suggested. "Without him, I won't be able to bring any lumber down to saw up."

I was surprised at that remark. "Oh, I thought you raised animals."

"That I do, but I also cut lumber in the barn for the people around here," he explained.

"Well, I'll be happy to look at this horse," I said as I motioned for him to lead me.

We got out to the field and I checked the horse over. I patted him down and he didn't budge an inch. I then checked out his teeth and had the feeling this animal had been on the ark with Noah. I told Mr. Schmitt, "If I didn't know better, I'd say this animal is older than the two of us put together. I'm surprised he can pull his own weight, let alone logs or a wagon."

"He is getting old, I know. I guess I'd better make a deal with someone for another horse." He motioned for us to go back. "Thanks for looking at him."

"My pleasure," I said. As we walked neither of us said anything. I realized I had left Raymond and once again had missed out on whatever he came to do. When we got within sight of the house, he was on the wagon, which was now bare of any hay. Mr. Schmitt must have bought it this time.

As we got to the wagon, Mr. Schmitt said, "Tell your father thanks for the hay."

"I'll do that," I assured him as I got onto the wagon. I waved good-bye as we pulled away.

"At least it wasn't a wasted trip this time," I said to Raymond.

"No, it wasn't," he replied.

Turning my head, I saw some wood in the back of the wagon. It was cut to length and had hinges mounted on the pieces that were nailed together. I asked, "Where did the wood come from?"

"Billy has to build something for the master, and I thought he could use it. Mr. Schmitt had it in his barn, and his brother said I could have it," he answered.

"That was generous of him." Leaving it at that, I looked out over the meadow we were just passing and saw a couple of riders, obviously riding for pleasure. They were talking and the horse's gait was slow. That reminded me that I needed to take my horse Prince out and give him a run. I hadn't been riding for a couple of weeks, which wasn't good for Prince or for me

I looked back at the wood in the wagon. I tried to imagine why we would need this wood for a project for my father. We surely had all the wood that Billy would need to build whatever it was. I tried moving the pieces around mentally. I tried to come up with something that didn't need cutting any of the wood to size. I saw there were four large sections, all the same size. Then a fifth piece was the same width as the narrow end of the big pieces. Suddenly I knew that if I put them together, they would form a rectangular box. I remembered there was hay on top and in the hinges when I first saw the wood, so I knew the wood didn't come from the Schmitt place.

"We've been transporting slaves," I said to Raymond as we rode on. I tried to sound casual. "That wood back there forms a box they can hide in. The hay covers all of it, keeping it hidden from sight."

"You've always been too smart for your own good," he replied as he shook his head. With a grin, he added, "Don't let your father know. If he thought I told you he would have my hide."

To confirm my suspicions I asked, "So we are part of the "Underground Railroad" and our house is a "Station" for escaping slaves?"

"Yes. And we're the "Conductors" that lead them down the road a ways towards a safer place for them in Canada," he said.

"And all of my relatives in Ohio are part of this Underground Railroad," I suggested, fearing I knew more than I wanted to.

"That's why your people have to move. I know from what my parents have said that the Quakers don't believe in slavery. Their neighbors disagree and are out to kill them."

I asked, "How long has this been going on?"

"They've lived with this fear for a few years now. Pan Face's grandfather was the first Conductor. That was with your father's backing. When he got too old to handle the team, I took over." With a smile, he added, "Maybe I'll be the next to go north. I hear it's not as hot as it is here."

"And leave me without a friend? Thanks," I replied.

"You do have Ida to keep you company," he reminded me with that same dumb smile.

Over the years I had heard the Underground Railroad quietly mentioned several times, but no one seemed to know much about how it actually worked. It was shocking to think that Father was part of this scheme, yet I realized that since Father had freed all of our slaves years ago, it would make sense for him to want to help them go north. Occasionally I would catch hints that our field hands were in touch with slaves who had left. I had always found that interesting, but I'd never had the slightest idea that Father and Mother were a part of it all.

It was the same with Mother and Elsie making uniforms. I never knew Mother to have any interest in sewing or anything of the kind. Mother had always been interested in entertaining, giving parties, but not in doing domestic work such as sewing. This was an indication of how dedicated my parents were to their beliefs. The thing that was really puzzling to me was the fact that they wanted to support the South if we had a war, yet they still wanted to free slaves.

Raymond interrupted my thoughts. "You know you almost got us killed last time, don't you?" He frowned. "You never talk back to someone with a gun aimed at you."

I didn't understand what he meant. "What do you mean, I almost got us killed?"

"Your big mouth and getting upset about him calling me a Darky," he explained.

I defended myself. "Well, he made me mad. And besides, I didn't know we were hauling slaves, you know. If someone had told me I would have handled it differently."

"Be more careful the next time. You never want to talk back to the Slave Police. It might get you or someone else killed," he said as he snapped the reins.

"What makes you so blasted smart?" It upset me that for the first time, one of my best friends had talked down to me. I realized I had it coming, but it should have been Father correcting me, not a friend.

Home was just over the next rise. I couldn't wait to see Mother and for Father to come home.

"Because I'm a Darky, I had to learn. Your father taught me more than just how to shoot," he answered.

"I don't ever want to hear you call yourself a Darky again…. You're better than that," I reminded him. I was getting more and more irritated at hearing the term "Darky."

"If only the rest of the country felt the same way you do. I'm free, but even though I am, I still can't go anywhere without fear of getting shot," he said under his breath.

We got home and had a bite to eat. Raymond went to do his chores and left me on my own. With Mother and Elsie occupied with their sewing and Mother not wanting to talk, there wasn't any reason to hang around the house. Again, I thought about doing some shooting but decided I needed to take care of my horse. I prayed that Father would be home soon so we could talk.

"Good morning, Master Edgar," Freddy, the stable boy, greeted me as I entered the stables. Freddy was the one who had taught me about horses.

I looked towards my horse's stall and asked, "Good morning, Freddy. How's Prince? I haven't seen much of him lately."

"I think he's in need of a good ride," he told me. With a grin, he added, "Going for a ride is the way the master works out his problems. It might do the same for you."

"I do have a few," I told him as I picked up a currycomb.

"I'll leave you alone. If you need anything just give a shout. I'm glad you got those people to safety," he said as he left.

"Thanks, Freddy…Ah, you're welcome," I told him finding it hard to talk. I was both upset and mad that everyone but me knew what was going on around the place. Father had to have others around the place helping him in his work with the Underground Railroad, and surely one of them could have said something to me.

I brushed Prince and was about to grab my saddle, but I stopped when I heard someone come into the stable. Figuring it was Freddy returning, I reached up to grab my saddle.

"Raymond told me about the past two days," Father said from behind me. Maybe we should take a ride and talk."

"And work out my problems or yours… Freddy said that's how you solve your problems," I answered as I took my saddle down. "Yes, I'd like to go for a ride with you."

"Let me get my horse and I'll meet you outside," he replied smiling. I looked at Father and realized he was getting older. His short hair was turning gray, but from the rest of his body you would never have guessed he was in his late fifties. He was strong and could outwork any three men I knew.

"Be right there," I said. I threw the saddle onto Prince and strapped it on him, then led him outside to where Father was waiting. I knew a change was coming, a change between my father and me. I was already standing straighter and taller as I approached him. My anger was giving way to a feeling that I was now a real part of the family.

Father was already astride his horse. "Took you long enough," he said.

"I'm only a child, remember?" I replied as I got onto Prince.

"Not anymore," he shouted back as he rode off ahead of me.

"I do know I can outrace you," I shouted. I kicked Prince lightly and we were off and running. Soon Father slowed down to let me catch up with him.

"Raymond told me about the Blue Coats coming through. I have him hiding all of our weapons," he said.

I asked, "You think that's needed?"

"Yes, I do. I don't want them to have any excuse to hurt anyone on the place." Pulling his horse to a stop, he added, "If we need them I know where to find them. I guess we don't have to talk about what we have been doing around here."

"I guess not, but I would just like to know why no one told me," I said.

"To keep you from getting hurt," he answered.

"I'm not sure I understand. If someone had told me, I wouldn't have said anything," I assured him. I rode off thinking about the different questions that I wanted to ask. Then I noticed that he wasn't riding beside me. I brought Prince to a stop and waited for him. I shouted back, "I thought we were going to ride. I haven't had Prince out for a month and he needs the exercise."

"I'm coming," he called out.

As he came alongside, I told him, "I hate to admit this, but I haven't paid any attention to your talks with Mother. There seems to be a strong possibility we may be fighting the North. Would you explain to me why? I don't understand why, after all these years of having slaves, we suddenly have to fight."

"It doesn't have anything to do with the slaves. Those newspaper stories and articles are for people in the North. The real problem is that they want us to change our lives to match theirs. If we don't, they won't give us financing to grow different crops." Bringing his horse to a stop, he added, "In reality it costs us more to have slaves than it does for them to hire people. The northerners don't understand that we feed, clothe and house our slaves. Most of us even give them medical attention in exchange for their work. The average workers up north don't get half of that. In fact, they have to work sixteen-hour days six days a week for almost no money. To add to that, over the years your grandfather gave over half of the slaves their freedom and land on which to make a living.

I asked, "Can't they see what we are doing?"

"It's a shame the people in the North don't know the truth. If they were to come here and see for themselves, it might be different. Most people can't come here and see for themselves… Even then, they would see the open spaces and compare it to where they live. They don't understand what it takes to plant and harvest crops. All they know is their way of life and, what they hear. It's the Abolitionists that spread those lies with the help of the newspapers," he told me.

"That's not right. The hatred they are spreading is about to start a war. Don't they realize that many of their men and boys will lose their lives?"

"I know." Father shook his head. "No, the real problem is financial. With the North wanting to tell us how to live, they won't loan us the money we need. But if we become a country of our own, we can govern ourselves. France will help finance us. They are even willing to finance the war if it comes to that."

I asked, "Do you believe we really need to go to war?"

"If the northerners were to keep their nose out of our business, we probably wouldn't be going to war. If I didn't need the loan from the banks up there, it wouldn't be so bad. I wouldn't be borrowing money from them if I didn't have to. I also don't think it's right for them to tell me how to live my life. It's their forcing us to be like them that will likely make us secede from the Union. The northerners certainly are not going to take lightly to that idea, and will threaten us with war. To think that this was a country of the free and now they're telling us how to live, trying to take our freedom away from us. I hate to say it, but that will make us slaves to the people up north. I don't care what it takes, I won't stand for it," he answered.

"Maybe that's what we deserve," I replied. "We kept slaves for many years in a free land." It surprised me that Father didn't act as usual or tell me he would talk to me later and then never tell me anything. This was the first time Father had talked to me as if I were a man. I knew he had simplified his explanation, but I got the idea. Even with his short explanation, I got a clearer picture of the situation than I had out of all the ranting and raving I had heard at our get-togethers.

"Our way of thinking has had flaws in it for a long time. The biggest flaw is taking the land for granted. We need to rotate crops and take on less land. All of this is valid and we have started to change. After living this way for so many generations, I'm surprised we've changed as much as we have. I know it will take a while for everyone to make the change, but we've started already. My worst fear is the hatred I see coming, if everything works out the way I think it will," he answered.

"If we go to war, will you fight?" I asked him. I knew I wouldn't like the answer he might give me. With his having only one arm, I couldn't imagine him fighting in a war. Nevertheless, I knew he would fight for what he believed in.

"No, not with one arm missing… Like you, I'll do my best to protect your mother and our place" he said. "And you won't be fourteen until next year. I'm not letting you go to war as young as you are. It would kill your mother if I did. Having been in one war myself, I would have to agree with her that you are too young."

Having finished our conversation, we headed back to the house.

From that day on, Raymond and I took many coloreds to the station north of our place. Some went to Mr. Schmitt's. On a few trips to his place, our excuse for going was to haul logs. We used the logs to cover the box where the slaves were hiding. Whoever had created this box was clever. They cut logs the exact length from the box to the end of the wagon.

One trip I remember well, for we didn't take the wagon. We had a family of six come to our place, and since we were not able to haul six at one time, Raymond and I took them along the creek to Mr. Schmitt's place. We had to hide in bushes several times before we got there. After the slaves were safely on their way, Mr. Schmitt brought us home.

Then 1861 came along, the year that I turned fourteen. Tension in the area was getting heavy. In Richmond we found disgruntled people everywhere we went. As we would go into a shop, everyone would stop talking until they were sure who we were. The conversation would turn to what everyone thought we should do.

We knew the days of speculation were gone in April of '61, when we heard the news from Mr. Davis that a group of Confederate soldiers attacked Fort Sumter, South Carolina, and the war began.

It had been in January the Southern States had officially agreed to secede from the Union. When our decision was announced other states joined our protests against the North. When Lincoln began talking about sending troops into the South to bring us back into the Union, things changed.

On April 17, 1861 we learned that on the 10th of the month our lives changed. In answer to Lincoln's threat Brig. Gen. Beauregard, the commander of the provisional Confederate forces at Charleston, South Carolina, demanded the surrender of the Union garrison of Fort Sumter in Charleston Harbor. From what I gathered there was no bloodshed over the three day affair Major Anderson on the 13th did surrender. In firing a cannon salute the cannon exploded killing one soldier and wounding three more. This takeover was to officially start the War Between the States.

It surprised me that Father and Mother didn't show any satisfaction in hearing it. Instead, my father told Mr. Davis, "We're not ready."

Mr. Davis asked him, "Would we ever be ready? Now with half of the state refusing to secede, we have a mess on our hands?"

"I know that they're part of the North, and they now call that part of the state West Virginia. I have to agree we will never be ready." Father answered. When are people or a country ever prepared for war? I'm just worried about what might happen to our young people, our young men who will have to fight."

"That has always been one of our fears. As with everything else, it's something you have to contend with," Mr. Davis said.

"What about Robert?" Father asked. "Now he lives in the north and has the opportunity to be the commander of the Army of the North."

He meant Robert E. Lee. It was interesting to learn what Lincoln had offered him. Having known him all my life I knew of his ties to both North and South, and would have to decide which side to be on. Despite his position in the Union Army, he would surely come back and help defend the South.

"He's in Richmond right now. However, as you know, he isn't in favor of this war. But he feels he can't fight his friends and relatives here in the South, either," Mr. Davis told him.

I left to fill Raymond in on the war that, as Father had predicted, had finally come to be. It didn't take long for the information to spread among our group of workers. Within weeks, the only ones left were Raymond, Elsie, Billy, and Freddy. With everyone heading north, planting crops almost ended. The Marshes, too, were suffering.

Through the Underground Railroad, I learned that most of the coloreds had to join the Union Army, which sent them out west to fight the Indians. It was fortunate for them the Union Soldiers came east to fight the war. If this hadn't happened, I don't know what the north would've done with them. I felt sorry for them, but thought it was better for them than fighting the war here.

We had also lost all of our horses when a Confederate troop came through and took them. I knew the Army needed them, but I didn't want to lose Prince. I also knew we couldn't survive without a horse for working the fields and getting supplies. Father and Mother discussed their concern many times that week. They didn't care if they were losing their pride or position. Their fears centered around putting food on our table.

As I thought about how everything would change, memories from my past year came back to me. One was of talking to some of my school friends about the troubles between the North and the South. I told them "I would think the courts and Congress could settle our differences." With the attack on Fort Sumter, I realized how futile my dreams of peace were.

We had discussed the idea of going to war. My school friend, Edward too had dreams of peace. He had asked, "But why would we have to go to war? Can't we just be two different countries?" I wondered how many of my friends were going to fight in the war.

The Fort Sumter event is easy for me to remember because my mother's birthday is in April, but another event took place a few months later that stands out even more. One morning we heard the Union Troops were marching our way with the intent of taking the Southern States back. We also heard that Mr. Marsh had joined the Confederate company that had been formed in our area. After telling us, Father held Mother in his arms as she cried. I knew she was afraid Father might follow Mr. Marsh's example and join himself. My concern was how Ida was taking it, since she worshipped her father.

"Enough of this bad news… Let's go for a walk," Raymond said, motioning for me to join him.

"Why not…? I've heard enough bad news for one day," I answered as I ran down the steps. The two of us walked and talked for an hour or more. We worked out our frustrations by skipping rocks in the creek. Neither one of us could find answers, so we went back to the house.

"Bet I can beat you to the house," Raymond shouted.

Being taller than he was, I knew I could beat him but I didn't feel like running. I shouted, "I'll catch up with you later."

"Fine," he called back.

After a short pause, I decided I would try to catch up with him. I did my best but he had too big a head start. I still ran until I got within sight of the house. As I was coming through the trees, I heard a shot ring out. I looked around but I didn't see anyone. Looking back at the house, I saw Raymond slump down on the steps. I ran as fast as I could, and I saw Elsie running to him also. Father and Mother came running out of the house. When Mother saw him lying there, she screamed.

"Raymond…Raymond…Don't die," I heard Elsie cry out.

When I got there, Elsie had his head on her lap. She was crying and stroking his head. She looked up at me as if she was pleading with me to help her, but I didn't know what to do. Raymond had a large hole in his chest big enough for my fist to fit into it. Blood was everywhere and now it was covering Elsie. His body lying there was nothing like the Slave Policeman father had killed. I could see Raymond's condition get worse with each gasp of breath. The pool of blood under him grew with each breath he took. I was in shock and wanted desperately to be able to do something to help him. I wanted to plug the hole in his chest, but I knew that wouldn't help.

Elsie didn't say anything more as she held his head in her lap. I got the feeling she was dying as he was dying and there wasn't anything we could do. She was doing everything she could by making him comfortable during the time he had left.

I couldn't believe what had happened. Over and over I said, "Raymond… Why you? Why did this happen to you?"

"Did you see anyone?" I heard Father ask me. Then he said to Mother, "Just sit here for a while and you'll be all right."

"No," I answered him. I was still looking down at my friend dying in his mother's arms. I knew I should be comforting Mother, but I knew Father was taking care of her.

As I knelt down beside Raymond, he managed to smile at me. It was a gruesome smile with blood running out of his mouth. I could see he knew the end was near, and I knew he wanted to say something. With a gurgle, he finally managed to say, "This is…one… Darky, that's not going north."

"Is there anything I can do?" Father asked. When he saw Raymond's chest, he shook his head. Looking up he added, "I guess not."

"Don't talk like that," I told Raymond. I saw his eyes go blank. Elsie screamed and I knew my best friend was dead.

Through her sobbing Elsie moaned. "Raymond…Oh, my little Raymond, why did you have to die.

I Don't Care Anymore

For one of my teachers I'm still making more entries in my diary. I'm not sure how interesting or important it is, but somehow it's a friend. I can write what has happened in my life without worrying what others might say. Today I was writing an entry with tears staining the pages. I wish I didn't have this to enter:

With Raymond lying in his mother's lap dead, I looked around again. I didn't see anyone who might have fired the shot. All I saw were Freddy and Billy running towards us. On the porch, Father was helping Mother to her feet. Before I knew it, Freddy was pushing me to one side so that he could help Elsie. I moved to one side and let them take Raymond's body away.

To this day I can't tell you if I was crying or not, but I was mad. Not knowing what to say I managed to tell Elsie, "I'm sorry."

"We'll take care of him," Freddy said.

"Take him into the house," Father offered. He gave Mother a hug and added, "You can put him on the dining table if you want. I'll go after the Reverend for you."

"Thank you, Master. I would hate to have him in the stable with all the flies," Elsie answered through her sobs.

Freddy and Billy carefully folded Raymond's arms over his chest and carried him inside the house. Father and Mother followed, motioning for me to join them. None of us said anything as we stared at Raymond's body. I knew I couldn't find words to express how I felt. I went to my room and lay on my bed.

I had probably been lying there for an hour when I heard the door open. I rolled over onto my back and saw Father enter the room. He was wearing a Confederate uniform with a sleeve designed for a man with part of one arm missing, so I knew someone had made the uniform especially for him. My heart sank and I couldn't say anything.

"Take care of your mother. I can't sit back and take any more of this. Like I said some time back, you're not a child anymore," he said. He shut the door behind him. Then he reopened the door slightly and added, "The guns are under the board next to the staircase. Oh, yes, the Reverend and a man are coming to take care of Raymond's body."

I lay there in my bed in complete shock. It was bad enough that someone had killed my best friend, and now my father was off to fight in the war. And he hadn't given me a handshake, or a hug, or a goodbye. He had just stood there telling me what to do and left. I was stunned, so I just lay where I was nearly all afternoon until I heard a noise downstairs.

I figured the Reverend had arrived to take care of Raymond's body. I was glad that he would give Raymond a proper burial. I knew I should go down and help them but I didn't, because I couldn't accept the fact that he was dead. And besides, I didn't know what to say or do. Knowing what Elsie must be going through, I didn't feel brave enough to be around her.

Later that evening I learned that the Reverend hadn't come by. I never learned who came, and it didn't matter. My mind was on my father and the loss of Raymond.

"You have to get something to eat," Mother said as she stood in the doorway of my room.

"I'm not sure if I feel like eating right now." I turned over, away from her.

"He does love you, you know," she said.

"I know… I saw that in his gray uniform… It said it all," I told her. I looked away. I didn't feel like doing anything, especially eating. Rolling back over I said, "He told me he wouldn't fight in this war."

"That's what I understood him to say too," she said as she left my room.

I finally sat up and looked out the window. Storm clouds had moved in, which seemed fitting. I asked myself repeatedly "What do I do now?" It seemed that all I could do was cry.

After a while, I was dry of tears and I just sat on my bed staring into space. I finally went down and found that Raymond's body was gone. Going into the kitchen I found Mother preparing food. "Elsie's upstairs," she told me.

"I figured as much," I replied, not feeling like talking.

"This is a sad day," she said as she stirred something in a pot.

"In many ways, I replied, as I got up to get a drink of water. Mother looked over at me and stopped talking. She dished up some stew and set it in front of me. I sat there trying to decide whether to eat or not. I finally looked up at her and said, "I don't know who I'll miss more. I know I should miss Father more, but Raymond was my best friend."

Mother either didn't hear me or didn't know what to say. She just stood there staring into the pot. I knew how scared she was at having Father take off as he did. Knowing Mother as I did I felt it best that I didn't ask her if she was crying. I picked up my dishes and set them in the sink.

As I left the kitchen, I remembered what Father told me about where the guns were. With my fingernail, I managed to pry up the board beside the stairs. I pulled out the Remington and a Colt, and remembered to grab a powder flask, caps, wads, and mini balls. I didn't want to find myself unprepared for whatever I got into. Before I did anything, I had to see Ida. The only problem with that was that I had to look after Mother.

The next morning the Reverend came by and arrangements were made for Raymond's burial in the family plot. Mother tried to console Elsie, but it didn't help.

"I'll miss him," I managed to say to Elsie. Her answer was to give me a hug, which I found hard to handle. Mother motioned for me to go outside.

I was restless and paced up and down the porch. I don't know how long I had been walking around the porch when I saw Freddy, Billy and other workers staring at the house.

Freddy walked up to me and said, "The Reverend is here."

"Yes… I think he wants to bury Raymond today or tomorrow," I answered. Once I had answered him, I knew it didn't matter to me I would still miss him.

I couldn't remember when any of the workers hadn't been a part of my life. I also couldn't remember a time they wouldn't talk to me. It seemed the workers felt as if Raymond's death only affected them and not me. From Freddy's actions and short to the point comment I got the feeling he didn't want talk to me. I also got the feeling that I wasn't a part of their lives anymore and it hurt. As I looked around, I got the feeling none of the other workers were going to be talking to me either right then. I finally left them to themselves and went to my room. At supper that night, I learned we would be burying Raymond the next day.

The burial was a simple affair. Only six of us, counting the Reverend, watched as the homemade coffin containing Raymond's body was lowered into the earth. That wasn't unusual, because no one ever took much notice when a Darky died. In our family, our help was part of our family. Since Raymond and his mother lived with us, it made him more family than the others. As I watched Freddy and Billy fill the grave, I knew I had to quit thinking about his death. I had to find some way to put the experience behind me and take care of Mother. My life had already changed without going to the war. I would soon learn that everything would change and the change would be forever.

For the next few days, Mother and Elsie discussed how we would get through the crisis. Elsie pointed out that we still had a cow, and she had planted a garden that would supply us with vegetables over the winter and into the following year. Mother assured us that our root cellar had plenty in it. Freddy, Billy and I could shoot game to provide meat. With all of this, it looked better than I would have guessed at first.

Then several days later, I couldn't bear to hear any more about Raymond's death, so I went to my room, leaving Mother and Elsie to talk in the kitchen. In my room I had a book Father gave me to read and I thought it was time to read it.

I had been reading for an hour when I heard gunfire. I began to worry about the women when the slug broke through my window. I inched my way to the window and saw a Union Soldier riding his horse through Mother's flowerbed. I grabbed the Remington. As I raised the rifle, he and his horse jumped the fence and took off towards the back of the house.

"Did you fire one of those guns up there?" Mother called up to me.

"No, Mother, not yet at least," I shouted down to her. I was glad to know she was safe. No matter where the bullet went, someone could have captured her in the meantime.

Carrying the Remington, I headed towards the other side of the house. Quickly opening a window, I looked out to see if I could see the soldier and the direction he was traveling. To say I was mad wouldn't describe how I felt. Someone had shot and killed my close friend, a Union soldier had trampled my mother's flowerbed, and now he was shooting at the house. It was too much. It was time to do some shooting myself.

The soldier was coming around the trees. I put the rifle to my shoulder and began to follow him with the sights. When he got between two trees, I breathed deep then releasing it, I squeezed the trigger. I was so nervous I wasn't sure if I had missed my target or even if the rifle had gone off. It was as if everything was happening very slowly. Then I remembered seeing smoke coming out of the barrel. I thought I had missed him and began reloading. Before I could lower the rifle, I saw the rider slowly fall from his horse. I decided to get the horse before I did anything else. From that point on, fear controlled every thought and action that was to take place.

Mother called out again, "Did I hear a gunshot up there?"

"Yes," I answered. I knew I should tell her what I had done, but I didn't want to scare her. I also didn't want to hear a lecture from her.

I ran to Mother's sewing room and grabbed a pair of gray pants and a jacket I thought would fit me. I threw them onto a blanket from my bed and rolled them up together. I couldn't see anything else I needed, and was too dazed to think. I tucked a pistol into my pants and with the bundle and the rifle I headed downstairs.

As I ran into the kitchen, Mother asked, "What are you doing?"

"Going after a horse," I told her as I went out the back door. Catching my breath, I ran out to where the soldier had fallen. He was dead. The bullet had pierced a hole in his skull. What was I going to do with his body? I had to do something or the soldiers might take their revenge on Mother. In disgust, I found myself saying, "At least we have a horse now."

"I don't know if you killed Raymond, but anyway you won't be shooting at anyone's homes again," I told the body as I gave it a kick.

Another soldier was approaching on the road in front of our house. Instinct told me he was coming after me. Not giving it any thought, I grabbed the soldier's rifle and threw it to the ground replacing it with my Remington. Taking my bundle, I jumped onto the horse and took off across the cotton field. I heard gunshots, and I knew I was in trouble. One of the shots whizzed past my ear, and I bent down until my head was right against the horse's neck. I kicked the horse in the ribs and prayed I could make it across the field into the woods.

I wanted to pull my pistol out and shoot back at him, but something told me my chance of hitting him was slim. I decided it would be better to save my ammunition than to waste it firing at air. I had to do something. If he were to get me, he probably would go back and take revenge on Mother for my killing of his friend. With this thought, I tried to picture the terrain. I decided to ambush him. Good locations for that came to mind, but none was in the direction I was going. Then I recalled a clump of five low trees not far ahead. I headed for them in hopes of getting there before he caught up to me.

I wasn't sure, but I thought the soldier had fired his last shot at me. I turned and saw him coming at me at a full gallop. I was at the edge of the field and he was half the field behind me. I felt a smile cross my face knowing I had enough time to do what I had to do. I turned back and found the clump of trees and went around behind it. Dismounting, I tried to decide whether to use the rifle or the pistol. I felt more comfortable with the rifle, so I pulled it out of the scabbard. As the rifle cleared the scabbard, I could hear the hoof beats were getting close to me.

I raised the rifle to my shoulder and took aim between the trees. For the first time I had second thoughts about pulling the trigger. It might have been easier if I hadn't looked at him. He looked like he might have been a year or two older than I was. A quick vision of his parents and brothers missing him came to mind. Then I thought of what might happen to Mother if I didn't kill him, and I pulled the trigger. He fell to his horse's neck. He was trying to pull his rifle out of its scabbard, but it looked as if he couldn't keep his balance. As his rifle cleared the scabbard, I shot him again. With my second shot, his body slid off the saddle and fell. One boot was caught in a stirrup. The horse took off and ran a short distance. When it stopped, the soldier's body fell to the ground.

"I'm sorry. You should have stayed home," I muttered from my position by the trees. I looked around to see if there were any other soldiers. I didn't know anything about Army procedures, but it didn't make any sense to me that two soldiers would be riding past our place alone. I wondered what I should do next. As I looked at the dead soldier, I said, "Sorry, but I can't give you a formal burial."

I decided to use the rocks that were piled up near me—rocks the workers had cleared from the fields. I removed the saddle and bridle from the horse and piled them on top of the body. I thought about crossing his arms on his chest and straightening out his legs, but didn't risk taking the time to do that. If there were other Union soldiers around, I was in danger. I left his bloody body as it lay and continued to cover it with rocks. I prayed though it wasn't a proper burial it would at least hide it for a time.

"You ruined a beautiful day," I told the body in the makeshift grave. Looking up, a few birds were flying in the cloudless sky. Other birds were singing in the woods nearby. They didn't care that two people had just died; they just went on warbling their songs. I felt as if I had disgraced my parents' place instead of defending it, and I prayed Mother would forgive me someday.

Then getting onto my newly found horse I rode off towards Richmond. As I rode, I prayed Freddy or Billy would bury the other soldier's body. I didn't want one of his friends to find his body in the open field. If one of the Union soldiers found the dead body, who knew, what they might do to Mother?

"What am I doing?" I asked myself after riding halfway to Richmond. After I had killed two men, I was more in a daze than ever and didn't know what to do. I knew I should've gone back and taken care of the first soldier's body before I did anything else. I also knew I should have said good-bye to Mother. She deserved to know what I planned on doing. Since I didn't have any plans, I would not have been able to give her an answer even if I had wanted to. To justify everything I muttered, "Father didn't bother to tell her."

I didn't want friends of those soldiers to catch me, so I avoided riding on the road. Usually fences were a problem but I had seen the horse could jump them when the soldier was trampling through Mother's garden and cleared the fence coming out. I gave the horse a chance to get more experience and I jumped a few.

After another half hour of riding, I found what had been an open field. Hundreds of tents had been erected there, and soldiers were walking around. There were horse-drawn wagons and cannons. The tents took up more area than some towns I had seen.

"I heard they're taking 287 prisoners to the Libby prison this afternoon," a soldier told a companion as they walked past me.

"I'm glad they put the prison on Belle Island rather than here in town," the other replied.

It was interesting that also on that island was one of the largest ironworks in the country. Mr. Marsh had told my father how that factory almost went out of business when the railroads quit laying track.

I looked off in the distance and saw a Confederate flag waving in the breeze. Someone had called the flag the Stars and Bars. Inside the blue square in the upper left-hand corner were silver stars for each state in a circle. Then there were three alternating stripes of red and white. It is no wonder it got that name. I decided to head for the tent with the flag first.

Reaching behind me, I felt my bundle containing my blanket and uniform. I wondered whether I should change into the uniform, but since I didn't want to change out in the open, I decided to go in as I was.

Most of the soldiers were walking around without their jackets. Their suspenders were hanging off their shoulders as if they didn't have a care in the world. None of them were carrying arms. In front of their tents, their rifles were stacked like a tripod.

As I approached, some of them pulled their rifles and gave me a questioning look. Getting still closer to the flag tent, I saw armed soldiers were marching back and forth across the road leading up to the tent. Cautiously I dismounted and began to walk the rest of the way. As I walked between the tents, I could hear soldiers talking.

"I didn't join to sit here to do nothing," one soldier said to his friend.

"Don't worry; we'll be seeing plenty of action soon enough," the other assured him.

From another tent, I could hear someone playing a mouth organ with someone singing along. I recognized the tune being "Dixie." Hearing it, I began to sing with them:

I wish I was in the land of cotton…

Old times there are not forgotten…

Look away, look away, look away, Dixieland.

Then I heard the men sing out words that weren't familiar to me.

Southerns!

Hear your country call you…!

Up! Lest worse than death befall you…!

Hear the Northern thunders mutter…!

Northern flags in South wind flutter…

Send them back your fierce defiance…!

Stamp upon the cursed alliance…!

In months to come, I would learn this song would become popular with the men. Then I heard someone playing a drum as a dog barked.

The tents looked new. The uniforms the soldiers were wearing were a crisp gray without a speck of dirt on them. Knowing the Confederate Army wasn't that old, I wondered how long the men would look that clean and neat. From what Father had told me of the Mexican-American War, cleanness and neatness wouldn't last long.

A few men were wearing guns or carrying rifles. There were a few colored soldiers who probably weren't armed. As Raymond would have done, they had followed their masters to war. During the war, they would take care of the masters' horses and equipment. Some of them drove wagons or helped with cooking the meals. The Army officers were afraid the colored people would shoot their own soldiers and did not give them a chance to fight.

Someone shouted out, "Would someone shut that dang fool dog up."

Patting the nose of my horse I told him, "Everyone seems happy… after a fashion."

To my pleasure, my horse let out a neigh.

"Halt!" a soldier shouted. Then his partner and he crossed their rifles, keeping me from going any further. He then said, "State your business."

"I've come to see Mr. Lee," I told him.

"The General isn't seeing anyone. The General has more to do than just see anyone that comes along," he told me.

"I have to see him. Tell him Edgar Buchanan would like to see him. He has known me from the day my birth," I told them.

They both looked at each other as if they didn't know what to do or say. Then the second guard said, "Stand where you are."

"Yes, sir," I replied as he turned and walked towards the tent. I did as they told me to do, but I did look around. In front of the tents, men were tending cook pots over fires. Between the tents were ropes with clothes drying. The tents were in groups of twenty or so across the field to my left. In each group, one tent had a flag with a letter on it. I had no idea what it meant for sure but I was sure there was a reason for it.

"You can go on in to see him," the soldier said.

"Thank you," I answered as the two separated for me to pass between them. I smiled to myself at the expression on their faces now, for apparently they thought I was someone important.

When I got to General Lee's tent, another soldier took the reins of my horse.

"Go right on in, sir," he said.

He caught me off guard, calling me sir. Apparently, he too thought I was someone important. As I went into the tent, I managed say, "Thank you."

"Good afternoon, Edgar." General Lee stood to greet me.

"Good afternoon Mr… I mean General." He had always been "Mr. Lee" to me, and the idea of calling him General was a little hard to get used to.

"Right now, Mr. is fine. I'm Mr. Davis's adviser right now, but most do call me General," he answered with a smile. "I hope you haven't come to join," he said as he pointed out a stool for me to sit on. Meanwhile he took a seat in front of a desk.

"I have. I don't know what I'll need, but I have my own horse, pistol, rifle, pants, jacket, and blanket," I answered, suddenly feeling strange hearing the words coming out of my mouth. I was afraid I would regret my decision to join the army, for I didn't like the idea of me killing more men. But my anger had driven me to join, and it seemed too late to change my mind. As I played with the idea, I realized I would carry through with it. Maybe I could justify my actions by thinking of the number of men the Union soldiers had already killed, and about the fact that others might have had to do what I had done.

"At least you came prepared. I don't mind telling you I'm against someone of your age joining. I could make you my aide, and that would keep you out of the fighting for a while. But I guess you would rather fight with your father than be part of my staff," he said.

A little hesitant, I asked, "So Father's here?"

"Company B," he told me. He looked down at his papers and then back at me. "Why are you joining? Is it because you're missing your father?"

I told him what had led up to Father's leaving to join, and about the two Union soldiers I had killed. I tried to sound like a man rather than a child, for I didn't want him to tell me to leave after all I had been through.

"That explains how you came to have a horse. I'm the one that told them to take your stock. I wish you were a little older and trained in the ways of the army, but I guess you'll get enough experience in the field." He shook his head. "What about your mother? Shouldn't you be home protecting her?

"She has Freddy, Billy, and Elsie," I told him.

"Then I guess it's up to you and your father. Lord knows we'll need everyone we can get. You could be your father's aide, or if nothing else you could be a drummer for your father's company," he told me. As he spoke, he set some papers from one stack to another. He got up and extended his hand. "It's good seeing you again. Your father's tent is the one with a "B" on it to the right of my tent."

"Thank you, sir," I replied as I shook his hand. It was the first time he or any other man had ever shaken my hand. As a child, I had gotten nods and waves but never a handshake. As Father had said, I wasn't a child anymore. The way the General treated me seemed to indicate he was right. I wondered if General Lee would feel the same if he didn't know I had killed the two Yankee soldiers.

I left the General's tent and took the reins to my horse. This horse wasn't Prince, but he had served me well so far. I told the soldier, "Thank you sir."

"My pleasure," he said with a smile. "Major Buchanan is a good officer."

"Thanks; he's my father," I told him. I looked to the right of the tent and saw a flag with the letter "B" on it. I began to head that way and realized I was hesitant to see Father. I wasn't sure whether that was because of the way he had left so abruptly, or because of the guilt I felt at leaving Mother alone. I wasn't too worried about his reaction to my killing the two soldiers, but I wondered how he would react to the fact that I had just left without saying good-bye to Mother or explaining anything to her. I also wondered what Mother would say if she knew I was here.

At the front of the tent, I said in a hesitant voice, "Excuse me."

"Enter," my father answered.

"Good afternoon, sir, I said as I entered." He was sitting at a desk with his back to me.

He dropped his pen and turned. With a shocked look, he said, "I was afraid my ears were right and it was you. What are you doing here?"

I told him what happened earlier that day, and that I had spoken to Mr. Lee. His expression never changed. He just listened with his elbows on the desk and his head propped in his hands.

"I wish General Lee was commanding the armies rather than General P.G.T. Beauregard," he said as he stood up.

After talking it over, he agreed to take Mr. Lee's suggestion and make me his aide. He suggested making me his drummer, but I didn't care for the idea.

He finally put me in with the other trainees to learn how to handle myself in the army. All I learned from the training was the chain of command, saluting, and how to stand at attention. Once training was over with, I wondered why they bothered. To my way of thinking, I didn't learn anything of use.

I did learn that I would be under Sergeant Owens and the platoon was under the command of Captain Fredrick. With Father being a company commander, I was to become his aide. It all sounded like a joke, but I knew there was protocol that I had to follow.

What I didn't have, Supply would equip me with. I was thankful that I had good boots, and when the Supply sergeant saw them, he allowed me to keep them. Father had my boots made for me by a boot maker, and they were a perfect fit. All the boots the Supply officer had were one size, and if they were too large the soldier had to stuff them with rags to make them fit. I had no desire to wear boots stuffed with rags.

While I was in Richmond, I wrote Mother and Ida to let them know I was still alive. I tried to write them daily but I didn't always get around to it. When I did write, I tried to keep my letters on the light side. I didn't see any reason to tell them about the gore.

In July of 1861, we were fighting at Bull Run under Brigadier General Joseph E. Johnson. Though I was there, I can't say I did much fighting. Father did his best to keep us behind the lines out of harm's way. In the end, we won the battle without me, or Father's help. It wasn't until a few days later that I wouldn't just hear gun and cannon fire but experience the sensation. We were on a march north away from the battle we had just won.

As we were riding along, we heard gunfire ahead of us. The captain leading our company brought everyone to a halt. As we kept low, orders reached us to circle around and take the Yankees from their rear flank. Reaching their flank was easy when we left the wagon behind. Once we were there, Father had the men stretch out across a ridge.

"Probably stragglers from Bull Run," Father told me as he stood up in his stirrups. Then as commanded, he jerked the reins of his horse to go through the woods.

"I thought the battle was over," I replied. I followed him, with the rest of the company behind me. I didn't pay any attention to where we were or what was going on. My main concern was not finding myself in the sights of a sniper. As we rode, I thought about the trees on our place and wondered which tree was more beautiful, a willow or a pine. Shaking those thoughts from my mind, I got back to the fighting.

Because of the woods and fallen trees, we couldn't fight on horseback. When we were in position, Father gave us the silent signal to dismount. I dismounted, pushing my horse away from me and grabbing my rifle at the same time. Before Father gave the command to charge, one of our men fired a shot at the Yankees, revealing our position. The battle was on.

"What do you think you're doing?" he shouted out as he took cover. He turned to me and added, "Keep your head down. There's no sense getting shot over something as small as this."

Meanwhile I looked around and marveled at the trees around us. Below our position was a lush meadow with a few boulders. Some of our forces would be firing at the Yankees from below us. We would be above them, firing towards both forces. The whole scene looked wrong and I knew what the outcome would be. In whatever time it took us to win or lose, men would die.

With us attacking from both sides, the Yankees still had enough firepower to keep us busy. Lead was flying over our heads as heavy as bees going after honey. I pulled my pistol out to be ready for the charge. Rather than having us charge as a unit, Father signaled for the furthest squad to go around and attack from our right flank. From my position behind a log, I fired a shot or two. With the brush between the Yankees and us, I couldn't be sure whether I hit anyone. Meanwhile I saw men fall on both sides of me. The reality of war was setting in. I knew there was no way I could desert, but I wished I had stayed home with Mother. As I let off a round, I wished I could be eating a piece of Elsie's peach pie. I would have given anything to be somewhere else.

As he fired a shot, Father commented, "Not what you thought it might be?"

"No, it isn't," I answered as I fired another round.

"This isn't getting us far." Father fired again. Lowering himself down out of sight, he added, "I think we need to charge them."

He gave the signal to charge. With him, I rose and began to attack. As I jumped over a log, I felt something hit my hat. I didn't feel any pain, so I didn't worry about it. I ran towards the enemy by running from tree to tree. After a little way, I began to worry as the trees began to thin out. I knew it wouldn't be long before we were face to face with the enemy.

"Ooh," I heard someone shout out in pain.

I quickly turned and saw it was Father. I asked him "Are you hit?"

"Just my stump, he replied." He held the end of it up as we ran.

As I dove for cover, I replied, "At least it didn't hit anything worth mentioning."

"True," he said as he fell beside me.

With all the bullets flying around us, I didn't think we were going far. As I thought about the two Yankees I had killed, I found it hard to shoot back. To save face I did fire off a shot or two.

After firing one round, I forgot to reload my rifle. I saw a Yankee stand up, leveled my rifle at him, and pulled the trigger. The hammer hit the percussion stem and nothing happened. The soldier fired a round at me and lay down. I had the feeling he knew he had gotten lucky.

"Ooh," I heard one of our soldiers cry out.

I dropped my rifle when I turned to look at him. I saw blood running down from his neck. I turned back to the fighting as I heard bullets flying around.

I heard a "thud." I knew from the sound it wasn't a bullet hitting a tree. At my left, I saw a soldier fall. He had a hole in his chest. I wanted to run to his aid but I knew there wasn't anything I could do. As I swallowed a lump in my throat, I was glad I wasn't the one bleeding to death.

"You have to load it first," Father said. As he lowered his rifle, he pulled out his pistol. He suggested, "At this range a pistol might be more effective. At least you won't have to reload after each shot."

"I think I'll try a percussion cap first. I don't want to double load it." I put a cap on the nipple and fired at a soldier below us. The soldier fell over, his blood spilling out.

"That was good thinking. Better to make sure than blow your gun up," Father said as he ducked down out of sight.

"And I hit him," I added.

"Be careful. I don't want to take you home with a blanket over you. Your mother wouldn't be happy with me," he said as he reloaded his rifle.

I had noticed how dirty everyone was now. The men's faces were covered with dirt and sweat. There was no comparison with the clean uniforms I had seen in the camp when I first got there and at the beginning of this battle. I knew I had to be as dirty as the other men were, and I thought of Ida—how she wouldn't want anything to do with me, as dirty and smelly as I was. The air was filled with gun smoke, making it difficult to see and breathe. The smell of blood was nauseating. At one point, I was coughing so hard I couldn't breathe. If anyone was to ask it wasn't a place I would suggest being.

"Good idea" and I felt like vomiting.

We got up and headed towards the enemy. With only six shots left, I tried to pick my targets carefully. Luckily for us, their shooting wasn't as accurate as their weapons. In practice, I had tried shooting at different targets at a distance and had found my success was due more to luck than to my ability, but if my target was less than fifty yards away, I didn't have any problem hitting it. We finally overpowered the Yankees and brought back the captives for deposit in the prisoner camp.

A few days later, I went into Father's tent to talk to him. Saying hello when I entered, I waited for him to say something, but he didn't. I walked over to him. He was lying on his cot, hot and soaked in sweat. His face was pale so I asked, "What's wrong?"

"My stump," he muttered, obviously in pain. He raised the bare stump for me to see. I had seen it many times, but now it looked terrible being bright red and swollen.

"Have you seen the surgeon?" I asked. I figured it was the wound received in our recent skirmish, and I wondered why there wasn't any salve or a bandage on it. Why had nothing been done for him?

"No," he answered with a groan. He added, "I haven't had any problem with it until this morning." Again, he groaned and turned over, away from me.

"I'll get the surgeon," I told him. I couldn't remember Father ever having been sick, and I was scared to see him lying there sweating and his face as pale as it was. I had an idea it was from what I thought was an infection of the wound. I couldn't do anything but pray he wouldn't die before I got back.

I made my way towards the surgeon's tent through mud that was so deep that I was unable to run. I decided to cut across the parade grounds to save some steps.

"Corporal," a soldier called out.

"Yes, sir," I said as I looked around and didn't see anyone. I decided that he was talking to someone else and went on my way.

"Corporal Buchanan, hold up," the voice called out again.

I turned and saw a sergeant of Mr. Lee's guards running towards me. I stopped and waited for him to catch up. When he was a few steps away, I said. "Yes, sir. What can I do for you?"

"Mr. Davis and Mr. Lee want to see you," he said.

"I have to see the surgeon first. My father is suffering from a bad fever," I told him as I began to walk away.

"I'll get the surgeon. You had better see Mr. Davis…He was insistent that you come as soon as I found you." He motioned for me to go to Mr. Lee's tent.

"Tell the surgeon it's an emergency," I said as he started running. I didn't want to neglect Father but I had to answer the call of our President. On my way over there, I looked around to see if the surgeon was on his way, but I got to Mr. Lee's tent before the surgeon got to Father.

"Go right in. They're expecting you." The guard told me as he held the tent flaps open.

As I walked into the tent Mr. Davis asked, "Come in, Mr. Buchanan. Or should I call you Corporal?"

"You could call him Edgar and he wouldn't mind," Mr. Lee offered. With that, he motioned for me to join them at a table.

"As you might have guessed…," Mr. Davis began. He looked at Mr. Lee. Turning back to me, he added, "I might let Robert tell you."

"Excuse me, gentlemen…," a sergeant interrupted.

Mr. Lee replied, "Yes, Sergeant?"

"A message for the corporal" he answered.

"Make it short, Sergeant. We have some important business to discuss," Mr. Davis shouted at the Sergeant.

I was surprised hearing Mr. Davis raise his voice to the sergeant. I had never seen him get upset with anyone. When at our house or the Marshes' he was firm but always in control. With this passing thought, I waited for the Sergeant's message.

"The Surgeon wanted me to tell the corporal that his father will be all right. The Surgeon does suggest he go home to recuperate, since it's so close," the Sergeant told me.

Mr. Lee asked, "What's wrong with your father?"

"A bullet nicked his stub in the skirmish after the battle of Bull Run... From what I gather, he didn't see the surgeon about it, and it's infected. When I checked in with him a half-hour ago he was burning up with fever."

"I guess we had better send him home," Mr. Lee replied.

"Johnson can take his place until he is fit to come back... Sergeant, take care of that this afternoon," Mr. Davis ordered.

"Yes, sir," the Sergeant answered, giving the two men a salute. With their acknowledgment, he left the tent to take care of Father.

"I'm sorry about your father and I know you would like to take him home. Unfortunately, we have another problem. I know your father thinks you can take care of yourself. With your father being ill..., I don't know," Mr. Lee said.

"What's this problem you're talking about?"

"I don't know how much your father has told you...but we weren't ready for this war," Mr. Davis said. Pausing as he looked at Mr. Lee, he added, "We don't have any money in the treasury. If we don't get some money soon, our troops will starve."

"But everyone is supporting them," I reminded them.

"We know, but it doesn't work that way," Mr. Lee responded.

I thought about that for a moment. "I see. If the army has all the horses, the farmers can't grow anything," I said. As I waited for his response, I thought of Mother and Elsie.

"That's right." Mr. Davis said. With his hand on my shoulder, he added, "As I see it, our people have a hard enough time taking care of themselves..."

I remembered Father visiting with a representative from France. "What about the French?"

"That takes time. Meanwhile they can't supply us with everything we need. We have to buy some of it," Mr. Davis explained.

"Such as meat, we have never raised enough beef to feed everyone in the South. All my life our beef has come from the North. Unlike your family, the people in towns and cities like Richmond don't raise their own meat," Mr. Lee said.

I hadn't realized how my life had been so different from everyone else's. I knew I didn't understand as much as I might have. On our plantation, we had raised nearly everything we needed. We never thought about having to go to a store for meat or vegetables. I realized that city people didn't have as good a life as we did or that we had before the war changed everything. Looking at the two men, I asked, "What can I do to help? Is there something you want me to do?"

"We need someone young to visit our supporters up north," Mr. Lee told me. It seemed he had more to say but didn't.

"Why did you pick me?" I asked him "I'm not old enough to do much...or am I?"

"You would do better than someone my age. I hope you know I trust you more than most. What I need for you to do is more important than fighting in a battlefield," Mr. Lee went on.

"Your father is the one who suggested you make the run," Mr. Davis added.

Feeling that I had no choice, I agreed to go. Mr. Lee opened a bundle full of clothes. One of the articles was a lined jacket similar to one I owned. The difference was that inside the upper half of the lining was a map and names. The map showed me the route I was to take and the people I should see along the way. With the map, there were notes written on cloth I was to pass along to those people.

"Even if they capture you, I doubt that anyone will open the lining and find any of this. It's far better than you carrying notes in your pocket that someone could find and read," Mr. Davis told me. He straightened out the jacket and handed it to me.

"As dirty and worn as it is, no one would want to check it out," I answered as I put it on.

"You should see your father off. Then later this afternoon Mr. Marsh and a few of his companies will help you on your way north," Mr. Lee told me. He added, "Here is some money to use on your trip."

"Thank you." I took a money belt from him, wondering how much was in it.

"Use it wisely," he smiled. "That Yankee money isn't worth much around here."

It surprised me that I hadn't seen Mr. Marsh. I asked, "No, sir. You were saying something about Mr. Marsh?"

"Like family around here," Mr. Davis replied with a smile.

"I'm not sure whether it's good to have so many friends and relatives around. Keeping them in one's thoughts can detour battle plans that could make a difference," Mr. Lee said. I got the feeling he wished I weren't there. With a shrug, he pointed to a chair and gave me a smile.

"Almost," I said, smiling to myself at the thought of Ida. I was looking forward to seeing Mr. Marsh and then writing Ida about seeing him. Thinking about her, I realized it had been a few days since I had written to her or Mother. Now that Father was going home, he could at least tell her how I was doing. Not waiting for either man to say more I started to leave. As I pushed the flap open, I told them, "I'll do my best."

"I'm sure you will. Give your father our best," Mr. Davis said

"Remember, the Confederacy is counting on you" Mr. Lee reminded me. Then looking up from his map, he added, "Leave your pistol, holster and uniform here. I wouldn't want them to catch you with them."

"Yes, sir, and I promise to do my best." I headed towards Father's tent. I began to worry again about Father and if he would be alright.

I had heard stories of men dying from a simple gunshot wound. Infections were killing men off as fast as the miniballs were ripping limbs off. I was just a few feet from Mr. Lee's tent when I saw the Sergeant boarding the wagon. I knew he would take Father home. Rather than walking, I began to run as fast as I could in the mud. A couple of times I almost slipped but caught myself before I made it to the ground. I shouted out, "Wait a moment… I want to say good-bye."

"Don't worry…I'll wait," the Sergeant called back.

"Thanks," I shouted as I slowed down to a walk. I wished I could go home with Father but of course I couldn't. From what I saw on the map, I knew Mr. Marsh was going northeast. Where he was to leave me was only forty miles from our place. If I were to go home with Father, I could easily catch up with him. But I knew there was no use in thinking about that.

As I walked up to Father in the wagon he asked, "Did you accept the mission?"

"Yes," I said, without adding any explanation.

"That's good. At least you'll be out of the fighting for a while," he replied. He sounded relieved.

"I couldn't let you down. You are the one who recommended me," I reminded him.

I thought briefly about what some of the notes said.

"Don't take any chances," he warned me.

"And you tell Mother I'm sorry for leaving as I did. Also tell her I…," I began to say.

"Don't worry, she knows you love her," he added as he took my hand and gave it a squeeze.

"Oh, if you see Ida, tell her hello and that I'm thinking of her."

"I understand. After all, you're Ida's little Edgar," he replied with a smile.

"That's enough of that. And tell her I'll write soon," I told him with a laugh. I wished I could see her on my trip north.

"I had better get going," the Sergeant said.

"Get well, and I'll see you when I get back," I told Father, still wishing I could go along. I knew I could be there in less than an hour, then thirty minutes back if I rode alone. The only problem with the idea was Mother. I knew she would hold me up for a while so I wouldn't get back until evening. So, I said. "Take him home, Sergeant."

"We are on our way," he said as he snapped the reins.

"Take care of yourself, Corporal," Father said as the wagon pulled away.

Reaching up to feel my stripes, I felt a smile form on my face. I had forgotten all about my promotion or mentioning it to Father. Since he referred to me as "Corporal," I knew he had seen my stripes or had known about my promotion. I waved good-bye.

It Doesn't Get Any Better

U nlike most, fighting the battles of this war hasn't been that much of my life. The only way I can cope is by writing. Without thinking, I'm continuing to make entries in my diary:

I stood there watching Father's wagon carry him home and felt jealous. As the wagon grew smaller, the more I wished I were going with him. Then trying to dismiss that thought, I looked around to find Major Marsh's outfit and felt something hit the back of my leg. I shouted out, "What the…"

"Excuse me, Master," a colored water boy replied. He looked as if he expected me to kill him.

"No problem," I said as I brushed off some of the water. I looked up at him and added, "I'm not your master. We are both soldiers now. Just call me Corporal."

"Yes, Master… Corporal," he uttered as he ran off, spilling water as he went.

Feeling the jacket on me, I knew he didn't know my rank. Inside my jacket, I was feeling a little warm. Unlike him, I knew its importance but I still would have liked to take it off. Seeing everyone else running around in their shirt sleeves made me feel warmer.

Once again I thought about how everything had changed. I remembered coming to Richmond and how it had never before looked like it had for the past month. The South had changed dramatically over the previous few weeks. All the clean tents and uniforms now showed the scars of war. There were more of my fellow soldiers with clean bandaged limbs and heads. The earlier look of hope on the faces of my fellow soldiers had faded, and they looked tired and fed up with everything. Whenever anyone looked at me, I could see the question of "Why are we here?" in his eyes. Even though I hadn't seen as many battles as some, I was asking the same question.

"Don't let it get away from you," someone shouted to one side of me.

Turning to see what was going on; I saw two soldiers were chasing a chicken. Trying to escape from them, the chicken ran under a stool and through the tent ropes. Watching the two men tripping over themselves, I found myself rooting for the poor bird. When a colored man joined in the chase, the bird lost the battle. I knew what was coming next and understood why. Nevertheless, I felt sorry for the bird after its bold effort to escape the frying pan, but I also knew the men had to eat.

The colored man that caught the bird handed it to one of the soldiers. The soldier took it and picked up a hatchet at the same time. He took the bird over to a stump and chopped its head off. It flopped around on the ground, then lay still. No one said anything, but I had a feeling supplies were short.

"Now we can have a decent meal," one soldier announced with a look of pride.

"We have to pluck it first," another reminded him.

"What do I know about cooking," the first said with a laugh.

Everywhere I looked someone was doing some chores, and the injured were sitting around idle. The blacksmiths were making new rims for wagon wheels. Other men were cleaning out pots from cooked meals. Others were washing clothes or mess kits and others were brushing their horses down. In the background, men were firing cannons. The biggest annoyance was the men on horseback and in wagons coming and going. They didn't seem to care whether they ran over you or not. As with the men on the parade ground, they had commands to fulfill and nothing would stop them.

"Watch out," a wagon driver shouted out.

"Yip," a dog cried out in pain. It appeared a wagon had hit him or had run over his tail.

"Got to watch what's going on. Otherwise, you might lose your tail," I told the poor dog.

A couple of cannons passed by making enough noise to make one think a herd of horses was running through the city. The noise made it difficult to hear your own voice.

"That's Mr. Lee's dog," a passing soldier told me.

"Oh," I said. I found the information interesting. I didn't remember hearing Mr. Lee talk about a dog, but then I had never been to his home. As with everything else in my life right then, I was beginning to realize I didn't know everything.

If that wasn't bad enough my arm was sore from swatting flies.

A soldier sitting beside a tree asked, "You're not going to eat that, are you?"

"I don't think so," I told him as another fly buzzed my head. I wished someone would move the camp's garbage a little further away.

"It seems everyone is killing whatever they can to get a meal," he said.

"That's what I hear," I replied as I continued to look around. I knew from what Mr. Lee had said that Major Marsh was around here somewhere. If not, he wasn't far off. No matter what, I was to wait for him.

Off to my left I saw something that made me feel sad. What had once been a school was now a stockade. Someone told me the building was holding Yankee prisoners. As I looked at the building, I wondered how many of my relatives were inside.

A soldier asked, "Up to a game of baseball, Edgar?"

"Don't think so…I'm waiting for Major Marsh," I told him.

"You could always play for the other team," he suggested. With a smile he added, "We're willing to win any way we can."

"No thanks, maybe another time," I answered. As he walked away from me, I thought of Ida, and the memory of the day we had sat talking when we watched the others play a game of baseball. I was glad I hadn't gone down and played with the others. Feeling her hand in mine, listening to her was better than playing some silly game.

As I looked around, I could see a cannon across the parade field from me. I had to smile for the cannon didn't look threatening sitting there with no one around it. The most noticeable part of it were the wheels; they almost blocked my view of the barrel itself. It was the big carriage wheels and the toolbox on the rear that made the cannon look tame to me, while the smaller cannons with a single axle looked menacing. Someone had told me that when soldiers fired a cannonball at a Navy vessel, they would heat the cannonball first. By doing this, on a direct hit, the hot cannonball would start a fire. I knew from experience that the ball by itself was bad enough, for I had seen many buildings torn apart by cannon shot. I also knew what it could do to a person when it hit anywhere near them.

"Are you Corporal Buchanan?" a Lieutenant asked as he walked up to me. With a smile, he added, "Without a uniform it's hard to tell."

"Yes, sir... Sorry about being out of uniform sir," I replied as I came to attention.

"I understand... Major Marsh is waiting for you...Once you are ready to move out, we'll be on our way," he told me.

"Yes, sir," I said. I saluted him and headed for the stables.

"I'll wait for you here," he told me as he returned my salute.

"Yes, sir," I said. I ran to the stable area. Nearly out of breath, I wondered if I would make it.

A colored boy called to me, "Your horse, Master?"

"Yes," I called back. I wanted to remind him that he didn't have to call me master, but I was so exhausted I didn't care. Bent over with my hands on my knees I watched him grab my horse. Then with perfect efficiency, he took my saddle and bridle down. Puzzled, I wondered how he knew which was my gear, then I remembered that mine probably was the only set with "US" stamped on it rather than "CSA." I doubted that there were too many soldiers in the Confederate Army had a Union saddle and bridle. Breathing easier I went on into the stable smiling.

"Once I get my horse and the Lieutenant's… I'll be ready," the colored boy said as he handed me the reins of my horse.

"What do you mean…, your horse?" I asked him as I took the reins. I was more than a little confused. I could understand him getting my horse and the Lieutenant's but not one for himself. It didn't make any sense but I figured it wasn't up to me to worry about it.

"Yes, sir" he said. Meanwhile he slipped reins around the head of another horse. He added, "We're going north together."

"No one said anyone was going with me" I replied with interest. I walked outside to wait for him. I wondered if he was even able to mount a horse. I wasn't that tall myself but he was half my height. He didn't even have Pan Face's bushy hair to give him some height. I had to smile, for his height didn't seem to matter, he could handle horses.

He hadn't said anything and I guessed there wasn't much he could say. With Mr. Davis and Mr. Lee in charge, he was like me, just a soldier doing a job. I figured Major Marsh would fill me in. If they wanted me to have company, it was all right with me. I just wondered why Mr. Davis or Mr. Lee hadn't said anything in the tent. Still surprised I watched the little colored boy work at saddling the two horses. Then smiling he brought the two horses out to where I was.

"I guess I'm ready," he announced as he brought out the two horses. He then asked, "You have more than just your horse?"

"Up by the Lieutenant," I told him.

He asked, "Then you're ready other than that?"

"Guess so," I replied as I gave the reins a tug. Noticing his smile as we walked our horses towards the Lieutenant I asked him, "What's your name?"

"Freddy…Freddy Rein," he announced proudly.

"Did you say Freddy Rein?" I asked him not being sure I had heard him correctly. The colored people I knew only had one name. I had never heard of any that had two names and I found it interesting.

"Yes… Now that I'm free, I thought I would take on a second name," he answered. Then with the big smile, showing teeth from one side of his face to the other he added, "Working with horses all my life what better name than Rein?"

"Sounds like a good name to me," I answered. I resisted the impulse to laugh, though I liked the way he thought. Now with his freedom, I didn't see any reason why he couldn't take any name he liked. My interest was more in what part of the trip north he would play.

I was moving my shoulders around because the jacket just didn't feel right. I could feel the notes sewn on the shoulders and the map hanging down my back.

I heard someone playing a song on a mouth harp, some distance away. Though I couldn't make out the song, it sounded sad. The only cheerful thing around the camp was a few dogs playing with each other.

"This is some trip," Freddy said, breaking my train of thought.

"I guess it is," I said. "I'm just curious, but why do I need you to go on the trip?"

"I know the way," he answered.

"I know the way…That's all you have to say?" I asked. I was also wondering what he knew that I didn't as well as why two people as young as we were be chosen for the mission? However, since I was sixteen now, I figured I was a man, and he probably he felt he was a man too. It bothered me they would want someone to escort me. Didn't they trust me to get the job done?

Turning back to him, I asked again, "That's all you have to say?"

Giving me a funny look, he answered, "It's not for me to say."

"So you're ready," the Lieutenant said as we walked up to him. Taking the reins, he added, "Let's get going."

"Let me get my belongings…and then I'll be ready," I said as I reached down to pick up my bundle. There wasn't much inside but a little food and a blanket. Without my pistol and uniform, there wasn't much to stow on my saddle.

I sensed a feeling of hesitation in Freddy but he followed my lead as I mounted my horse. I didn't know about Freddy, but I had expected to meet Mr. Marsh in camp. The way it looked, we were to ride out and meet him. It didn't upset me, just surprised me. I said to the Lieutenant, "I take it Major Marsh isn't in camp."

"No," the Lieutenant answered. He spurred his horse and rode out ahead of us.

Watching him leave us behind, I spurred my horse to catch up with him. Protocol dictated that due to my rank Freddy and I should follow rather than ride alongside. When I got within a horse length, I reined my horse back. It pleased me to see, Freddy follow my example. I would have felt funny if he had stayed behind us. Watching the Lieutenant, I admired the way the Lieutenant sat as he rode along. He rode as my father did, erect in the saddle as if he owned the world.

Riding in silence, I looked over at Freddy. As I looked at him I thought of Raymond and Pan Face and felt lonely. I wondered where Pan Face and his grandfather were living. I wished I could tell Pan Face about that Yankee killing Raymond. I knew he would have a hard time accepting the idea Raymond was dead. I also wished I could see Ida for a moment or two. Just the thought of her usually brought a smile to my face.

After riding for half an hour or so I was getting a little sore in places I didn't know I had. I began to wonder if we would ever find the Major. Just then the Lieutenant signaled for us to leave the road. Scanning the area as I followed him I saw some banners through the trees. I had a feeling the banners belonged to Yankees.

"Get down and keep your horses quiet," the Lieutenant said as he dismounted.

"Yes, sir," I replied, as I dismounted and grabbed the muzzle of my horse. I prayed he wouldn't let out a sound. I saw Freddy muzzle his horse and he looked scared. I wondered whether I looked as scared as he did. I couldn't see anything in the direction of the Yankee banners. From behind the clump of bushes where we were hiding, we had difficulty seeing.

"We'll wait a while and let them go on past us," the Lieutenant told us in a hushed voice.

"Since you're the only one armed, it might be wise," agreeing with him. From the sound of the horses, we knew some soldiers were passing by. I was worried more about hiding where we were than I had been at Bull Run. If any of them saw us, we were as good as dead. We were all stroking our horses' noses praying they wouldn't neigh or whinny, or even snort.

"That was close," the Lieutenant said as the last horse was out of ear shot.

"I'm worried about not making it to my seventeenth birthday," I confessed.

"If I understand what you two will be doing…, you're apt to see more action," the Lieutenant warned me. "We've lost enough time… The Major isn't too much further north."

"I wonder if a company of Yankees have attacked them," I said as I got onto my horse.

"You never know," the Lieutenant said as he rode off.

"I believe they could talk me into going back to the stables," Freddy said with a half grin.

"Understandable." I told him riding off to catch up with the Lieutenant. Then behind us, I heard gunshots. It was unlikely they were firing at us, but we still spurred our horses. Looking down at my empty scabbard, I wondered what had happened to my rifle. I wouldn't have minded as much if it weren't for the fact that it was Father's. I knew the Remington was far better than the ones most of our soldiers were carrying.

"Freddy… what happened to my rifle? I asked. "I know it's my fault for leaving it in my scabbard, but I didn't think anyone would take it."

"Mr. Lee asked me to bring it to him," Freddy answered.

"Then it's safe," I answered. He gave me a look that said, "And you doubt that?"

I called up to the Lieutenant, "Just in case something happens to you, where are we meeting Major Marsh?"

He answered, "Gain Mill…Do you know where that is?"

"If he doesn't I do," Freddy said.

"I know about where it is…I would think it would be on the map I have," I confessed to him.

"Good, then if anything does happen to me, you might find him," he answered with a laugh.

We then turned and headed east. In that direction I doubted that Major Marsh had met with the Yankees we had seen.

"I'm glad he thinks it's funny," I told Freddy as we rode off.

Continuing to ride at a moderate pace, I had plenty of time to think and I wondered once again whether I wanted any part of this war. I didn't like what I had heard about our soldiers. I had heard reports of soldiers burning down farms and fields, not those of northerners but of our own people. There were stories of men molesting the women on the same farms. It seemed these were the spoils of war. If this was what I was fighting for, I didn't want any part of it. I had always considered my fellow Southerners to be honorable, and I didn't see any honor in these kinds of actions. It made us seem no better than the northerners.

"I see them just ahead," the Lieutenant announced.

"Good… I want to get going and get back so I can see my father," I said under my breath.

"You know it will probably be a few months before you'll see him, don't you?" Freddy said as we neared the camp.

"What…? I hadn't thought about that." I confessed, speaking a little louder than I should have.

"Afraid so," he said giving me a worried look. As we stopped, he added, "Even if we could do everything in the open, it would take a while."

"I guess I should have thought about it before I agreed to the mission," I told him.

"Might have been a good idea, though there is one good thing about it," he told me.

"What's that?" I asked. I thought I knew what his answer might be. I could hear him say, "You'll be with me."

"You won't have to worry about being in any battles," he answered as he got off his horse.

As I dismounted, I asked, "Getting caught and shot by one man or a hundred…what's the difference?"

"I'll keep you safe" he assured me.

"And who'll keep you safe?" was my response.

"You, Master," he replied with a smile.

"I feel so much better." I answered not feeling like smiling. I knew that Freddy was just trying to be funny. But having seen Father carried off, as I had a few hours before; I didn't feel like laughing. I wanted to make sure he would be all right. In truth, I also knew I was thinking of a visit to him as an opportunity to see Ida.

"Corporal," the Lieutenant called to me.

"Yes, sir," I answered as I walked towards him.

"I'm sure the Major is waiting to see you," he told me.

"Yes, sir," I returned as I followed him. It was hard to believe the Major was waiting just for me. He had to have more important concerns than any that involved me. I figured Mr. Davis had enlisted his help somehow.

A soldier asked as I walked past him, "What's new…? Have you heard any news?

"I haven't heard anything," I answered.

"Do you know Jim Antrim…? Is he all right?" another shouted.

"Sorry, but I don't know him," I shouted back to him.

With a grin another asked, "How are the girls in Richmond? Have they missed me?"

"They don't even know you're gone," Freddy said.

"Shut up, Darky," the soldier answered.

"You had better shut your mouth, or I'll shut it for you." I told him raising my voice. I didn't give Freddy a chance to say anything. I decided I would take care of them because I didn't like their attitude or the term they used. Father had taught me to show respect to everyone.

"I doubt if any women would want me right now," Freddy confessed.

"I said to shut up," the Lieutenant shouted back to the soldier.

"If the two of you don't shut up, I'll sit on you," the Lieutenant shouted at Freddy and me.

"I'll have you know there are more women out there that want me…than you," the soldier shouted at us.

"I would love to see it," Freddy said, just loud enough for me to hear him.

"Me too… That guy is three times the size of the Lieutenant," I added with a laugh. As we walked along, I added, "I agree with you… I doubt any woman would miss him."

"Unless they are blind," Freddy said.

It wasn't long before we were looking for something else of interest. When the Lieutenant entered a tent with a flag flying over it, I knew we had reached Major Marsh's tent.

"I'll take your horses," a soldier said greeting us.

"Thank you," Freddy and I answered.

"Good afternoon, Edgar, I mean Corporal. It's hard to break old habits," Major Marsh said with a laugh. Then he returned my salute and nodded to Freddy. Sitting down he suggested us to do the same. He also motioned for the Lieutenant to leave adding, "Thank you, Lieutenant Crawford."

"Yes, sir," the Lieutenant answered with a salute, and left the tent.

"A good man" the Major said as the tent flap closed behind the Lieutenant. Turning to me, he asked, "I take it Robert filled you in?"

"You mean Mr. Lee…Everything other than telling me about Freddy here," I answered.

"I hate this when friends hold positions like he does. I have a feeling it won't be long before he'll be the commander of the entire Confederate forces," he told us.

He explained why Freddy was part of my party. Because Freddy was so small, they didn't think I would want to take him. There was the fact, that he had many contacts with the Underground Railroad that might be useful. If people connected to the Underground Railroad were still around, it would make it easier for us to move about for the first half of my trip. My concern was that having another person with me would make it easier for us to be spotted. I held onto my dream of going home to Ida in one piece and I didn't want to take any chances.

After hearing what the Major had to say, I told Freddy, "I guess I'll look after you if you look after me."

"You'll see…it'll work out all right. I promise you'll get home in one piece," Freddy returned.

"I'm not sure if Ida could handle two pieces of you," the Major added with a smile.

"Have you seen her lately?" I asked. I sat up straighter waiting for his answer. Down deep, I was waiting to hear her anxious to see me. Knowing she cared meant more to me than I wanted to admit.

"No…I haven't been close enough to stop by," he answered sadly. As he got up he added, "I miss her more and more each day. I know joining was something I had to do but…"

"They understand," I told him not knowing what else to say. Having grown up with them, I knew his wife and daughter meant a lot to him, but of course he felt a strong need to stand up to the North. Like Father, he was willing to give up his life for his beliefs.

"Well, I'll see them soon I hope. Right now, we have to get ready to move in the morning. I want the two of you to get a good night's sleep. It might be the last chance you'll get for a while," he told us as he stood up.

"Thank you sir…We'll do our best," I answered as I gave him a salute.

After returning my salute, he asked, "By the way, how's your father doing?"

I filled him in and we left his tent. Lieutenant Crawford met us outside and showed us where to take our horses. From there he took us to a tent set up just for the two of us. It wasn't large but it did keep us out of the weather. After getting something to eat, we went back to the tent to get some sleep.

The Lieutenant went back with us and told us "We'll be leaving at first light."

"That's all right with me," I assured him, I was ready. I was almost looking forward to it, since I hadn't been in a real battle.

"I don't know if you know it, but there are Yankee's everywhere," he warned us.

"I've heard that Sherman is on a march and no one is sure where he's headed," I said.

"There's even talk that Mr. Davis is planning on leaving the city," Freddy said.

"I've heard the same rumor," he said.

"We'll be careful," I assured him. As I thought about taking off again I remembered my other missions. In taking them on as others had, I found blowing up and burning bridges wasn't as easy as it might sound. It wasn't just the climbing the trestles to set the charges there was the dodging the enemy. I have to say it got exciting when we blew up a train on one trip. We came upon a company of Yankee's that chased us almost all of the way back to Richmond.

"I'll be ready," Freddy told him.

"We had better get some sleep…what little we can get," the Lieutenant suggested.

Our night's sleep that night was short but that was all right with me. I was ready to go before anyone else was up. As soon as I was awake, I woke Freddy. We rolled our bedrolls up and set them outside the tent.

Since the camp was breaking up, we began taking our tent down. As I began pulling tent pegs, I heard someone approach us. I looked up and saw it was Lieutenant Crawford coming towards us.

"I see you're ready to go…No need to worry about the tent, someone else will get it," the Lieutenant said.

"We almost have it done, so we might as well finish," Freddy told him as he began to fold it.

"It's up to you. The cook has some coffee and mush on if you're interested," he told us. Then as he turned to leave, he added, "We should be leaving soon."

"We're ready" I assured him. I noticed that a blanket of fog was covering the area, and a chill ran through my body. I turned to Freddy and told him, "I doubt the mush is as good as our cook Elsie's, but I could use some coffee. This fog is giving me a chill."

"Coffee sounds good," Freddy answered. He looked out at the dense fog. He said, "at least the Yankees won't be able to see us."

"And we won't be able to see them, either" I reminded him. It sounded good to travel through fog but it also had its bad side. You couldn't move that fast because you can't see the terrain, and when the enemy is in the area you can't see him. I had already learned it was better to see your enemy before you engage him. Finding yourself in the middle of the enemy because of fog wasn't a good idea.

"I wouldn't know… I've never been in a battle before," Freddy said.

"Here's hoping you never will be," I told him. I laughed to myself. Here I was sounding like an expert when I had only been in a few skirmishes. Even so, I had seen a few men maimed and die.

We rode along in silence for a while.

For those who have not been to war, it's hard to explain what it's like. One way I can describe it is that it's like imagining you walk over to your mother, thinking she's asleep. You touch her hand and her arm falls off. On the battlefield, it's something you come to expect. I had had that happen to me once. A soldier was lying on a litter and I went over to comfort him, only to find that he had been dead before they took him off the battlefield.

"I hate this fog," Freddy said, breaking the silence.

We had been riding for an hour at a snail's pace. I was bored looking into the fog. "Me, too," I answered.

Freddy didn't say any more about it. I then asked, "Why?"

"I'm used to seeing the sky no matter if it's cloudy or clear. I can look at the sky and watch the birds fly over, and look around me to see the trees and the land, and watch the leaves change color in the fall. This fog is nothing but white and its boring," he answered.

"I know what you mean." I was praying as Freddy was for at least a touch of blue in the sky. The fog was so wet that I could almost taste it, and it was getting to be too much. I asked, "How much further do you think it is, and how much longer do you think it will take to get there?"

"At this pace, another month if we're lucky," he said, sounding irritated.

"You could have lied… and said another hour," I said.

"Tell me the next time you want me to lie," he told me.

Before we went too much further a shot rang out. Everyone in the march stood up in his saddle looking for the sniper. I wasn't sure but I doubted that anyone saw him. Then I began to worry that a sniper might shoot at me.

Freddy asked, "See anyone?"

"Not in this fog," I answered as we continued to ride along. I heard another shot and thought I saw Major Marsh fall from his saddle. Knowing it wasn't proper, I broke ranks anyway and rode ahead to see if it was true.

Freddy shouted out to me "What's wrong?"

"The Major…" I shouted. As I dodged everyone, I could hear the sound of shooting, it was coming from the general direction of the sniper. I didn't know whether anyone had hit the sniper or not, but everyone was trying.

It wasn't hard to find where the sniper's victim had fallen. Everyone around had dismounted to look after the downed man. I pushed part way through the crowd, but still couldn't see if it was the Major or not. All I knew was that he wasn't anywhere to be seen.

With everyone around the wounded man, I shouted out, "Is it the Major?"

"Yes," a quiet voice answered.

"Let me through" I demanded. Before anyone could make room for me, I asked, "Will he make it?"

"I don't know," a soldier answered.

"I'm an old friend of his... Let me through," I shouted out. My worst fear drove me through two rows of soldiers to get to him. Major Marsh's chest was a mass of blood. I didn't have to be a surgeon to know that if he were still alive, he wouldn't be for long. I knelt down and asked a stupid question, "How are you doing?"

"I doubt if...I'll make it," he uttered as he coughed up blood.

"Don't say that," I said as I felt tears rolling down my cheek.

He could barely answer. "I know the truth...I can feel... death... around us" he answered with a cough. With his eyes closing, he uttered, "Tell Annabelle and Ida...I love them."

"I will," I promised. The words just out of my mouth I knew they lay on deaf ears. His expression and his eyes went blank telling me, but he probably didn't hear. He was dead. I felt as if a part of me had died right there in front of me. I took a silent vow to get even with the North for his death, even if it meant killing every Yankee in the country. My only fear was who would break the terrible news to his wife and Ida? For as close as the three of them were, I knew this would be hard for them to accept.

"Pick the Major up... and get him back to Richmond," someone shouted out. Then the same voice added, "We had better get behind some protection. It's hard to say where the sniper is."

"There's nothing you can do for him now... You had better get your horse and head for safety," the familiar voice of the Lieutenant Crawford suggested.

Wiping my eyes, I looked up at him and answered, "I guess not." As I stood up, I remembered the major and his wife giving Ida a bad time at one of the socials. He would be standing there in his white suit and hat, looking as if he owned the world. Then he would break into a smile as he gave his wife a hug. I hadn't ever thought what it might be like if he were to die.

I began to worry what was going to happen to Ida and her mother. I had heard stories of what happened to other women and their children while their men folk were away. Hardships weren't only on the battlefield; sometimes the ones left at home had to endure worse. I knew then I had to live up to my promise to Mr. Marsh.

I asked, "What should I do now?"

"Captain Taylor will get the two of you to your destination… The Major told me everything about you and your mission…He was afraid this might happen," he answered. He motioned for everyone to move to the side of the road.

I didn't say anything, but I was unprepared for this outcome. Out of the corner of my eye, I saw Freddy looking concerned. Everyone else had gotten out of sight. The only ones on the road were the Lieutenant, Freddy, and I. There wasn't any gunfire so I wasn't too worried. "I guess the trip is still on," I said to Freddy.

"I'm sorry about your friend," he said. We walked our horses off to the side of the road.

"I grew up thinking of him as being my second father… I knew he had been waiting for me to marry his daughter Ida," I told him. My voice began to tremble and I knew I was losing control.

"Yes, you have mentioned her once or twice" he replied.

"I wish I had a rifle or something… I would go after that sniper," I said as I scanned the area. The fog was lifting, but I still couldn't see much beyond the road. I watched as two men with a litter finally got to Mr. Marsh's body. They carefully lifted his lifeless body onto the litter and carried it off. I knew they would be taking him to a wagon for his last trip to Richmond. Mr. Marsh and my father were going home by wagon, but Father was alive.

For a second I thought about taking off and going to tell Ida and her mother about his death, but I knew I couldn't do that. Once again, the map and notes inside the lining of my jacket reminded me of my mission and I had to carry on.

"I wish I had a rifle to give you… I wouldn't know what to do with one," Freddy said.

"What?" I asked. The idea of going on this mission with someone who didn't know how to defend himself didn't make any sense. I wanted to laugh thinking about it as a birthday present to me. I had almost forgotten but this was my birthday and I was going on a mission with this ex-slave.

"I'm sorry," he replied.

Another shot rang out. It seemed the sniper was across the road somewhere, with everyone on our side firing back at him. I reached up to a soldier's horse and grabbed his rifle.

"What are you doing?" the soldier demanded.

"Watch," I shouted. Looking at his rifle, I asked, "Is it loaded?"

"Yes," he answered as he watched me closely.

With the rifle in my hands, I took off across the road. I didn't think about someone shooting me, I just ran. I couldn't think of anything other than finding the sniper.

As I entered the woods, I tried to get some clue about the sniper's whereabouts. He had to have a horse, a bedroll, or something to leave on the ground. I knew if I could find some of his gear, he had to be near.

I heard a horse somewhere nearby, but because of the thick fog I couldn't be sure where.

I stood waiting in case the horse whinnied again. As I waited, I kept an eye on the trees and bushes around me. The sniper fired another shot. I didn't see where it came from but I noticed some movement in a bush not far from me.

As I lifted the rifle to my shoulder, I realized I only had a single shot left. I muttered, "I won't have time to reload anyway."

For safety, I dropped to the ground and cocked the hammer. I figured that if anyone came out of the bush, they would have their pistol or rifle ready to fire. If I were standing, I'd be an easier target. Lying flat on the ground would give me a better chance for a good clean shot. I lay there for a minute and then began crawling a little closer to the bush, but moving across the ground wasn't that easy. I knew that getting closer might save my life. If the rifle pulled to the right or left at a distance was a concern. This was as important as the distance between the target and me. As I moved, I looked up into the trees wondering if the sniper was above and not in the bush. If so, I could be in serious trouble.

Suddenly I saw a head come out of the bush. Then I saw an outstretched arm on the ground, suggesting the sniper was crawling out of his hiding place. I shouted out, "Halt right there."

The sniper looked around bewildered. Then his mouth dropped and he answered, "What?"

"I said halt," I repeated. Then before he could do anything, I fired at his mouth. A soldier across the road began shooting in my direction. I shouted out at the top of my lungs, "Quit shooting…! I've got him."

I stayed down to be sure the soldier wasn't going to fire another shot. As I laid there I wondered if I had gotten the sniper. I tried to get up but a root had caught on one of my suspenders, keeping me pinned to the ground. I finally untangled myself and rolled over so I could get up. Lying on my side, I could see the sniper's body slumped half out of the bush. I knew I didn't have to check, for I knew he was dead.

I got up and headed toward the men across the road. Halfway there I heard another shot fired in my direction. Falling back to my knees I shouted, "Stop the shooting… the sniper is dead."

As I waited on my knees, I rehashed the day's events and found them hard to believe. I had found my father burning up with fever. Then not that many hours later, a sniper killed Mr. Marsh. Now I was in the woods with a dead body. I knew this was only a start of what was to come. I had to get out of the woods and on my way. Without any more thought, I got up hoping the shooting was over. Ignoring the body, I walked back to my group of soldiers.

Out on the road a voice asked, "What's going on here?"

"I took out the sniper…He's in the woods back there," I said. Then I held the rifle up and a soldier took it from me.

"Thanks," the soldier said.

"No…, thank you. Your rifle performed well," I told the soldier. Then I saw the Captain coming towards me.

"All right, tell me what's going on over here. I know the Major was a friend of yours but…," the Captain said walking up to me.

Everyone began coming out from behind trees and bushes and turned their attention to the Captain and me. As I was about to answer him, I saw Freddy pulling our two horses over to me.

In a hushed voice Freddy asked, "Did you get him?"

The Captain talked right over Freddy saying, "You had no business going in on your own."

"Sorry sir… I didn't want anyone else killed." I said not caring whether he approved or not.

"Don't you realize how important your mission is…? You, son, are the one who needs protection. The Confederacy may hang on what you do or don't do," he screamed at me. Then in a calmer voice he added, "I'm glad you got the Major's killer, but let us do that. Once you leave us, then you'll have to do whatever it takes to stay alive."

"He was a young lad not much older than the Corporal here… There wasn't any information on him," the Lieutenant told the Captain.

The Captain asked, "Did he have a uniform with him?"

"No, none on him or on his horse… All I can tell you is it looks like a Yankee rifle," the Lieutenant answered.

"Either a supporter… or someone just like the Corporal, traveling disguised," the Captain replied. Then looking at all of us, he ordered, "Saddle up."

Freddy handed the reins to me and asked, "What was it like?"

"The same as whenever you kill another human…sickening. The only difference this time was a feeling of revenge," I told him as I mounted my horse.

A soldier rode up alongside me. "Good work," he said. He gave me a slap on the back and continued down the road riding beside me.

"Thanks," I said. I wanted to tell him I appreciated his approval but I didn't think it mattered. The way everything was going, I wasn't sure if I wanted to go any further.

"Here," the same soldier said offering me a silver flask.

"No, thank you," I said. On my last trip, I had tasted what someone told me was the best whiskey available. I didn't like it the first time and I doubted that I would like it now. As he took the flask back, he took a swig with a nod of his head, indicating he thought it was good. I explained, "I never gained a taste for the stuff...but thanks for the offer."

"More for me then," he said with a laugh as he rode on ahead.

"He didn't offer me any," Freddy said with a laugh as he spurred his horse to get ahead of me.

"You can have my share," I shouted to him. I had nothing against alcohol, for I had seen my parents having a drink occasionally, and whiskey was always kept around for medicinal purposes. I just didn't like the taste of it.

It seemed to me the men were drinking more than I could remember a few months earlier. One soldier told me it made him forget what he saw in battle. I couldn't see how anything could take those memories away.

"If we make it back I'll buy you a barrel of the stuff," I told Freddy.

"I don't know what I'll do with it... I might sell it," he said.

"All I know is that I won't want it," I told him.

"Then I guess I will sell it," he replied.

"If we're where I think we are, we should only have another hour of riding," I told him. The slow pace we were moving at was tiring, but at least the fog was lifting, making it possible for us to see the enemy. I looked up to see if I could find the sun, and all I could see were clouds and more clouds.

"Now we might be able to pick up a little speed," Freddy said sounding hopeful.

I looked at the sky again and added, "If it doesn't start raining"

"That might be better than fog... I don't know of any soldiers that like fighting in the rain," he said.

"At least riding feels better than sleeping on the ground last night," I told him, feeling a knot in my back. I realized the knot might have been the result of crawling across the ground trying to get the sniper, but whatever the cause it was a little bothersome.

"Don't get too used to riding," he warned me.

"Why?" I asked. Then I remembered Mr. Lee telling me that most of the trip would be by wagon or train. I hadn't given it any thought until Freddy said he hadn't ridden before. With a shrug of disappointment, I added, "At least they could have left us some firearms."

"I'm not sure I like not having a horse or rifle. That's just what Captain Buchanan told me yesterday," he said.

"I know…we're supposed to be young kids that have nothing but each other. So I'm praying that having you is enough," I replied.

Just then, a raindrop hit me on the forehead. The rest of the morning, we rode in the rain, making the ride a gloomy one. I prayed Freddy was right that soldiers do not like fighting in the rain, because I had had enough killing for one day.

Messenger and Spy

It has been a while since I've made any entries in my diary. I haven't found anything worth writing about for some time. I have realized I'm not the man I once was, but now I have to make the following entries:

"Ooh… what happened to me?" I heard myself cry out. My head hurt like it had never hurt before. My heart was beating through my head, driving the pain out through my ears. It felt as if blood was running down the back of my neck. I lifted my hand to the back of my head and felt a lump as big as a boulder. I couldn't remember anything that could have caused my head to hurt as it did. In fact, right then it hurt too much to think. All I knew was that I wanted to scream but knew I couldn't if I wanted to stay alive. I slowly brought one hand to my head in hopes I could find out what was wrong. Touching it, I let out another, "Ooh."

I must have lost consciousness, for everything went black. As I regained my senses, I was lying on my back in an uncomfortable position. I couldn't get the strength up to change my position. I was just too weak to move. I tried to calm my breathing, I wondered what had happened. No matter how hard I tried, I couldn't remember anything and it made my head hurt to try. Vaguely I heard some commotion around me, and then I heard screams. Nothing I heard made any sense to me so I stayed motionless. It sounded as if the two sides in the war were still fighting.

Not being able to move, my thoughts went back to Freddy. Where was he? Since we were traveling together I knew something must have happened to him. I'm in poor condition, I wondered in what condition he was. I prayed that with some luck he might have gotten away. Even if he had something was wrong. I knew we weren't close yet, but I didn't think he would have abandoned me.

As I slowly became more alert, I knew I wasn't in the leaking barn anymore. How had I gotten here? I was in the open and there was a battle going on. I tried to open my eyes to confirm what I was thinking, but I didn't have the energy to get one eye open, let alone both. I finally stopped trying and waited for the throbbing in my head to stop.

I remembered that Freddy and I had left the troops a few days earlier in a torrential downpour that made the fog seem like nothing. I wasn't sure that we had found the station, but Freddy thought we had. The trouble was that no one had been there to meet us. It looked as if everyone had pulled out and taken everything with them. It was hard to believe they wouldn't have stayed a little longer, and I couldn't understand why.

"Since I know the way, them not being here isn't a problem," Freddy had assured me.

"I hope so," I told him as I curled up in my blanket in the barn. I asked, "How long do you think we should stay here? I don't see us staying more than another day."

"I agree…We have a good distance to cover," Freddy said. Then flipping up the bill of his wool cap he added, "At least we're not fighting."

A big puddle of rainwater was forming in front of us. "And if we stay here much longer we might drown," I remembered saying.

As I lay there with my eyes closed, more of my memory began coming back to me. I vaguely remember we had heard gunshots off in the distance. A faint picture came to my mind of Freddy's very worried look on his face. I felt lonely, hesitant and afraid because of not having a weapon to protect myself.

I remember Freddy asking, "What do you think is going on?"

"I'm afraid both of us know what's going on. I suspect one or the other raiding party is fighting it out," I said.

"We had better find a place to hide," he replied as he looked around the barn.

"There isn't any place here that's safe," I remembered telling him. As I got up, I added, "They've been known to burn buildings down for the fun of it."

"That's true…I guess we should get out of here then," he said as he headed for the barn door, carrying his bedroll.

I picked up my stuff rolled it up in my blanket and followed him. I opened the door slightly to make sure the way was clear. Still hearing the distant gunfire I realized that the enemy wasn't on the farm. It sounded as if the shooting was a mile or so away.

I told Freddy, "Their shots sure are echoing through the woods…, not close but closer than I would care for them to be. It might be wise to get out of here. I have a feeling, these soldiers are likely to burn the place down, and I don't want to find myself in this barn if they set it afire."

"Me neither," Freddy answered. He pushed me to one side and looked out. With a grin, he suggested, "Let's get out of here before they over run the place."

"I'm right behind you… You have a better idea where we're going than I do." I didn't know whether he had a better idea or not, but I knew any place would be better than where we were.

"We need to forget about the horses. They may bring us more trouble than they are worth. Only soldiers have horses and we don't want to attract any more attention than we need to," he reminded me. "And we'd be easier to spot, sitting up on our horses where they could see us over the brush making us a better target."

"Sounds like we're in for a fun trip," I said commenting as I listened to the gunfire in the distance.

Out of habit as we left the little farm, we crouched down running across the open areas. Soldiers around or not, we weren't taking any chances crossing the field. Because of this, a distance that should have taken two or three minutes took us fifteen. Part of the trouble was that we were also fighting the rain and the mud. If my memory serves me, as we made our way across the yard, I said, "Seems as if the farmer took everything, not even a rake or shovel laying around."

"Master Billings was that kind…He was tight with his money," Freddy replied as he climbed through a fence. Turning back to watch me he added, "It should be easier now."

"If it would ever stop raining it would be easier. I've almost fallen more times than the steps I have taken," I told him as I cleared the bottom bar of a fence. Then thinking about Billings I remember adding, "As clean as the place is I guess he moved by choice. If they forced him to leave, he wouldn't have been able to take all that he apparently took with him."

"I suspect he knew what was coming and got out, expecting to be burned out. I just wish he had waited for us," Freddy said as he pushed aside a tree branch.

The gunfire was getting louder with every step. We couldn't hear the echoing anymore, so we knew we were getting closer to the fighting. A couple of times I saw what looked like a flash from rifles. Cautiously, I grabbed Freddy's arm and motioned for him to lie low as I pointed where I thought the battle was.

As I waited for my head to quit throbbing, a memory came to mind that I resisted. The image kept coming, and the harder I tried to stop it; the more I knew I had to let it come.

"I think we might be able to get past them," Freddy said as he looked back at me.

"I don't know about that. I have a feeling they're coming this way," I answered.

We got to a grove of trees and saw blue and gray uniforms running behind us. An open field was ahead of us. We looked at each other, unsure what to do. Afraid someone might see us, we made our way across the field in silence and keeping low. The battle was on top of us by then, with the gunfire so loud my ears hurt. I knew there was a chance a stray mini ball might find its way to us. Soldiers from both sides were charging each other. Probably neither side had noticed us, and if they did see us, they would think we weren't a threat to them.

Nevertheless, I was so scared that I didn't take my eyes off Freddy. I kept within a footstep of him as we ran at full speed across the field. Looking at his back, I wondered how I had gotten myself into this mess. Then I remembered how it all began when I killed the Yankee who had shot Raymond.

"With any luck we should be safe in a few more steps," I remembered Freddy telling me in a hushed voice.

Suddenly I heard a shot fired not far away; and I could have sworn I heard someone behind me. As I stumbled and fell, I thought I saw Freddy fall face forward. I called out in a hushed voice, "Freddy… are you all right?"

When Freddy didn't answer, I slowly rolled to my left side. With my eyes barely open I saw smoke rising and men fighting in the distance. I rolled back onto my back and relaxed for a second. Then rolling over onto my right side, I saw a couple of bodies on the ground. It wasn't hard to pick out Freddy's black-skinned body. I asked again, "Freddy… are you all right?"

Still I got no answer and a lump formed in my throat. I crawled over to see if he was still alive. To get to him I had to crawl over a dead soldier and downed branches. Reaching out I grabbed Freddy's foot and shook it. There was no response. He was dead.

I lay there not knowing what to do. I was feeling as sick at Freddy's loss as I had at losing Raymond. Although I had only known him a few days, we had become friends. It was through him I was to start my mission up north. Now I had to make it on my own, if I could get myself out of this mess. I wasn't sure whether I could finish the mission. I had never been in such a position and I didn't have any idea what to do.

A twig snapping brought me back to reality. A Yankee about my age was taking aim at me. I quickly reached out and grabbed the rifle from the dead soldier. I hoped I could fire off a lucky shot and get him before he got me. As I picked the rifle up, I saw him and knew I had no chance. Then from behind me, I heard a shot and the Yankee fell back. As I relaxed, I said aloud, "Thank you Lord, for saving me."

"I've been, called many…" a familiar voice announced from behind me. Then before I could say anything, the same voice added, "I would get out of here and to safety if I were you."

The familiar voice belonged to, of all people, Pan Face.

"My exact thoughts, Pan Face, what on earth are you doing here?" I managed to get up and head toward his voice. Still stooped over, I struggled to move the branches to one side. I had to say it was rough going but I knew it wasn't as bad as getting a bullet to the head. As I saw him, I added with a smile, "You might not be the Lord, but He sent you."

"Get out of the line of sight," he told me. Then he offered his hand to help me through the brush. Seeing my old friend, for a moment I forgot my other troubles. He nodded towards the action, and when I looked in that direction I saw both sides swinging their rifles at each other, like clubs. Some were trying to reload as others were swinging. Men were falling right and left, and I couldn't tell who was winning or losing. Men fell down either dead or crippled. Both sides had downed soldiers covered with blood. Even worse were the screams of the dying mixed with the sounds of battle. I had seen similar sights before, but I knew I would never forget what I had just witnessed.

"It's good to see you," I said as I turned back to Pan Face. To my surprise he was wearing a makeshift Yankee uniform. I came close to laughing when I asked, "What's with the uniform?"

"It was either join the Yankees or starve…Grandpa and I couldn't find any work," he explained. Looking away from the battle, he added, "We had better get you out of here."

"Let's go…I was to be at the next station by now…wherever that is" I replied. I was a little out of breath and hurting. I began to run but my knees were wobbly. I stumbled a few times before they began to work properly. As we made our way to what I thought was safety, I told him "I have some bad news."

As he continued to run, he asked, "What's that?"

"Some Yankee killed Raymond," I told him. It had been a while back but suddenly when I said that, the memory of seeing him die came back so vividly that it seemed as if it had just happened. "But I got him with the first shot…He won't be killing any more of our friends."

Once he stopped, he asked, "Did Raymond suffer?"

"No," I told him. I didn't know for sure, because I hadn't hung around.

"That's good…I'll miss him. We shared a dream where we would marry on the old place and raise our children together…We used to talk about that a lot" he replied. Then laying his hand on my shoulder, he added, "I also have something I need to tell you."

A Yankee officer walked up to us. "What's going on…? Oh, so you caught one of them Rebels. Good job, Darky," he said. Behind him were two other soldiers watching every move. The officer told his two companions, "Might as well as put him in with the rest of them."

"Yes, Master… I do my best," Pan Face replied to the officer.

Then as a signal, he gave me a nod, I nodded back to him. He was obviously up to something and I needed to stay alert. As I waited, the soldiers continued to get closer.

"Yes, sir," one of the soldiers said as he headed for me.

For a moment, I took my eyes off Pan Face and the officer. I watched the soldier coming toward me. I felt I could take him as long as he didn't bring his rifle up. All I needed was the right opportunity. Then from the corner of my eye, I saw Pan Face move. He brought his rifle butt up catching the officer on the chin. Seeing the movement, I caught the soldier off guard slamming into his stomach. We fell down and as I rolled with him, I managed to grab his rifle. I fired at the other officer, dropping him where he stood. Turning on my knees, I saw, just as Pan Face caught the soldier who had come for me with a rifle butt to the head.

"Now we had really better get out of here," Pan Face said as he helped me up.

"I wish I could get out of these long johns," I said as I took his hand. I was sweating so badly in them I was beginning to itch.

He asked, "What was that?"

"Never mind," I answered.

As I began to get up, the officer also began to rise. I didn't want to waste a round, so I hit him in the head with the butt of the rifle. The rifle stock splintered in my hands as if someone had used it as a club more than once. Throwing the broken rifle down, I took off with Pan Face.

"That was close," I said as we tried to sneak off.

"Closer than I want to have happen again," he said. Just then, he motioned for me to get down. Turning back to me, he added, "We might have more trouble coming our way."

I took a quick peek and saw five more uniformed Yankees coming. I could tell three of them had seen a skirmish or two from the way they looked; they were sporting bandages and limping. I wasn't too worried about them, for they looked tired of it all. The other two looked as if they hadn't killed enough of us and were looking for more. At Pan Face's suggestion, I got down quietly hoping they hadn't seen us. I listened for their footsteps. At first they were coming towards us, and then they stopped for some reason. Luck was with me and they headed off in the other direction. Their change of direction gave me enough time to get out of sight. Both Pan Face and I smiled at the parting soldiers from our hiding place.

"Another close call," I told Pan Face.

"Again… too close" he replied. "What do you think? Should we get out of here before they come back?"

"I'm right behind you," I said as I began to follow him. Then for the next half hour or so, we crept from bush to tree and then to another bush. We finally made it to the top of a rise and looked back to the battlefield. I couldn't see much but it was more than I wanted to. I saw the flag bearers on both sides were down. They either were dead or wounded for neither man was moving. Most of those alive were on their knees swinging their rifles at each other. The entire scene was sickening so I turned my head away. I turned my attention back towards Pan Face and ran after him. No one seemed to notice us and we decided to stop for a break.

As we looked around, I said to him, "Swinging that rifle wasn't something father taught us."

"I learned it on my own," he answered, sounding a little sour.

"No matter, it worked," I commented, wondering what was bothering him.

"Let's rest for a while," he suggested as he sat down.

"Sounds like a good idea," I said, keeping a lookout for snipers.

"As long as you're standing don't let them catch you," he advised.

"I'll try not to…What was it you were about to tell me?" I asked as I looked towards the battlefield. It seemed the battle was over for there wasn't any more gunfire or screaming.

Once dusk fell, I knew they would take care of the carnage left behind. If both sides were to follow standard protocol, they would each pick up the dead and the wounded. The first time I saw this it shocked me. It seemed that moonlight meant an automatic truce. To my surprise, both sides put their rifles and pistols down and worked side by side taking care of their wounded. Many times, I wished night would fall and never let the sun come up again, for a permanent truce meant I could go home to my family and Ida.

I asked, "What was it you were about to tell me?"

"I don't know how to tell you," he said as he sat down. Removing his hat, he added, "You had better sit down yourself."

"I think I understand why you joined the Yankees," I replied as I sat down beside him. Then looking over at him, I added as I tried to grin, "I even forgive you."

"I wish it was that easy… What I have to tell you… I don't know how to put it into words. In fact I don't understand how or why it happened," he said as he looked off into the trees. He looked back at me with a tear in his eye he added, "Some of our men came back from a raid. In hearing their jubilation, I went over to see what had happened that had them so excited. I expected them to tell us about getting feed for their horses or stopping a train… What I heard was something I never expected."

I knew whatever he had to say wasn't easy to tell me. I couldn't remember ever seeing him cry, but he was on the verge of crying right then. He wanted to get it off his chest, but the enemy might be closing in on us. I reminded him, "We don't have long. I don't want our men to find and kill you, and I don't want a Yankee finding me and killing me."

"I know… It's just that it isn't that easy," he confessed. Then wiping his eyes he added, "You know how I feel about your folks…. Mama died giving birth to me and Pappy got killed, so your folks were like the parents I never had."

"What about my folks?" I yelled at him wanting him to hurry up and say what he had to say, but I wasn't sure I wanted to hear it.

He reached into his pocket and pulled out a piece of wood. Taking his knife he began to whittle slowly. Looking at me, he continued, "The men began telling us about their raid… then… they said they had taken care of some Rebels. They went on to say the Rebels would never see another battlefield. My ears perked up and I began to listen. It was then I began to get mad but there were too many of them for me to do anything."

"What are you talking about? What happened that made you so mad?" I asked him still worrying about my folks. Having grown up together, I had never seen him at a loss for words before. Ordinarily, he would make his point in just a few words, unlike Raymond who could beat around the bush better than anyone I knew of. In fact, Elsie many times gave up on getting answers from him. I said to him, "Get to the point before someone takes one of those triangular shaped bayonets to the two of us."

"I'm sorry…but I love all of you so much," he said looking down at his feet. Putting the piece of wood back into his pocket, he added, "They began describing a house with white columns. As they went on, I knew they were talking about the master's house… They described your mother and Elsie saying they saw them women taking a Rebel officer out of a wagon. They killed the driver first…Then they said…"

"They killed Father…? What about Mother?" I shouted as I stood up.

"From what I heard they had their way with the two women before…," he began to answer before I interrupted him again.

I wasn't sure what he meant at first. I asked, "They did what…? What do you mean that they had their way with the women?"

"You know what I mean…They…, uh, had their way," he answered.

I stood there, petrified, unable to speak. I wanted to ask him more but I was afraid of what he might answer. After a long pause, I asked, "What did they do with them then?"

"They tied the two of them…to the columns and either torched the place or blew it up…I'm not sure, because I wasn't close enough to hear exactly what they said amid all the laughing and cheering. For all I know they might have done both," he answered. The tone of his voice said he was glad to get it off his chest. He still held his head down and looked at his feet.

"They burned them after they tied them to the columns of the house?" I asked. I could hardly believe that a human being could do something like that. But maybe that's what war did to people by turning them into something not quite human. The shock of visualizing what they had done to the women was worse than just realizing that both of my parents were dead.

I sat down and I was getting mad as I sobbed. I had lost my whole life. My grief was so deep I couldn't put it into words.

Looking over at Pan Face I didn't know what to say. Everything I held dear to me was gone and I felt empty. Finally, I shouted out, to God or whoever might be listening, "Why? How could you take them away from me like that?"

Then some of my grief was replaced by anger. Fury! I had to get even.

"War is cruel," Pan Face replied in a hushed voice. Then hesitating he added, "You have to understand I'm not sure…I wasn't there to see it, but it sounded like home to me…If I had been there, I would have tried to stop it from happening."

"Not many places like ours in the area…. If you had been there, you would have gotten yourself killed," I said.

"I wouldn't have been able to just stand there doing nothing," he assured me.

"They didn't have to do that to Mother…She never did anyone any harm," I said, still weeping. To take advantage of my mother then tie her to a column to burn, was too much. I could see her tears and hear her screaming. Yes, I would get revenge! I didn't care about politics or anything that had caused the war. All I wanted to do was avenge my mother.

Someday, someone would pay for what those men did. I would serve them a plate of justice if I ever met them. If I found them, I would make them suffer as they made her suffer, one stroke at a time. I would cut them up into little pieces with my knife. Thinking of the men suffering at my hands made me feel a little better. It was one way to cope with the awful news Pan Face had brought.

A Yankee suddenly appeared. As he lowered his rifle at us, he asked, "What are you doing?"

I remember getting up quickly but nothing more. Vaguely, as if from a distance away, I heard Pan Face shouting out, "No more… That's enough; he's dead."

I realized I was still swinging and asked, "What?"

"He's dead. You don't need to beat him anymore," he answered.

I didn't understand what he was saying. Then feeling something between my legs I looked down on the ground and stared at the soldier in shock at what I had done. Seeing him covered with blood and seeing the flesh on his face torn made me sick, but I still felt some satisfaction. Soldiers like him had killed my mother and father. With that thought, I felt justified. I was just getting even for what they had done. I lifted up my hands they were covered with blood. Seeing, his condition and knowing I had done it to him, I got sick. Killing the soldier earlier had been bad enough, but this was horrible. I have to be honest I was glad I had done it but I did feel a touch of guilt for what I had done.

"We had better get you out of here," Pan Face suggested. Then backing away to let me up he added, "Someone must have heard you…

More soldiers will be here soon to check out what has been going on. If they're Confederate, it might be all right for you, but if they're Yankees, I don't know."

"I guess so," I said agreeing with him." The whole area was quiet. From the soldier I had just killed there was a scent of death. With a sickening feeling, I knew I wasn't through. I knew I had changed and I didn't care. I was saying on a personal level, "This was what happens in a war."

"Let's get going," Pan Face urged me.

"I'm coming," I said.

"You realize I have to go back. If I'm listed as a deserter, they might take it out on Grandpa," he warned me.

I was listening, but bloody my hands hurt so bad I didn't care what his problem was. The flesh was torn from my knuckles. Not thinking of what I was doing, I began shaking them as if I thought that would help. Following Pan Face, I pushed a tree branch to one side. As I grabbed it, a pine needle caught a knuckle and I let out an, "Ouch!"

"We'll take care of your hands once we get a little further away," Pan Face said as he continued to walk.

I knew he had told me about his grandfather earlier, but I couldn't remember what he had said. I asked, "What were you saying about your grandpa?"

"I'd like to go with you," he said. "I don't have any use for this war or understand it. I know I don't care for the way the northerners treat me either…but I have to say it's better than the way we had to live… We had gotten to where we were eating dog meat. Now Grandpa's doing odd jobs at the base camp and I'm out here fighting. I would hate to think what they would do to him if I deserted. All he has is me."

I understood what he was saying. I still wanted to tell him all of us had our problems. I assured him, "I understand…I wouldn't want to think what I would do if I had to eat dog meat. Still, I am thankful you saved me back there… In fact, twice you saved me."

"That's what a friend would do," he smiled. "Let's sit down and I'll bandage your hands."

"All right," I said as I looked at my hands. I looked at my coat and saw nothing but blood all over it, and my hands were stinging.

Without a word, Pan Face ripped his shirt off. Tearing it into strips, he began wrapping my hands. Looking up at me, he said, "I can tell them I was bandaging men with my shirt. It won't be a lie because I did bandage you."

I wasn't sure what he did was good or not. He had wrapped it so tight it hurt worse than before he touched it. I managed to smile and say, "Thanks."

"As I said, that's what a friend would do," he said as he tied off the strip on one hand. Continuing with the other hand, he asked, "What have you been doing…? From the way you're dressed, it doesn't look like you have joined the Confederate Army."

With difficulty, I told him the details about how Raymond had met his death and how I joined the Army. I told him what I had seen and done since I had last seen him. Hearing the story, we both cried at the loss of our friend. We discussed the senselessness of the war, the sadness of losing a friend like Raymond. Like me, he felt the war was nothing but an excuse to kill people and take away what everyone had worked all their life for. No one would benefit from the war, no matter who won. I didn't have any idea what losses the North was suffering and I didn't care. I only knew the South was losing more than it could gain. I couldn't see the South regaining what it had lost in even two or three lifetimes.

He asked, "Are you going on, or will you go back to Richmond? This mission of yours might not be possible."

"I guess I'll try to go on. Some of what I'm carrying might bring this all to an end," I told him. I figured the more support we got; the less the North would want to fight. I knew there was one note among the others that might end the war.

He asked, "What are the notes about?"

"I don't know about all of them but let's see. I have to remove my coat to get to them… Mr. Lee was afraid I might get caught and they would end up in the wrong hands," I answered. As I removed my coat, I added, "I think I need to wash the blood off."

As he watched me taking off the bloody coat, he asked, "How are the two Generals?"

"The same as always," I said. "I think Mr. Davis has aged a lot with the war and all. Mr. Lee has aged too, and it has to be hard for him, with his emotional ties being with the North."

Thinking of Mr. Lee as a General was hard for me. He became a General after the Battle of Hanover Courthouse outside Richmond, Virginia, and his position with the Army was to change from that point on. Though that battle wasn't a major one, by winning it he showed he was able to meet the enemy head on and win.

Like me, Pan Face had grown up seeing Mr. Lee and Mr. Davis as regular visitors to our place. Both men were like uncles to us. It was hard to think what it must be like for him fighting the people he knew best.

"I remember hearing him talk about his feelings toward the North and how his family is in the South…It must be hard for both of them," he said. Looking at my coat, he added, "A map…Let's have a look at it."

"The proposed route that I'm to take," I said as I smoothed out my coat. Pointing to the notes, I added, "These are the messages I'm supposed to pass on. The money and supplies coming from France hasn't arrived. That being the case, Mr. Davis and Mr. Lee want to see if we can get some support from up north."

"This one isn't a note asking for support," Pan Face said, giving me a funny look.

"I know," I replied as I read it again. When I first saw the note, it troubled me. Now after what had happened, I didn't care one way or the other. If fulfilling my orders would help end to the war, I would continue.

"You know, if I didn't know better, I would think we were home," he said as he looked around.

I wasn't sure what he was talking about so I asked. "Why?"

"Looks like the woods between our place and the Marsh's," he explained.

"I guess it does. Now that Ida's father is dead, the place won't be the same," I said. I agreed that the woods did seem like the ones at home, if you were to forget about the deaths that had just taken place. The body lying at my feet didn't go with the trees and open fields around us. A bird flying overhead caught my attention and I could see the black clouds floating eastward. It was almost as if it was a sign saying the killing was over. For the first time that day, I was almost happy. Turning to Pan Face I calmly told him, "Yeah… a beautiful day and place to die. The hardest part of all is that this should have been a peaceful trip. I was thinking I would avoid the fighting."

"I know what you are saying," he said looking across the field.

"I pray Ida and her mother will make it without Mr. Marsh… I don't know what I would do if something should happen to Ida," I confessed.

"Ida and her mother are strong people" he assured me.

"Like an egg. Strong shell on the outside and soft in the middle," I answered. I didn't want to think about Ida's loss.

"Have faith they'll make it," he said.

"That's just my problem. I have faith, faith that it's going to get worse before it gets better," I told him.

"Pray they have more strength than you think they do. Something has to go right some time," he said as he stood up to leave. He then asked, "If I leave…, will you be all right?"

"I think so. Freddy wasn't traveling with me all the way, anyway. If I'm on my own here or in New York I guess it doesn't make much difference," I replied.

As he was getting ready to leave, I turned my coat right side out and put it on. It was getting late and I had to find a place out of the weather before dark. I wasn't looking forward to traveling alone but I had no choice.

A voice called out just south of us, "Is that you, Master Edgar?"

As he raised his rifle, Pan Face asked, "Who's that?"

"Sounds like Freddy," I answered. Turning around I shouted out, "That you, Freddy?"

"Me and a headache," Freddy answered as he came into view. Then seeing Pan Face he stopped halfway through a step. He asked, "Who's that Yankee?"

"Pan Face…the friend I told you about the other day. He saved my life back there," I replied. Looking over at Pan Face I saw him grin from ear to ear. "I thought you were dead," I said. "I reached out and shook your foot but you didn't move."

"It's going to take more than a tap on this thick head to kill me," Freddy answered as he rubbed the back of his head. As he brought his hand down he added, "To tell you the truth I wish I was dead. My head wouldn't hurt like it does right now."

"I'm just glad you're alive. I've lost too many in this war already," I told him as I gave him a slap on the back.

"Knowing Edgar as I do, I'm glad you are alive. He's always needed help, and on this trip of yours he'll need all the help he can get," Pan Face said.

"I don't know what has happened while I was lying there in the dirt, but I surmise it was something major," Freddy said. He looked at Pan Face and with a painful smile, he added, "I'm just glad you're a friend and not what you look like."

"Don't worry; he never looked like much even in his normal clothes," I said, smiling at Pan Face.

"Thanks," Pan Face returned. Then to Freddy he said, "See if I save his life again."

"We had better get going," Freddy said. In explanation to Pan Face, he added, "Our next station probably won't be there when we arrive."

"Sounds like more fun," I replied.

"I guess with Freddy back, I won't feel so bad about leaving," Pan Face said with a smile

"I can't tell you how glad I was to see you, and on top of that, you saved me…! Do me another favor and stay alive," I said as I gave him a hug.

"You too, Master Edgar," he answered as he let me go.

"None of that master business," I told him, knowing he was only joshing me when he used that term.

"Take good care of him," Pan Face told Freddy.

"I will do my best," Freddy promised. Turning to me, he added, "That is, if you protect me at the same time."

"We won't have to worry if we don't get going," I said.

Pan Face was already out in the woods. I called to him, "I plan to see you again, real soon."

He returned my wave as he disappeared through the brush.

Thinking of what he had told me raised my temper again. The only shred of hope I had was that he didn't know for sure whether the soldiers had been at my place or not. It still wasn't right no matter whose parents they murdered. A soldier knows he'll kill someone on the battlefield, but it's another matter to kill someone in their home for the sport of it. What those Yankees did to the women was inexcusable, to say the least.

Freddy asked, "What are you thinking about?"

"Everything," I replied. I wasn't in the mood to discuss what had happened to Mother and Father. I didn't feel like talking to anyone about anything right then. I could only pray Ida didn't meet the same fate. My fears began to rise as I thought about what the Yankees might do to her and her mother.

"Doing some heavy thinking? If you want to talk about it, I'll listen."

"Just thinking about a girl I know," I revealed part of it to him.

"Being with her has to be better than being here," he said.

"I think I could use some food right now," I said. Finding some food would help get my mind off her. So many memories were coming back that I felt I couldn't stand it anymore.

"We should only have another couple of miles and we'll be at the next station. Mr. Howard's wife is a good cook," he said.

"Even a bad cook… would do. Even some berries would be good right now," I told him.

"Wrong time of the year," he reminded me.

"Thanks… I know," I said as we walked. The wooded area mixed with farmland did look like home. The land the farmers had was nothing in size compared to our place. At best, they were only two to five acre plots. These farmers were growing some crop I didn't recognize. Whatever it was I could see the green buds looked healthy.

"The next farm is where the station is," he told me.

"I would even be willing to settle for a drink of water," I told him feeling thirsty. We passed many little ponds and a stream, but the water in them was so dirty I changed my mind. If any one of them had been the Chattanooga River, I had drunk enough of its dirty water when swimming I wouldn't have worried about it.

As the walk progressed we didn't talk much and the silence made the walk seem like a death march. I wondered whether Freddy really knew where he was going. I had a map to go by, but I didn't take time to look at it, and it wasn't that detailed, anyway. Freddy was supposed to know this part of the trip, so I relied on him. Once he got me to the last station, I would have towns for reference points. As Mr. Lee had suggested, I might be able to catch trains the rest of the way. I knew getting back would be another story. I wished someone had given me some ideas. I don't know why but something told me they didn't expect me to make it back. They may have thought someone would kill me or that I would desert.

After twenty minutes or so Freddy stopped and crouched down. Holding his fingers to his lips, he told me, "Get down…Let's make sure it's safe to go on in."

"All right," I returned. As I got down beside him, I saw the farm across the field. Looking through the bushes, I couldn't see much. There was a wagon in front of the house, but it wasn't anything special. I saw a cow and some chickens but I didn't see anyone moving. From Freddy's expression, I could tell he didn't like how it looked.

"At least there's no sign of the Army having been here," he said. Sitting down he explained, "They don't socialize much, so seeing that wagon worries me a little."

"I guess we can wait and see who it is," I said as I sat down. Off to my right I saw a pond, and thought about washing my bloody coat in it. With a shrug, I turned my attention back to the farmhouse. I figured I could wash it there just as well. Before long a couple came out onto the porch. I asked Freddy, "Is that them?"

"No… Must be visitors," he replied as he kept his eye on the couple.

Just then, a man came out onto the porch. It seemed the two men were having a cordial discussion. The first man kept shaking his head, but it was in a friendly manner. It seemed we didn't have to worry about the visitors.

"Even if they are friends, I doubt that he wants people to know what he has been doing," Freddy said.

I was ready to get up so. I asked, "Should we go over there?"

"Let's wait until they leave," he said.

Soon the couple left. I saw Freddy nod his head and we both got up. Approaching the house, we kept our eyes open for Yankees that might be around. I would have preferred leaving during the night, for the cover of darkness would likely provide us some protection. The occasion brought back memories of taking slaves to the next station from our place. I distinctly remembered the trip to the Schmitt place with Raymond. I had a feeling old man Schmitt wasn't around the place anymore.

"Good afternoon, Master Howard," Freddy shouted out as we got close to the house. Then cautiously he looked around.

"What?" Mr. Howard asked turning our way. As he saw us, he reached in through the door and brought out a rifle. Leveling the rifle at us, he asked, "Who are you?"

"Don't worry…His eyesight isn't all that good," Freddy assured me. He shouted, "It's me…Freddy."

"I hope his memory isn't like his eyes. I wouldn't want him to have forgotten who you are and that we were coming," I replied. I was finding that being in someone's sights was getting tiresome. It was hard to believe I would have to worry about that again, with us being on the same side. I prayed his eyesight was so bad he would miss if he did shoot at us.

Mr. Howard lowered his rifle and asked, "Little Freddy?"

"Yes, sir," Freddy answered as we got a little closer to the house.

"I wish I could say it was good to see you, but I can't see you," Mr. Howard said. Then as we got within an arm's length of him, he said, "Why, yes, it is you... Where have you been? You were supposed to have been here yesterday."

"A battle kept us busy. And we had bad weather. The two of us were almost killed earlier this afternoon," I told him.

He looked at me and asked, "And who are you?"

"Edgar Buchanan, sir," I told him. He appeared to be worried about me. It surprised me no one had told him I was coming.

"Oh, yes. You're the young lad that has to go north," he said. He motioned for us to go inside. As we entered the house, he added, "I hate to give you this news..." he added, "but your ride just left. They waited as long as they could and you didn't show up, then with Lincoln's making that speech of his."

Freddy asked, "What speech is that?"

"At Gettysburg...or the Emancipation Proclamation...or something on that order," Mr. Howard answered.

I didn't say anything but I knew most of his thinking was wrong. As with most people he only heard bits and pieces of the truth.

"I don't understand," Freddy said.

"He's finally taken a stand on slavery. He's made all slaves free men," Mr. Howard explained.

"After what..., six months of war and who knows how many thousands dead, he finally takes a stand," I pointed out to the two of them.

"Most people in the South never had any problem with freeing the slaves... I've been free for years, not that I left or anything," Freddy, told us.

"What I would like to know is…what will you do now? I don't care about Lincoln and what he has decreed," I shouted. We had gone through so much I couldn't sit there calmly. With the likelihood that the Yankees had killed my parents, with seeing Ida's father die, with the fog and rain and the gory battles, it was getting to be too much. Then he tells us that our ride has just left. I couldn't believe it.

"I'm sorry, but the Yankees are trying to get all of us that support the South. In fact, my son is due here any time to help me get out of here," Mr. Howard explained. Then, rubbing his chin, he added, "You can go with me… The only problem is that I'm heading west."

"That won't work for me," I said. "I need to get to New York and into Canada, not west.

"I'm sorry but the Phillip's waited for you for almost two days… They also fear for their lives," he said. "I can offer you something to eat."

"Sounds good to me," Freddy told him. Then to me he said, "It'll be a whole lot better than the dog and rats they're eating in Richmond."

I wasn't sure I heard him right so I asked, "What?"

"You probably didn't know it, but our soldiers don't have much to eat. Crops had been poor and all they have to eat is whatever they can find," he explained.

He turned to Mr. Howard and described everything that had happened over the past two days. Then he added, "If it hadn't been for all that, we would have been here on time."

Mr. Howard asked, "So you're saying this battle took place five to ten miles from here?"

"Yes, sir," Freddy replied.

"That worries me… I can understand why you didn't get here on time," Mr. Howard said. He paused as he looked around the house. He then added, "Even though your trip wasn't that far, it sounds like it was a rough one… I just don't understand why the North and South can't get along. Too many good men are losing their lives for nothing… and the saddest part is that most of them are kin to each other. Families have been split apart, never to get together again."

He shrugged his shoulders and told us, "Make yourself at home… There's some stew on the stove if you like. My wife should be back shortly."

"If he only knew how rough as it was," I said to myself. I wanted to ask him if the killing of women and children weren't just as bad as losses on the battlefield. I had an idea that, like most people, he was under the misunderstanding that casualties came only from fighting, which certainly hadn't been the case for my mother and Elsie who weren't on any darn battlefield when they died. Over the next few years, I was to learn how bad the women had it. Not only losing their loved ones, they were to suffer even more than their men folks. Turning to Freddy, I asked, "What now?"

"That depends on you," he replied. He motioned for me to join him at the stove. Then looking at Mr. Howard and back to me, he added, "It's just a little setback. We'll get you there somehow."

"You might be able to catch a ride on the train twenty miles from here," Mr. Howard suggested. With a smile he added, "I might worry about my accent if I were you… Northerners will pick up on the fact you're a Southern boy."

"What's this about you killing a Yankee with your bare hands?" Freddy asked as he took a bite of stew. Then putting his spoon down he added, "That friend of yours seemed shocked when he told me about what you did."

"I don't remember much about it… I would rather think about how we're going to get out of here," I answered as I took a bite myself. I had been honest with him and I didn't want to dwell on it. I knew the soldiers weren't the only ones who would pay for Mother's death.

Soon Mrs. Howard returned, driving her wagon into the yard. With her was their son on another wagon, ready to load up all their belongings.

"Ma…, these are the two boys we have been waiting for," Mr. Howard said to his wife. He added, "With all the stew gone, I think I can say they liked it."

"It was good, Ma'am," I assured her. Freddy nodded in agreement.

Mr. Howard made the introductions. "Boys, this is my son George…Ma, George, these are Edgar and Freddy."

"Good to meet you" I said, and again Freddy nodded.

"Good to meet you… I'm sorry you missed your ride "George said. He turned back to his father and told him "If you want to get out of here we had better start loading up the wagons."

"He's right, Pa…We don't have much time," Mrs. Howard said. Turning to us she suggested, "Perhaps the boys can give us a hand?"

Mr. Howard asked, "Would you mind?"

"We'll be glad to," I said. With that, Freddy and I helped them load the wagon up for their journey west. I didn't like the idea of using precious time helping them, but I didn't know what else to do. They had done so much for the Underground Railroad; I felt it was our duty to help them escape the danger they were in.

After we had everything loaded, Mrs. Howard suggested, "Pa…, we could take these boys north a ways."

"I guess you have a point," Mr. Howard answered. After a short pause he added, "If it weren't for them, we wouldn't be getting out of here until morning…There's a rail line not that far out of our way."

"We would much appreciate it," Freddy told them.

"Why don't you and Ma go on as planned?" their son offered. "I can take them north a ways to the railroad and catch up with you later… I'll be able to hide them with the stuff I'm hauling better than you."

"Anything would be bett er than getting caught here…The farther away we get, the safer it's likely to be," Freddy told them.

I didn't care what happened as long as we got on the road. I was afraid I wouldn't get my assignment done since we were two days late. With a little rearranging, we got his son's wagon set up for Freddy and me to hide in.

"We'll see you somewhere along the road tomorrow," Mr. Howard told his son. He snapped the horse's reins without waiting for a reply.

George waved to his parents, he told us, "Go ahead and get in… I'll run you north a ways and then east to the railroad. That should get you close to where you should be by now. I should be able to catch up with Ma and Pa without too much trouble."

From there onward, no one paid much attention to us and the trip was uneventful. I left Freddy in Philadelphia and continued on to upstate New York. As we parted, I told him "Once this is over, come back home…, and thanks."

"I will, and take care of yourself," he said as my boxcar left the train yard.

Other than being a long trip and food was scarce, the rest of my trip was uneventful. I dropped off the three coded messages. No one gave me a clue as to their meaning. The fourth and most important note I delivered to a doctor in Montreal. Getting that message to him took me six weeks but it gave me the most satisfaction. Whoever wrote the supposedly coded message must not have reread it. I couldn't imagine anyone reading it and not understanding it. The message was short and to the point:

> *Someone has to stop him at all costs. Get men together and do it as soon as possible. We cannot hold out much longer at the rate its going. Everett is waiting for you. Get him the date and he will be there to help you with a group of men. He will report to us.*

I knew it must be a plan to assassinate Lincoln. If it were anyone else, I couldn't think who it might be. I didn't understand how the doctor in Canada was involved. We had more than enough of our own men that knew the Capital inside and out and who could assassinate him.

Since I had given Freddy half the money I had, it was harder getting home. I had to work a few times for food and a way to get transportation. Mr. Howard was correct, a few people did notice and ask questions about my accent. I explained to them that my now deceased parents had sent me north a year earlier in fear of the war. To make it worse I had lost my grandmother in an accident, leaving me homeless. I was amused when people listened to that story and began feeling sorry for me.

After eight weeks, I was feeling poorly but I was just forty-some miles away from Richmond. I was looking forward to reporting to Mr. Davis and Mr. Lee.

It felt as if the last forty miles were the longest I had ever traveled. To my surprise, neither Mr. Davis nor Mr. Lee commented on my report. I asked them if there was a plan to assassinate Lincoln and neither would comment. I left the meeting wondering if my trip had been worthwhile. I went back to camp and to the battlefield, not knowing much more than before I left.

The End Was Near

I have picked up my diaries and I'm starting to make entries again. As a young man, I had found writing was the best way of getting everything off my chest. If Ida was around I could talk to her. Thinking of the past few years I know her opinion of me wouldn't be good. I decided I was glad she wasn't here to talk to me. This gave me time to add to my diary:

It was the first week of March of 65' and it had been a wet and cold winter. I found myself heading back to Richmond from another trip north and I was sick again. Sometimes my vision was blurred and every part of me hurt. All that kept me going was the fear that the Yankees would find me and kill me. If they didn't kill me, they would put me into one of their prisons and I would die a worse death. I had heard many stories about them and I didn't want to end up in one of them. With that in mind, I kept on walking in hopes of finding a faster way back.

Then as I approached a bush, I heard something. Cautiously I crept toward the bush and pushed the branches aside. I saw movement not far from me I froze in fear that I had been detected. After taking a couple of painful breaths I spread the branches of the bush open a little more and saw it was one man.

"What are you doing?" I shouted at the man in front of me. The way I was feeling, I didn't want any more interruptions. I would have loved to take on a company of Yankees if I had been stronger, but I didn't have the strength to fight even one man. I just wanted to report in and get a good night's sleep.

"I'm getting dressed," he answered. From his expression, I got the feeling he thought I was stupid not seeing what he was doing.

Holding the rifle on him and talking was taking all the energy I had left. I was burning up with fever and didn't know how long I was going to be able to stand, let alone fight anyone. Still, here was a soldier wearing a Confederate uniform changing into a uniform of the North. I knew I was suffering from the fever but I didn't think I was seeing what was before my eyes. Was I hallucinating because of my fever? Using the rifle as a crutch, I lowered myself to the ground. I managed to ask him in a softer voice "What are you doing…? You seem to be changing uniforms."

"I don't like being on the losing side… so I'm putting on this Yankee uniform to be on the winning side," he said.

"Are you a Southerner or a Northerner?" I barely got the question out.

"A Southerner, of course," he answered with a note of pride in his voice.

I asked, "Then why not fight with your own side?"

"I want to get even with some of my friends," he answered with a grim smile on his face. "My so called friends, that is. It looks as if they're going to lose everything, anyway. Why not take part in destroying what they have?"

I knew that Confederate soldiers had done some things that were as bad as what the Yankees had done, though I didn't like to think about it.

"I can almost see some sense in what you are planning to do," I replied. At that point I didn't care very much. All I could think about was how terrible I felt. Managing to gather a little more energy, I asked, "What's your name?"

"Wilbur Marsh" he told me.

Hearing his name I was a little more than shocked. I asked, "Are you related to Harold Marsh?"

"He's my brother…Do you know him?" He asked. He seemed surprised by my question and stopped changing clothes as he waited for my answer.

"Yes, also his wife and daughter, Ida…You knew he was killed three years ago?" I said. I wondered why I had never seen this man visiting his brother's family.

"Yes, I heard about that," he answered as he sat down. He had a sad expression on his face. Obviously, his brother had meant something to him. He continued, "Annabelle was to have been my wife…or that was what I thought. Then she married Harold and I never had anything to do with him after that. Through the years, I realized that my judgment of Annabelle was wrong. With the three of us growing up together, I never had the chance to spend time with her alone. I thought she loved me, but what she felt for me was just deep friendship, because her love was for Harold. I realized I had been mistaken, but I couldn't bring myself to tell the two of them. I ended up going away, searching for the right woman for me."

"Did you ever find her?" I asked being more than curious. Once again, our conversation made me think of Ida. Numerous times during the four years of fighting, I had dreamed about being married to her. I wasn't sure whether that was love, or simply a need for an old friend to comfort me during those terrible experiences.

"Oh, I found her… She wasn't Annabelle, but she was a loving wife," he told me." He looked even sadder than before.

I had expected more than what he told me. I asked, "Was…?"

"Our own troops raided our place while I was fighting somewhere else… I don't know all that happened, but they took everything… even what she had to offer. I found her the next day and she had killed herself," he said. Then he got to his feet and pulled his pants up. As he buttoned them, he added "Another reason I don't mind changing uniforms."

"This war seems to have started out with hatred and is ending with the same feeling," I said to myself. A few years earlier I had come back from my first mission north and checked out the old place. I had to see if there was anything left of Mother and Father to bury. What

I found confirmed what Pan Face had told me. The place had been blown apart and burned to the ground. There wasn't enough left of the place to recognize it. All I found was black ash where the house had been, and later the wind blew the ashes away. All that remained were my memories of days long gone. Like Wilbur, I felt hate and when I thought of Mother and Father's death, my hate at times had turned into an uncontrollable rage.

Finding what I had at home, I continued to the Marsh place. The Marsh place was in almost the same condition as ours. The only difference was the soldiers hadn't been as thorough as they were to our place. The Marsh place still had a few columns and parts of walls standing, though there certainly wasn't enough left to rebuild. I recognized the Marsh factory, the church, and the school. Everything else seemed unfamiliar. All the crops were gone.

I didn't even see animals on any of the places that someone could use to work the fields. Then it hit me; the war had changed everything and not for the good. I felt sick at the sight of the destruction. I was afraid that Ida and her mother had lost their lives as my parents had.

Wilbur interrupted my thoughts of home and the Marsh place when he asked, "You don't look good… Are you all right?"

"I don't know…I think I need a surgeon. I feel as if I'm burning up" I told him feeling sick.

"I didn't get your name but I don't think it matters now. I'll try to get you to a camp nearby," I heard him say. He sounded far away, though he was standing right there beside me.

I couldn't have told him my name or anything else. For some reason I couldn't remember it nor did I care. I didn't know what was happening to me. I felt as if I was burning up and the world was spinning around. I couldn't focus my eyes or my thoughts on anything. Then slowly the world began going dark.

The next thing I felt was the sensation of being lifted onto a horse. At first I was a little concerned, but then, I felt movement and not much else. I was glad someone was taking care of me. Friend or enemy, it didn't matter as long as they were getting me help.

Later I woke and I knew I wasn't on the horse anymore. I felt as if I were in a bed or at least covered up. I tried to open my eyes but didn't have the strength. Giving up, I lay there and I listened to what was going on around me. I could hear cannons moving and the sound of troops marching not far away. I sensed I was back in Richmond.

In my semi-conscious state, I heard a pleasant female voice ask, "Are you awake?"

"I think so," I muttered. Managing to open my eyes, I mumbled, "I'm not sure if I want to be. I don't feel all that good and my eyes don't want to open."

"You're doing better than most of us thought you would be doing," the voice said.

"What do you mean?" I said as I opened my eyes.

"Obviously you had typhoid fever. Most of the soldiers who caught it haven't survived," the woman said. Smiling she added, "It seems you have worried some important men in the camp."

"I bet," I replied as I tried to sit up.

"Don't worry about getting up. You're fine right where you are" she advised.

"At least you can tell me your name," I said.

"Just call me Bonnie," she answered as she straightened out my covers.

I began to feel cold. I pulled the covers up and realized I wasn't wearing much. I hoped Bonnie wasn't the one who had undressed me. She was about the same age as my mother and attractive. As I lay there admiring her, I found myself blushing and praying no one saw me. I began wondering what it might have been like if she had undressed me.

"You're not the first man I have seen naked, Mr. Buchanan," she said with a grin.

I was feeling a little warmer now.

"How long have I been here?" I asked. I vaguely remembered Wilbur changing from a Confederate uniform to a Yankee uniform. With this memory, I asked, "Did Wilbur bring me in?"

"I don't know anything about Wilbur. I heard you were found on the edge of the road." She picked up a few pieces of clothing from a nearby cot. "I guess I'll let you sleep. I have others to take care of."

"Thanks, Bonnie," I said, not sure what I was thanking her for. Every muscle in my body was screaming. I had tried to get up a few times and each time, I fell back, exhausted.

As Bonnie turned to leave, I realized she had called me "Mr. Buchanan." She had also mentioned some important men had been worried about me. "Who were these men who were worried about me?"

"Mr. Davis and Mr. Lee for starters," she answered. Pausing, she turned and added, "I'm afraid they won't be around for awhile. From what I hear, Mr. Davis has moved his office and Mr. Lee is campaigning with his forces."

"Oh," I replied softly. I think I was supposed to be impressed. What she didn't know was that I had known these men when I was growing up.

Looking around I saw I was in a hospital tent. Except for the bed next to me, the tent was full. Almost everyone was moaning and wearing bandages of one type or another. A good many of the men had amputated limbs. I tried to imagine which was worse, seeing wounded men in this hospital tent or spread out on the battlefield. The thought of all these wounded men was depressing. It seemed such a shame that these men had to sacrifice so much for their beliefs.

With the sides of the tent pulled up, I could see part of the camp from my cot. I could see the camp wasn't as large as the last time I had been to Richmond. I had heard the number of fronts we were fighting on had increased and I figured that's why this camp was so small. Even so, it was still busy. As I tried to get a better sense of what was happening, Freddy came to mind. I was just happy that he was away from all of this.

From my spot I could also see some of the city. Around the buildings, I could see people milling around aimlessly. For what I had grown up knowing of the city, it seemed dead to me. All I could see were wagons coming and going through the camp. I didn't see any wagon or buggies passing between the buildings. It was difficult to look at the city and contrast the way it looked with memories of the lively setting it used to be, with carriages, wagons, and men on horseback filling the street. There were no children playing as one might have expected. I had a feeling everyone in Richmond knew the Yankees were planning to attack the city and most had left, nearly turning it into a ghost town.

"I wish I felt as good as it looks out there," a soldier beside me said.

Looking up into the sky, I saw the sun was past the halfway point. I figured it was two or three o'clock. Unlike the city, the sky was full of life with all the birds flying around. The sky held a few little puffy clouds, but mostly it was a beautiful, clear blue. The light breeze wasn't unusual for May. Turning slightly towards the soldier I replied, "I agree."

"Why did you take my leg off?" a soldier screamed from somewhere nearby.

"You'll be all right," Bonnie responded in a comforting tone.

"Would you shut up? They took both of mine last week," another soldier cried out.

In the distance I could hear others screaming. A surgeon was working on someone, probably removing another limb or two.

"I don't know if I would rather be them or the way I am," a soldier not far from me said.

I managed to get out, "What?"

"I have all of my limbs…I just lost an eye," the soldier answered.

"A good question," I said. As I tried to see who it was that had spoken to me but I was unable to turn over. So, I finally gave up trying to identify the speaker.

I turned my attention back to the campgrounds and city. I spotted a woman and a soldier coming toward the camp from between two buildings. At first, I didn't give them much attention. But then I looked at them again because I thought the woman looked familiar. As far away as she was, I couldn't be sure. The more I strained to see her more clearly, the more my eyes watered and the less I could see. As they came closer, I was sure that she was Ida's mother. As she entered a tent with the soldier, I managed to say, "What are you doing?"

From that point, I don't remember much. I went to sleep wondering what she was doing going into the tent with the soldier. I wondered where Ida was and what she was doing. I wished Ida would come to visit me. So much had happened I couldn't make out what was or wasn't real and I fell asleep.

I had no idea what was going on but something woke me up.

"I see you are with us again," a female voice sounded in my dreams. Before I could reply, the voice asked, "Are we getting up today?"

"What?" I answered. I could only see the back of my eyelids. I tried to open them but I couldn't manage the strength. Trying as hard as I could, I told her "My eyes won't open."

"I'll get a wet rag and wash them for you," the voice offered.

"I need something. I don't know what," I said as I pulled the blanket over me again. As I lay there, the image of Ida's mother came to me. The memory of thinking I had seen her in the camp puzzled me. I was shaking my head as I told myself that it must have been someone else...

As a wet rag was rubbed on my face, a female voice asked, "It couldn't have been who?"

I didn't recognize the voice it wasn't Bonnie's, but the rag felt good on my eyes. As I enjoyed the sensation, I realized I was starving. I opened my eyes and saw a big woman standing over me. She was an older woman who looked tired and bedraggled. Her clothes were spotted with blood and mud, and her hair was escaping from its bun she had arranged on the top of her head. I tried to smile as I said, "Thanks."

"I'm Marge," she said.

I asked, "Where's Bonnie?"

"She died the other day," she told me. Tears were welling up in her eyes...

With a lump in my throat, I was afraid I might not have heard her right over the noise of the moaning and the cries of pain all around me. I said, "She what?"

"Typhoid got her… With so many of you infected, it was a risk she took working here," she answered. Then wiping her eyes, she added, "She was my firstborn."

I knew I should say something to comfort her but I didn't know the right words. Realizing that I might have had something to do with her death, I said, "I'm sorry. She seemed to be a pleasant woman."

"Always cared more for others than herself," she replied, still crying. As she wiped a tear away, she asked, "Do you feel like eating?"

"Yes…if it's not a bother." I answered feeling hungrier than I could ever remember being before that day.

"Ouch…! What do you think I am a piece of beef?" a soldier screamed out.

"Don't tempt me. You'd probably taste better than the mess we've been getting," another said.

"Won't be much, but more than you've had for some time," she said as she turned to leave.

"How long have I been out this time?" I asked. As I moved, I felt worse than I remembered the last time I woke up. Even with my muscles aching, I managed to sit up. Thus, in position I looked onto the campground. The tent I'd seen the woman enter was gone. Again, I wondered if it had been Ida's mother

"A week," she answered as she continued to walk away.

From what they told me, I had been there for weeks. If I understood her right, I hadn't eaten anything. Looking at my body, I realized I had certainly lost some weight, for I felt downright skinny. I chuckled, knowing that after almost four years of the war I had reached my full height. During those years I had also put some meat on my bones that Ida would probably appreciate. Now here in the hospital tent, I probably had lost all of it. As I sat on the edge of the cot I muttered, "You have your skinny Edgar again, Ida… a little taller, but skinny again."

The soldier next to me asked, "What was that?"

"Just thinking how much weight I have lost in the past few weeks," I told him.

"On the food around here a person could die," he said.

"I would be happy with a bowl of mush… Anything to fill my stomach," I told him. As we were talking, I looked for my clothes. Not seeing them, I looked for any sign of my belongings. I looked around and I couldn't find Father's pistol or his Remington rifle.

"Looking for something?" Marge asked as she brought a bowl of something to me. She then reached out to give me the bowl. In doing so, she added, "It's not much but it's something your stomach should be able to handle."

"Where's my stuff?" I asked her as I took the bowl. Not bothering to look into the bowl, I continued to look for my belongings. As I looked I wondered what else there was of importance.

"Your clothes were burned. Because you had typhoid fever, we had to burn everything… to keep from spreading the infection. Mr. Davis had the surgeon take care of your pistol and rifle for you," she answered. Then pointing to the bowl she told me "Now eat that and get back under the blanket… I don't think you're strong enough to worry about going far."

I didn't mind them burning my clothes, but I wanted my boots back. I asked, "Did they burn my boots, too?"

The soldier next to me asked, "So if they burned your boots. What's the big deal?"

"They were custom made…and my father bought them for me. Not, some of those one-size fits all boots everyone gets," I explained.

"Better your boots than you," the soldier said.

"Remind me never to get the fever again," I told him feeling a little irritated. Looking at my feet, I remembered how my boots were getting a little tight as I was growing taller. I would take whatever they gave me. I just prayed someone else wasn't using my custom made boots.

"Best get eating," Marge said as she left us. Then a few feet away she added, "I'm not planning to go anywhere for the next few days."

"Yes, Ma'am," I said. I looked down at the watered down soup in the bowl. Looking at it, memories of my trip north came to mind. Without trying it, I knew my worst meal up north was better than what they were giving us.

"I'm Rodney Anderson," the soldier in the next cot said.

"A pleasure to meet you... I'm Edgar Buchanan," I answered without taking my eyes off the soup. I looked over at him for the first time and realized he was the one who had lost an eye to a mini ball. Luck was in his favor that it didn't hit him straight on. The ball had grazed his eye and taken part of his cheekbone.

I wondered why they had kept him here as long as they had, if his only injury was the lost eye. As he sat up, I saw his body was covered with bandages, so obviously his missing eye was not his only injury. Though it was hard to tell through all the bandages, he seemed a little thin. Around the bandage covering most of his head, I could see a few locks of his red hair.

"It's not as bad as it looks," he said.

With all the noise around, I couldn't make out what he had said. I asked, "What? Being wounded?"

"Well, that too...I meant the soup. There's some flavor to it," he said as he smiled.

"I wasn't expecting something like what Elsie our cook, used to fix...I would be happy even if it was something canned. To add some fun to it the labels could be missing. As I said earlier, mush would have been fine," I replied. I hesitated a little before I took a spoonful. I did my best not to think about what might be in the soup, because of what Freddy had said about men in camp eating rats. I was afraid to consider what the meat in the soup might be. Looking back at Rodney, I added, "You look like you took a beating."

"All this is from cannon shelling coming our way. One landed not far from me sending fragments everywhere. Fragments got me in the eye and five other places throughout my body," he answered as he looked down at his bandages.

"Ouch," I replied as I took another spoonful of soup. I couldn't say much for what I was eating other than that it was hot and filling. The flavor was questionable. Maybe because of how sick I was and the fact that I hadn't eaten in so long, I couldn't eat any more right then.

With a smile Rodney asked, "As bad as you thought it might be?"

"Worse," I said.

"I didn't say it tasted good, just that it had some flavor to it…It hasn't killed the rest of us yet," he assured me.

"I'm not sure if that's a good thing or not…With the taste that's in my mouth death might not be so bad an ending," I replied as I finished the bowl. I wasn't sure but I imagined the water from boiling my clothes would have tasted better. At least Rodney was correct, there was some flavor to the soup. I didn't recognize it and didn't want to. I had learned sometimes it's better not knowing than knowing. Setting the bowl down I said, "I think it's time to get some sleep."

"Watch out for the bedbugs," he said.

I laid back down and fell asleep instantly.

I was there for another month before the routine was to change. In the middle of the night I heard a male voice.

The voice said, "All right, Buchanan…You too, Anderson and Miller. Up and at it; we have a battle heading our way."

I raised my head to see what was going on and asked, "What?"

Rodney started to rise and asked, "What's going on?"

"The Yankees are moving on Richmond and we have to be ready," the voice of a soldier told us.

"We're not supposed to be up," I told him. I knew it was the middle of the night. Through the cracks of the tent, I could see it was dark and no one was about.

"Would you rather die on the cot or defending yourself?" The soldier asked. Then he added, "I'm Lieutenant Gordon."

"I guess…," I began to answer as I got up. Then feeling a draft I added, "I think I need some clothes and a rifle or something to fight with." Looking at him and the men in their cots, I knew I would rather go with him. Sometime during the night someone's screams had woke me up. A fellow patient explained that a soldier was having his leg sawed off. I had seen the surgeon do it a few times and my stomach still turned at the thought. At times I asked myself which would be better, death at the hands of the enemy or living to fight more battles.

"Here are some clothes and your firearms, sir," a doctor said, addressing me.

"Thanks," I answered as I took the stuff from him. Checking the rifle, I saw it was Father's Remington and I felt a little better having it back. To me it was as much of a treasure as what I heard Mr. Davis had taken off with. It was rumored that sometime before I got back, he had taken off with all of the money in the States treasury.

"A person can't even die in peace…Lose an eye, get punctures everywhere… and someone wants you to fight again," Rodney said as he got dressed.

"Like I said, you can die here or out there protecting yourself… Now get going," Lieutenant Gordon, ordered us.

"You don't have to tell me," Another replied as he dressed himself. He added, "My brothers as well as our parents were killed…They burned down the building on the farm and I still have to fight. I'm beginning to wonder what I'm fighting for with everything gone. If we were to win, what will I have to show for it? Everything is in ruins."

"I guess I'm ready," I announced. Hearing what the two had to say, I couldn't find anything wrong with their thinking.

My motivation was to make the Yankees pay for what I had lost. It wasn't just losing my parents and my home. I had lost old friends and new friends alike through death and moving to other parts of the country. All of it was becoming clear that it was for nothing. I had been up north more than most and learned what they had planned for us and it wasn't good. I had seen how they hadn't suffered as we had. They might have been short of farm animals but their fields were lush and green. All we shared was the regret that our brothers were fighting brothers. Like us, they also lost their husbands and fathers. I had a funny feeling that people out west were like the ones on the Canadian border. These people didn't seem to be aware of the war and its effect on their daily life. The war was just something they read about, not part of their reality.

From what I had seen in the big cities up north, you would never know anything had happened. The average worker had it rougher than our slaves ever did. Even so, everyone up there was still condemning us for having had slaves. Then Lincoln's Gettysburg Address speech saying everyone was equal seemed to have fired them up with more determination to kill us all. Somewhere they've forgotten the war started before his speech and it wasn't over slavery. The war was an economic statement more than anything else was. Some think it was a game of killing people for fun, not for a political or moral reason. I feel it was more of a jealousy of our way of life. If killing wasn't enough for them there was the bonus to be able to rape women, burn and destroy anything in their path.

"I have a feeling there isn't going to be many of us to greet them," a man said across the room.

As I waited, I wondered how many men I would be fighting with were going to be ex-slaves. I remembered someone telling me back in January that there were many men deserting. To solve the problem Mr. Davis had given his authorization to the army to allow slaves to carry guns and fight alongside us.

"I guess I'm as ready as I'll ever be," Rodney stated.

Lieutenant Gordon looked around the tent and said, "Let's get out there."

"Even if we win…, we won't have enough money to rebuild," Rodney added to my thoughts.

"After all of this we can't let them win," I reminded him.

"I don't know…Win and have nothing or lose and have nothing… What difference does it make?" he said as we followed Lieutenant Gordon out of the tent.

"What we need are the Cherokees from Missouri," I said as we made our way to the edge of town.

Rodney looked puzzled and asked, "What?"

"What he's talking about are the Cherokee Indians who are keeping a good part of the Union Army from invading us. If it hadn't been for them, we would have lost a long time ago," Lieutenant Gordon answered for me.

As they discussed the subject, I was thinking about the rumor I had heard to the effect that General Lee had abandoned us. I found it hard to believe, and thought he had left to support troops north of Richmond.

"Maybe it would be better if the Yankees had beaten us a long time ago. Then there might be something for some of us to go home to," Rodney said.

"I don't want to hear any more talk like that," Lieutenant Gordon shouted at Rodney.

"Well, it's the truth. Even if we do win, we won't be able to afford to rebuild," Rodney said.

"All I know is it seemed we had a chance when McClellan and Halleck were commanding the Union Army…Then Grant took over and it's been downhill since then," I added.

"That's true," he said.

"If it wasn't for the Indians and Lee we would never have lasted this long…If he had taken Lincoln's offer of commanding their forces we wouldn't have had a chance," I said. Thinking about what Mr. Lee had told my father that Mr. Grant, like himself, had owned slaves and both was in favor of freeing them, so they held a lot of ideas in common. Yet now, one is commanding the Union Army and the other became the commander of the Confederate Army, and they find themselves fighting each other.

"As for me, I don't care who wins right now…I'm going to kill everyone I see," I said.

"Other than you not caring who wins, I like your attitude… Now let's get out there and defend the city. We can't let them take it, or the troops' morale will fall more than it has already," Lieutenant Gordon said. He signaled for everyone to follow him.

Rodney asked, "What do these Indians do that makes them so good?"

"Their favorite time to fight is at night," I told him.

"We like to fight at night, too," he replied, sounding a little defensive.

"No…There've been a few skirmishes fought at night, but most of our fighting is during the day. On the other hand, the Cherokees go in at night and chase off the horses and mules. With the horses gone they attack the men as they are getting up to defend themselves… Most of the time, the Yankees don't even get to their rifles before they're dead. Those that manage to defend themselves find the Indians have made a run for it…Then the Indians hit again the next night, and so on, until the company is wiped out," I explained. With a grin on my face, I added, "These military types don't understand an idea that has worked for thousands of years for the Indians. They are bound to the formal way of fighting and don't recognize that it is ineffective."

"You have a point, Buchanan," Lieutenant Gordon said. "A few of us have given these ideas to our superiors. They think we have to fight one army against the other and it isn't getting us anywhere. All we have to show for our efforts are more dead men. We've been told our suggestions will be passed on to the ones higher up." But he sounded doubtful.

"At least the Indians are taking this war to the Northerners," I added.

"Don't forget Lee's battle at Antietam Bridge…With 23,000 casualties in twelve hours it's been called the bloodiest single day battle so far," Rodney reminded me.

"There still hasn't been enough fighting up there for me. If more battles had been fought farther north, the war might be going the other way," I added. I thought of Lee's battle up north in September of "62" and I remember the effect it had on our forces. It raised the morale of the South to the point where most of our soldiers were acting as if we had won the war.

"Ouch," Rodney uttered.

"Does it hurt to walk with all of those wounds?" I asked. As I watched him, I could see some of his wounds were bleeding. I couldn't see how he could manage this hike in his condition.

"If the wounds weren't bad enough, hitting one with a tree branch doesn't help," he answered sounding irritated.

"I can imagine," I replied as I caught a branch letting him go ahead of me.

"Thanks," he smiled.

The Lieutenant asked, "Everyone with us?"

"I believe so, Lieutenant," I answered. In fact, I didn't have any idea who was or wasn't with us.

"I know I'm here," a voice offered from the dark.

"It's the first time Richard has ever known where he was," Rodney commented with a laugh.

"I had a friend like that," I said as memories of Raymond came to mind.

As we walked, getting to the edge of the city, I saw a wooden barricade I didn't remember ever seeing before. Obviously, someone had been thinking in terms of protecting the city. I imagined their idea was to use the barricade as a shield during an attack, but apparently, they didn't consider the fact that one cannon shell would turn it into nothing but splinters. But after all, it was better than nothing. There wasn't anything else to protect us from the Yankees when they attacked. At least they would have to climb over it to get to us, and that would expose them to our fire. Lieutenant Gordon's order to hunker down was passed down the line of men to find a place. We will battle them here.

As we took our positions Rodney asked me, "What's wrong?"

His asking the questions caught me off guard. I asked, "What do you mean?"

"You keep touching your Kepi," he explained.

"Ooh…Just wondering why these caps are called Kepis," I answered. I hadn't realized I had been touching it. Only rarely had I ever worn a hat at all, and I had only worn my Kepi two or three times.

"I've heard the French military caps are called Kepis. I guess it means a cap with a flat circular top and a visor... Or something, like that," Rodney told me with a "know it all smile." Then grinning he asked, "Any other questions?"

"I guess they had to call them something," I said. "With the decoration on top and with it looking as if someone just sat on it, just calling it a cap wouldn't be enough." I replied as I looked over the barricade. Glancing at him I added, "I'm just wondering when they'll attack. I don't see any fires showing where they're camped."

"Those Yankee boys may not be the brightest but they're not so dumb to camp in sight of our lines" he replied.

"I guess not," realizing he had a point. I tried my best to get comfortable but couldn't. Then I began thinking about how Rodney and the other guys might be feeling and I couldn't imagine their discomfort.

"Would the two of you quiet down there," someone shouted.

"We can talk quietly and it's wrong… He can shout and that's all right," I replied. I then added in a hushed voice, "And that reminds me of something else…Most of our officers bought their position. If we had some experienced officers, the war might be going differently."

"Shhhh," someone hissed from not far way. I settled back for what I prayed would be a peaceful night. I had seen and heard enough death over the past three plus years that I wanted to scream. To make it worse my body had more blood splattered on it than it has in it.

"They could have left us in our cots for as much fighting as we're doing," Rodney said.

"At least we're not getting shot at," I reminded him. I didn't know for sure but I think we both had fallen asleep.

It seemed that as soon as I replied to Rodney's comment, I was rubbing my eyes and the sun shining faintly through dense fog. Then as Rodney woke up, I asked, "Did I miss something during the night?"

"If you did…, I did too." He yawned and sat up straight. "If those Yankees attacked last night, they were quiet about it," he answered as he sat up straight. Yawning he added, "Some coffee would be good right about now. Then they can attack."

"Yeah," I said as I looked around. All the rifles were propped against the barricade. Most of the men were lying around waiting. As I turned my head, I saw the cemetery behind us. Fog was heavy again that morning, making the scene especially eerie more than I knew it was. I asked myself "All of those buried belong to families that will never see them again. Is it worth it?"

"Enough of this daydreaming, Buchanan…We have more to worry about than sleeping," a Captain announced above me.

"Yes, sir," I said as I jumped to my feet.

"Major Hutchinson wants to have a word with you," the Captain said. He signaled for me to go ahead of him along the barricade

"Save a couple Yankees for me," I told Rodney as I walked away.

"All you want is two… not three or four?" Rodney shouted back to me.

"I don't want to be greedy," I shouted back. After hearing about Mr. Davis leaving and the news about the fall of Petersburg, I wondered why we were trying to hold Richmond. Was I the only one with a feeling of defeat. To see all the wounded in readiness for battle I was sure I wasn't alone with those feelings.

"Keep it down… Do you want every one of those Yankees to hear you? That's the best way to get yourself shot," the Captain warned us.

I followed the Captain on down the line for the meeting with Major Hutchinson.

The meeting was like so many others had been. Once again, they needed me to go on another trip north with another message. The Confederacy had to do something, or we would lose the war. Major Hutchinson wanted me to tell our supporters to do whatever it took to kill Lincoln. He said Mr. Davis's thinking was that Lincoln's assassination would demoralize the Union Army enough to give us the edge.

"You might want to wait until the present threat is over... Then leave," Major Hutchinson suggested.

"Yes, sir," I replied in deep thought. I had made the trip enough times to have made a few friends. My concern wasn't that the Yankees might catch me; it was trying to decide which route might be best.

I felt no guilt about being part of a plot to assassinate Lincoln. I had finally come to realize that war was war; and if it meant killing; that was the way it was.

"Good luck" the Major said, offering his hand. "You had better get back to your post... By nightfall the way should be clear."

"Thank you, sir…," I let my words trail because I thought I had heard gunfire. Gun flashes were coming from the woods in front of the barricade. I kept myself low so the enemy wouldn't get a good shot at me. Not having my rifle, I wasn't in any position to fight back. Before I did anything else, I needed to get back to Rodney.

As I came up behind Rodney, he turned and said, "Your timing's good. You're gone a minute or two and they begin shooting."

"I know my place," I said as I dove for the wall. I picked up my rifle and looked over the barricade. A Yankee was coming towards us. I took a slow careful aim and fired a round. Before I could lower the rifle to reload it, the Yankee fell. Rodney and I got into a rhythm in which he would fire a shot; and then as he reloaded I would fire. Most of our shooting was at what looked like puffs of smoke from a firearm in thick woods. At times the fog and smoke were indistinguishable. We didn't know how many Yankees we had killed, but at least the enemy wasn't advancing on us anymore. That changed as the Yankee cannons got into position and they began firing cannonballs at us. The first shot was a near miss. The debris rained down on us for what seemed like hours. The worst of it was the dirt in the air that made it hard to breathe.

After a few minutes, I heard a cry, "Why…, he was just a kid."

Later I was to find out the kid was the brother of one of the soldiers. The kid had come to the barricade to check on his brother. The cannonball had hit within a few feet and killed him. I felt sorry for the surviving brother for he would always feel responsible. If you get yourself killed, you halfway expect it, but losing a family member in battle is another matter.

The fog was still heavy. "I hate weather like this," I said quietly to Rodney.

"No, this fog certainly isn't helping." Looking over the barricade, I added, "This hour of the day doesn't make it any easier to fight."

"But it isn't doing them any good, either," I replied.

"They haven't got our range yet but it won't be long," Rodney shouted at me as he raised his rifle.

"When they do, this barricade won't do much to help us," I said as I got ready to fire.

"If this fog lifts, we might be in trouble," he commented.

"I agree…but right now it's bad enough that they're in the woods, without this fog making it even harder to find a target," I added as I fired a shot. Lowering my rifle, I said, "I'm beginning to think we're wasting our time. It might be better if we could find some way to take out those cannons."

"Do you have any suggestions? I won't be of much help being shot up like I am," he said firing a shot. Then lowering his rifle he added I agree we are wasting our ammunition.

"Other than praying, I don't have any right now. Give me a little time and I'll come up with something. I'm getting tired of crouching down behind this barricade wondering when a cannonball is coming through," I said as I fired. Suddenly I began to get an idea. Turning to him, I suggested, "Maybe we should blow them out of their position."

"Our boys are doing their best to do just that," Rodney said as he fired again.

"Without much luck," I reminded him. Just then, a cannonball exploded through a section of the barricade. We were a good twenty some feet from the impact but we still were showered with splinters of wood and dirt.

"If you're planning on doing anything, do it fast," he replied.

I had seen a keg of gunpowder sitting next to a tree. That had given me an idea. I had used a similar keg of powder on the bridge near the Marsh place. I thought it might destroy a cannon or two and slow the forces down a little. All I needed was a fuse and a way to get the keg near the cannons. I couldn't carry it through the lines, but there had to be a way. Picking up my rifle, I fired, killing a Yankee on horseback that was charging us.

"That guy wasn't smart at all," Rodney said as I began to reload.

I didn't understand what he meant. All I could see was the guy charging us. I asked, "What?"

"Riding out in the open like he did. He must have had a death wish or something," he explained, as he got ready to fire another round.

As I was listening to Rodney, a cannon shot went sailing over our heads. It exploded in the center of the cemetery, leaving a deep crater. It seemed I was the only one who had noticed it. Most of the men firing rounds at the Yankees were receiving cannonballs in return fire. Remembering the soldier, I had just killed I looked over the barricade at his body. Recalling the meeting with Mr. Marsh's brother, I had gotten an idea. The soldier had fallen not too far from us and his horse wasn't far off. I got the idea that I had this idea of wearing his uniform, like Wilber Marsh had, to help me get closer to the cannons. I told Rodney, "I'll see if I can get him… He might be the answer to our problems."

"What are you talking about? He's dead… you can't do anything for him. You can't even make him any deader than he is," he told me.

"I need his uniform," I explained. As I was talking, I looked over the wall to see if I might be able to get to him. After a few minutes, it seemed there weren't any Yankees within sight of our position.

As I put my hand on the edge, Rodney asked, "What's wrong with you…? Are you trying to get yourself killed?"

"I'll be right back," I assured him. Cautiously I leaped over the barricade. As I hit the ground, a bullet hit the wall above me. I grabbed the dead soldier's body and I picked him up placing him on top of the barricade. Then as another bullet hit the wall, I slid over the barricade. I was beginning to think Rodney was right in that I must have been trying to kill myself. It didn't matter. I wasn't going to quit yet. I reached up, grabbed the dead soldier and pulled him the rest of the way over the wall.

"That was dumb…What were you thinking?" Rodney said shaking his head.

"I told you I need his uniform…if I'm to take out those cannons," I explained to him.

"What do you mean?" He asked inquisitively. "Now that you have him and his uniform…, what do you plan to do?" Rodney said as he reloaded his rifle.

"I'm going to become a Yankee," I answered him, grinning.

Looking shocked at what I had told him, he asked, "What…?"

"Yep, that's what I'm planning to do, become a Yankee carrying a keg of gunpowder," I told him. I began taking the jacket off the soldier's body. I had already taken his belt and shoulder strap off and set them to one side. I knew the hardest part would be to get his pants on. With the barricade as low as it was, I couldn't stand up to pull them off. I wondered whether I really needed them; surely the jacket would be enough. I had already taken enough chances; I didn't want to die undressing him.

"Undressing a woman would be more fun…" Rodney chuckled. With hesitation, he added, "Great. So you're now risking having our own men shoot you. If they catch you, what will you do then?"

"Other than getting myself killed what else is there to do today," I joked. With a smile, I added, "And I wouldn't know about undressing a woman... I haven't had the pleasure."

On my missions north I had met a few women, but I hadn't had the time to get involved. On one trip north, I met Miss Bradfield. We rode the train for more than a day together. During that short time, we struck up an interesting friendship. I had feelings I had never experienced before. These feelings were strongest whenever I was near her or thought about her. As we continued with the trip, I began thinking of her often. One day I realized how much she reminded me of Ida. I then realized the only woman I wanted to get to know better was Ida. I just prayed she felt the same way about me.

Thinking about undressing, many years earlier a bunch of us boys stripped and went for a swim in the creek. All of us were afraid that some girls would see us and steal our clothes, but that didn't happen. I wondered what it would be like to have Ida join me in a swim. Something told me her mother wouldn't approve of the idea.

Even since I thought I had seen Ida's mother, I had worried about what had become of Ida. Was she still alive? Then if she was alive, had she gone down the same path her mother had been doing? Again, I began getting mad at what the war was causing women to turn to. I understood the whys but it still made me sick. It wasn't right for a woman to have to give her body to any man that walked by. Thinking of Mother and Father, I added, "My mother said I was too young to fight in a war."

With the words out of my mouth, a vision of Ida came to me. With a lump in my throat, I decided I didn't care. No matter what she had to do to survive, I wanted her. I couldn't think of anyone else that I wanted to spend the rest of my life with.

Right now, though, I was in the middle of a war. If we were lucky, both Ida and I would make it through. Then we could start again, even if it meant moving west. Having heard so many stories, I began thinking of moving west away from everything. I thought getting away from the destruction and hatred might be a good idea.

Rodney didn't say anything but from his grin and the shake of his head, I knew what he was thinking. I had to do something, no matter how risky it was. Mr. Davis wanted me to go north not go down fighting behind the barricade. There was no time to waste, so I concentrated on changing uniforms.

As the Captain walked up to us, he asked "What do you think you're doing?"

"He has this dumb idea that if they see a Yankee uniform, they won't fire the cannons at us" Rodney said.

"Also, it'll get me headed north as the Major asked me to do," I said. I scanned the area and then added, "Now that I have his uniform, all I need is that horse of his...I also need a fuse to set off that keg of gunpowder."

"I can get some fuse for you," the captain said. Before he turned around, he asked, "Why is it there's no blood on that jacket?"

I answered him by giving the body a kick, causing it to roll over. With the body on its back, it was easy to see where I had gotten him. The slug had taken out whatever teeth he once had. It then took out the back of his skull, killing him instantly.

"A clean shot," the captain commented.

"I doubt the dummy felt anything," Rodney said. "He rode straight towards us…It was as if he wanted to be killed and Edgar just cooperated."

"The fog probably had him confused," I suggested.

"Then let more of them have the same problem and get this over with," Rodney replied as he fired another shot.

"I'm beginning to hate this war," the captain said. He then muttered as he left us, "I wish I had gone into business with my father."

"A little late to think about that" I said to myself. I started thinking if Father hadn't joined, I probably wouldn't be where I was, and both of my parents might still be alive." But there were no guarantees that anything would have been different. I knew he would join no matter what anyone said or did. He had given his life for a cause he believed in which is more than some could say.

Rodney asked, "Are we going to stand around doing nothing, or are we going to get this plan of yours going?"

"What…?" I asked. It took a little bit and then I understood. I added, "Oh, yeah… I had better see about getting a horse.

"Watch out…! They're coming straight for us," someone down the line shouted out.

As I turned to see what he was talking about, I heard a shot. Out of the corner of my eye, I saw Rodney fall. Forgetting about the Yankees coming towards us, I looked to see if he was all right. I knelt down to give him a hand. I saw he had taken the shot in his blind eye. His good eyes were still open looking as if he was still in shock. I knew he was dead. Not knowing what else to do I closed his one eye and felt a tear run down my cheek. As anger welled up in me again, I reached to grab my rifle.

As I picked up my rifle, all I heard was the shouting and screaming. As I looked over the top of the barricade, I saw Yankees heading towards us. I could hear the cannon fire. The cannonballs were taking out sections of the barricade, allowing the enemy easy entrance to our lines.

"Get them, boys," a Yankee shouted out as he passed me.

"Retreat for safety," someone else shouted.

I was in shock as Yankee soldiers ran around me firing at my fellow soldiers. At first I didn't understand why they hadn't killed me. Raising my rifle, I saw my blue sleeve and realized why. Changing uniforms had saved my life. I realized I had better do something quickly because there wasn't much I could do but run. If I were to shoot any of the Yankees, I was sure to lose my own life in seconds. So rather than firing a shot, I ran for safety.

It wasn't long before my fellow Confederates surrendered. With me staying out of sight, I was safe. From my hiding place, I watched my comrades taken off as prisoners. As I watched them hauled off, I knew my trip north was out of the question. I thought about my feelings of Rodney and a Yankee shooting him as he stood next to me. He joined Raymond, Mr. Marsh and so many others that I had known throughout my life. I didn't know what else to do but I was tired of it all. I prayed that Mr. Davis and Mr. Lee would understand there were other issues more important than this stinking war. I was tired of the war and I turned my thoughts to Ida and one of her smiles.

As dusk came, the activity began to die down. I came out of hiding and walked around the streets of Richmond. I felt sick at what I saw. Buildings I had marveled at as a young man were now in ruins. The people wore ripped, dirty clothing and looked as if they had not had enough to eat. Many of them had blank expressions on their faces or looks of downright despair. I knew I had seen many men killed but I hadn't been through what these men had. It was easy to see in their eyes the war hadn't been worth it.

In front of me were the ruins of one of the most prominent buildings I could remember, the multi-story paper mill. The attack of the Yankee's had left it in rubble. What was left of the multi story building surely wasn't worth trying to rebuild.

Two emaciated looking men walked past me. I wondered whether they had been in Libby Prison. As thin as they were, matched the rumors that Libby didn't have enough food to feed the prisoners. It was a shame to think war could do what it did to people.

As Ida came to mind again, I murmured "I pray you are alive... If I ever needed someone it's now." At that very moment I saw Ida's mother again. She was with a Yankee soldier, hanging onto his arm and wearing a tired smile. She was thin and pale. Her hair was straggly, and she looked deathly sick. She had on a dress that was torn and dirty, and she looked as if she hadn't bathed in months. She was a total mess. She wasn't anything like the woman I had known growing up before the war.

A voice from behind me asked, "What are you doing, soldier?"

I turned around, startled and said, "What?" Taking my eyes off Ida's mother, I saw a Yankee sergeant was staring at me. My first inclination was to run, but I knew better than to do that.

The Yankee sergeant asked, "I asked you what you were doing?"

"I was told to patrol the streets to see if there were any stragglers around" I answered. I prayed he didn't ask what outfit I was with or the name of my superior.

He asked, "Have you found any?"

"No," I replied, hoping he wouldn't ask me anything else.

"Keep your eyes open. You can't trust those rebels," he said as he turned away.

"Yes, sir" I saluted. I couldn't remember if it was proper to salute a sergeant or not.

Just then, I saw Ida's mother and the soldier a block away. I picked up my pace to catch up with them. Though it wasn't any of my business, I needed to know what she was doing here. Could it be possible that she was selling herself to the Yankee soldiers? Fearing the worst, I didn't know whether I should approach her or stay away from her. I was afraid if I approached her, it might be embarrassing. I also knew it would be better than having her do what I feared she was planning. As I got closer, I wondered how many times she had sold herself to the men. As the thought began to form, I knew I didn't want to know the answer. With this realization, I almost turned around and went the other way.

As I stopped to consider my choices, I saw Mrs. Marsh and the soldier enter a wrecked out building. I followed, keeping a discreet distance and being careful not to alert them. From a room not far down a hall I heard them talking.

"It would be better if you undid the buttons first," the soldier was saying.

"I'm trying to" Mrs. Marsh said.

I couldn't stand to listen. I stepped outside, walked across the street and hid in an alley. From there I could watch the building and see them leave.

I was glad that from where I was I couldn't see the dead bodies piled up like cords of wood. The faint screams coming from the hospital tents made me cringe. There was still the smell of death in the air and I felt like it would be years before it left.

Seeing Richmond as it was that day, it was hard to believe that carriages with fancy dressed women used to travel down the street in front of me. I would never again think of Richmond as I had as a child. I would never again be able to look at the city without seeing all the corpses, so I would never return.

Soon Mrs. Marsh and the soldier left the building. Mrs. Marsh, walking slowly and occasionally stumbling a little, headed for the center of town, and the soldier went in the other direction. As the two parted, I knew I could never tell Ida what I had seen and heard. I walked on a little and nausea overwhelmed me. I began to vomit.

The Start of the Reconstruction

In going back over my diary, I realized I should have added a lot more. I hope historians record what I haven't, for these events are important to the country. My promise to my family in the months or years to come is to do a better job. My only fear is that my entries are only important to me, but I continue to write:

Over the next few weeks, I took care of a few Yankees as I did Mrs. Marsh's friend. I realize he didn't deserve to be killed but I was out of my mind. When I saw those Yankees take advantage of the women was something I couldn't ignore. I knew I couldn't do much for the cause but I still had to do something. It was the same with the other Yankees that took advantage of the women. In the end, I felt I was still part of the war doing what I needed to do. Thinking how we lost so few letting the Yankees take over the city I felt I was doing more than the rest of the men. I recalled the only big battle fought outside of Richmond, was a defeat for the North. I wished this could have been another they lost. But when Mr. Davis left Richmond, his defeatist attitude affected the others. I didn't want to admit it but I knew down deep that we had lost the war.

By this time, I had gotten to know more about the Yankees in Richmond. With the little information I had, I could bluff my way in conversations and go into a camp and get something to eat. Whenever possible I stuffed whatever I could into my shirt to give to the first hungry child I came across. My reward was seeing the smiles on the children' faces.

One afternoon while I was eating in a camp, an excited soldier walked through shouting, "Have you heard?"

"What?" I replied. Suddenly I could see excitement everywhere I looked. Men were laughing and dancing with each other. Off in the distance, soldiers were jumping around excitedly. Guns were being fired all over the camp. I didn't know what was going on but everyone looked pleased.

"Appomattox," he answered. I put my plate down and asked, "What's so big. "What about Appomattox?"

"Lee surrendered to Grant," he shouted.

"He did what?" I asked not fully understanding. I couldn't imagine Mr. Lee surrendering to anyone. Thinking about how I felt about the war I realized that maybe he, too, was tired of the war.

"He surrendered! We should be going home soon," he said, sounding elated.

"Really…? It's hard to believe," I responded. I remembered my parents. "I guess so. At least those that have homes to go to."

He asked, "What do you mean?"

"Nothing…Just thinking about people who lost their homes," I replied as I got up. He still looked confused, so I added, "I'm just tired."

"I know what you mean," he said. Then he ran off to tell others the news.

"I guess that's that," I said as I turned to leave, unsure of what to do or where to go.

A soldier asked as he rode past me, "What was that?"

"Nothing… just thinking to myself, I'm not sure what I'm going to do." I answered him.

"I know what I'm going to do. I'm going back home to my wife and little girl," he smiled. Looking at me closely he asked, "Where are you from?"

Knowing that saying "Ashland, Virginia" would give away the fact that I was a Rebel, I said, "I'm from Minnesota." I hoped he didn't detect my Southern accent.

"You're a long way from home, farther than I am," he replied. He sounded interested in knowing more about Minnesota…

"I wish I had a family to go home to," I said. Then under my breath I added, "Ida's even out of the question now that her mother's become what she has."

"Sorry," the soldier said as if he understood what I meant.

"I'll survive…I may head west and start a new life," I told him.

"Many of our men have been talking about doing that. Good luck," he said with a smile and a handshake.

"Good luck to you too…and enjoy your family," I said as I let go of his hand.

I watched him walk away. At that moment I thought that after knowing what had happened to Mrs. Marsh, I would never be able to face Ida or her mother again. In the past I had felt lost and alone, but never to the degree, I felt right then. Holding back tears, I went on my way and watched what was going on around me.

I began to think that leaving might be a bad idea. If my Confederate comrades found me, I might find myself facing a firing squad for deserting. On the other hand, Yankees might shoot me if they found out I was a Rebel…

Telling that one soldier that I might go out west made me start to think about it seriously. Mr. Marsh had made gold pans for the miners back in the fifties. I knew the gold rush was over, but I imagined there still might be some left for me to find. I laughed to myself and told myself to quit daydreaming.

But if I did head west, before I did that I wanted to see the old place and find out whether anyone was living there. I needed to know what had happened to them, not only Ida but other friends, and see whether they needed my help.

A familiar voice asked, "Still looking for stragglers?"

It was the same Sergeant who had stopped me earlier. "Yes, sir…," I said. "But I don't know why, since Lee has surrendered."

"Good point…I guess it's not up to us to know everything. As far as I'm concerned, we've done enough damage…Why not leave well enough alone?" he said as he shook his head.

"My thoughts exactly" I replied. I wondered how long this conversation would last. I was afraid standing around might ruin my chance of making my break.

"Anyway, you should be wearing an arm band," he said as he handed me a strip of black cloth.

"I didn't know I needed one," I told him as I took it.

"Not everyone has gotten the word," he said. "If I don't see you again…good luck."

He asked, "Where are you from?"

"I'm from Minnesota," I answered. I hoped he wasn't from there. I had used Minnesota with the other soldier and it seemed to have worked. This was the second time someone had asked where I was from. I guess everyone was more interested in going home.

"You're a long way from home," he said.

"Yes, sir… I'm looking forward to getting home" I replied.

"So are we all." He looked toward the center of town and added, "As I said…good luck."

"Good luck to you too." I replied as I tied the strip around my arm. I was feeling a little more comfortable having met, up with him. This strip of cloth might save my life, and if so, I owed this man a lot. As we each went our own way, I asked under my breath "I wonder what he would say if he knew I was a Rebel?"

Before leaving Richmond, I went back to see if I could find my old uniform. I wasn't planning to change right then but knew I would later. I also didn't plan to remove the strip of black cloth for a while either. I figured that once I was out of the city, people would accept me more easily as a Confederate soldier coming home than as a Yankee. For my own safety, I would have to change uniforms or run the risk of getting shot by one of my Confederate comrades.

I did find my old uniform, unlikely as that was. As I tucked the clothes under my arm, I thought of Mr. Marsh's brother and chuckled. Had he been wearing the right uniform?

I threw my blood stained jacket away, as well as my Yankee uniform. I had just changed into my gray pants when a wagon came along. I stayed behind a bush, looking out to make sure it wasn't a Yankee wagon with armed guards. As it approached, I saw it contained an older man with a woman sitting next to him. As it got even closer, I recognized the passenger and it was Ida!

I had mixed feelings. No matter how much I wanted to see her, I didn't feel like talking with her right then. I couldn't run the risk of blurting out what I had learned about her mother.

As the wagon passed, I saw what I knew was a body. I couldn't tell if it was a man or a woman. Down deep, I knew it was Ida's mother and I felt sorry for Ida. Like me, she had lost both her parents now. I thought it might be for the best that her mother had died, after what her life had become in her last weeks or months. I hoped that Ida had never found out about that, for I didn't know how she would be able to live with the shame of it.

Then I heard Ida's faint voice ask, "Is it worth it?"

"A good question" the man answered. Then before either could say anything more, they were out of range of my voice.

"I wish you luck, Ida," I said as they passed out of sight. I headed towards Ashland on foot; but unlike them, I would detour around our little area so that Ida wouldn't see me. As dusk fell, I was growing very tired.

Then I heard another wagon and I stepped to one side. I didn't look back to see whether it was a Yankee wagon, for I was too exhausted to care. I looked up as the driver brought the wagon to a stop. On the seat was an old man wearing a smile.

He asked, "Going far?"

"Ashland area," I told him, doubting that he knew where it was.

"Never heard of the town," he admitted.

"It's not much of a town… Just a church and a school north of here a few miles," I said. Having been away for as long as I had I wondered if there was anything left of it.

"Hop on board and I'll give you a ride," he offered.

"Thanks…I'm thankful for any walking you can save me," I told him as I tried to smile. I handed him my rifle and got up into the wagon. Sitting down felt really good, after having been walking on my feet all day. I reached over, took my rifle back, and propped it between my legs. I nodded my head to let him know I was ready. Before I could bring my head up, he snapped the reins and we were on our way.

We introduced ourselves. His name was Samuel Anderson.

"I'm a little surprised to see you with your firearms," he said. He sounded as if he approved of that. "I've been told all they allowed you to keep were the clothes on your back and a horse."

"What they don't know won't hurt them…Most didn't have clothes worth keeping and there's, not enough horses to go around. If any of them thought about it might be better to join the Union Army and go west to fight the Indians. Something tells me few of the farms around here aren't worth trying to save," I said.

I didn't feel like telling him I had been wearing a Yankee Uniform. He was right the Confederate prisoners could keep their clothes, horse, but not their firearms. It was me wearing a Yankee uniform that allowed me to keep my Remington. It was the only thing I had left of my father and I would have died trying to keep it.

As I settled back he said, "I guess you're right… I bet you're glad it's over?"

"Yes," I said, suddenly not wanting to talk anymore.

He asked, "I take it you're from this Ashland?"

"It seems like a lifetime ago…, but yes," I answered.

"I just came back from my brother's place on the south side of Richmond," he told me. Then not giving me time to say anything he added, "His wife sent some bread home with me."

"That was good of her," I replied." My stomach was hurting from hunger. I glanced toward the back of the wagon. I didn't see any sign of bread, but there was a lot of stuff piled high.

He asked, "Hungry?"

"I'm past that point," I answered. He reached between his legs and pulled a blanket back, revealing four loaves of bread, then grabbed one and handed it to me.

"I don't have anything to go with it, but you're welcome to this loaf," he said with a grin.

"Thanks," I replied. My hands trembled as I accepted it. I took a big bite of the bread, feeling a little embarrassed at my lack of manners.

"From the way you're going at it, I would say you're starved," he said with a smile.

It didn't take long and I pulled the loaf away from my mouth. As I let the flavor of the bread flow down my throat, I felt more relaxed than I had since the beginning of the war.

Suddenly I thought of Rodney. If that shooter hadn't killed him, he would have seen the end of the war only a short time later.

All around us the night was quiet. In spite of all I had experienced and all I had lost, I felt at peace. Finally, this terrible war was over.

"Thanks. I certainly was hungry, and this is the best bread I've had in years."

"Jim's wife's known for her bread," he replied as he snapped the reins. Turning to me, he added, "I would like to get home this evening."

"This is good," I commented as I put the rest of the first bite into my mouth.

"I guess the food they've been feeding you hasn't been all that good," he suggested.

"Not really…I never had to eat rat or dog but I came close a couple of times," I answered.

"In his last letter, my son told me he had to eat rat a couple of times," Mr. Anderson said.

I had a feeling I knew what he meant when he said the last letter. The "Last letter" usually meant the writer had met his death. Not knowing what else to say I told him "I'm sorry," I said.

"We don't know whether he was killed or not. With the surrender, he may still come home…It would make his mother and me happy," he said not sounding too convincing… "That's all we can hope for."

"What is your son's name?"

"Rodney," he answered.

When he told me his name was Anderson, I felt a little uneasy. I did not remember right then but Anderson rang a bell. When he said, his son's name was Rodney I put it together. I didn't know what to say, so I just looked off into the dark woods. I had to tell him but I didn't know how I would do that. Since I was with Rodney when he died, it was my duty to tell his father, but I couldn't find the words for that. After riding on in silence for a while, I asked, "Did he write that he had been, wounded?"

"Yes…but he said it wasn't serious," he answered.

"Oh," I managed to get out. I took a deep breath and told him how his son had died. After I finished he didn't ask anything or comment in any way. He just held the reins quietly as the horse clip-clopped and the wagon rumbled through the moonlight. The way he took the news drove a stake into my heart. I felt guilty about telling him, almost as if I had been responsible for the death of his son, for I had killed every dream he had of seeing his son again.

For the next twenty minutes, we didn't say anything. As we came to the top of a rise, I recognized the area. Without the moonlight, I wouldn't have been able to tell where I was. I told Mr. Anderson, "You can let me off here."

He asked, "Are you sure?"

"Yes," I told him. As I got off the wagon, I added, "I'm sorry about your son."

Sounding as if he wanted to cry, he asked, "Did he suffer much?"

"He didn't feel anything," I answered.

"That's good…Thanks," he said as he snapped the reins.

"Thanks for the ride," I shouted to him. Then I remembered the bread in my hand and added, "And for the bread."

I waved as he drove off, then I headed into the woods. My old slave friend Billy's place was only a quarter of a mile into the woods. I prayed someone would be there and would offer me a place to stay. It was pleasant to be away from the sounds of gunfire and men screaming in agony, and not to smell death in the air. In the blackness of the night, I couldn't see anything that resembled war. I prayed I would never see another war.

After walking a few minutes, I saw the outline of a house. My heart began to beat with excitement until I realized there were no lights shining through the windows. As I approached, I saw the house wasn't there anymore. Only one end of it was still standing and the rest had burned. Looking up at the one wall left, I said to myself "Another one you Yankees got."

With a shrug, I headed north towards Ashland and prayed Mr. Smiley and Jacob and his wife were still there. I knew I could find a bed or floor to sleep on. Anything was better than what I had right then. Though the moon was still shining through the clouds, I could feel rain was in the air and I was afraid I might be caught in a storm without proper clothes or a horse. I prayed I would make it the two miles to Ashland. Knowing I had only a few choices, I took the first step and headed north. With each step I prayed, "Be there, Jacob… Please be there."

Jacob had been the Marshes' stable boy before the war. When he wasn't cleaning out the stables and brushing down the horses, he was watching Jocko doing blacksmithing. Eventually Jocko taught him all he knew about that trade, and when the war broke out, Jacob was as good at blacksmithing as his teacher, if not better. When I went to the Marsh's with my parents, of course I always wanted to see Ida, but I also wanted to see Jacob. During the war, I had stopped at every opportunity to give him what help I could. I was lucky enough to be there when he married Molly. I didn't know her before the war but I had gotten to know her on my visits back while the war was going on.

I came out of the woods and looked out over the meadow. In the moonlight I could still see a cluster of buildings and knew I didn't have far to go. I could make out lights in the windows and my heartbeat with excitement. I was looking forward to enjoying the warmth of a fire. Feeling tired, I knew I could use something to drink and maybe a little more food. The bread Mr. Anderson had given me had helped, but it wasn't enough.

As I got closer, I could make out the steeple of the church, and then the school. The first house was the Reverend's place. On the other side was Mr. Marsh's factory and Smiley's place. Not far down the road to the south would be whatever was left of the Marsh place. The thought that Ida might be staying there made me start walking faster…

In the street between the Reverend's place and Smiley's, I stopped. Since Ida's father had left the manufacturing place to Smiley, she could be staying with them. Knowing Ida and Jacob were good friends she might be at Jacob's place. Curious as I was about where she might be, I wasn't ready to face her right then. I just wanted to get something to eat and then some sleep. I didn't want to see but a few friends. Being in the Ashland area wasn't where I wanted to be. With the Marshes' place to the south and my parents' place to the north, there were too many haunting memories around Ashland. I decided to go to Jacob's place. On my way over I remembered how small his place was, and I doubted that Ida would be there.

Jacob met me at the door. "I was worried you had gotten yourself killed…Molly, come here…It's Master Edgar."

"Did you say Master Edgar?" She asked. She was wiping her hands on her apron as she came to the door. "We have been so worried…We haven't seen you for over a year."

"Remember, I'm just Edgar… I'm no one's master," I reminded both of them, then added, "As Father used to say… about me, I don't have enough brains to get into too much trouble." I told them with a laugh. Then I asked them "Mind if I come in?"

"Forgive my dumb husband… Come in out of the weather," Molly answered as she reached out as if to help me. As Jacob shut the door, she asked me "Are you hungry?"

"I don't mean to put you out" I said. I knew they didn't have much themselves, yet I was hungry.

"We have a little stew that's still warm… Jacob came home late so we just finished. You're more than welcome to what's left," she told me as she went to the fireplace, where the stew pot was hanging over the embers.

"If it's no trouble," I answered. It was a little hard to say no as hungry as I was. The aroma of the stew filled the room making it even harder to say no. As I walked closer to the fireplace, I added, "Sure smells good."

"Might be a good idea to heat the back room," Jacob suggested.

"Do I smell that bad?" I asked seeming to be embarrassed. Now that he mentioned it, I couldn't remember the last time I had bathed.

"You do smell a little," Molly said with a smile. She ladled up some stew she added, "I'm sure Jacob has something you can wear."

"I've never been one to argue," I said as I took the bowl. Then not knowing how else to put it, I told her "It would be easier to eat if I had a spoon."

"Oh, Lordy… What's wrong with my head?" She asked sounding flustered. It didn't take long and she put a spoon in front of me.

"Edgar's smell is getting to you," Jacob said, smiling.

"Don't pay any attention to him, Master Edgar." Molly replied as she shook the ladle at him.

"Just Edgar, please" I reminded her.

"I'm sorry…Edgar" she answered, slightly embarrassed.

After I had eaten a second serving of stew, we talked for a while. I told them what had happened in Richmond and about how I was thinking of going west. I didn't say anything about seeing Ida. Jacob told me that if I needed money, he had a few dollars he would give me. I told him I would find a job and work my way west. He also said that Mr. Smiley might have some work that I could do. What would that be, I wondered, since all I knew how to do was be a soldier.

"I guess you wouldn't know… but Ida brought her mother back and buried her next to her father," Jacob said.

"That's what Mrs. Marsh would have wanted. A shame Ida had to lose both her mother and father." I certainly didn't want to tell them what I knew about Mrs. Marsh's life in Richmond. It didn't concern them, and besides, I didn't want to say anything that might make Ida look bad or make them think that I wasn't ready to see her because of it.

"She would love to see you," Molly said.

"Maybe he needs a bath first…I'm sure Ida doesn't want to smell him like he does now," Jacob replied.

"It would be good to get rid of this war smell," I said. Bringing up the idea of a bath changed the subject of conversation, which meant I wouldn't have to tell them I didn't want to see her yet.

"I'll put some water on," Molly said.

"I'll speak to Smiley in the morning," Jacob offered

"No that's all right… I'll talk to him" I assured him. It wasn't long and my bath water was ready. After the bath I felt as if I were in heaven, and glad I had friends like Molly and Jacob. Until Molly could wash my clothes, I wore a pair of Jacob's pants and one of his shirts.

Having slept that night on a pallet on the hard floor, it wasn't hard to get up the following morning. I went off to the factory with Jacob, and Mr. Smiley put me to work delivering and picking up supplies. He couldn't pay me much, but it was more than I could have had without his help.

Only three of us worked at Mr. Marsh's old factory. Mr. Smiley handled the business end, Jacob worked at the forge, and I did odd jobs.

I didn't think Mr. Smiley's business would be able to complete with the Tredegar Ironworks in Richmond, which had come through the war largely undamaged. If that was so, we wouldn't be in business long, and after that I would probably go west.

On the first day, I said to Jacob, "That training you got working in the stables on the Marsh place paid off."

"That it did… I used to dream of working a forge. I just didn't think it would happen as soon as this, with the war and all" he replied as he pumped the bellows. "Smiley has ideas of making more than horseshoes and rims for wagon wheels."

"I guess it will be a while," I said, eager to hear more. I wanted to see the old place come to life again and be the way it once was.

Silently I watched him and the glowing coals. The fire in the forge shimmered like a bucket full of the lightning bugs we used to catch and put in bottles. Watching it almost put me in a trance.

The big problem with working the forge or even doing the forming was that it was such a hot job. I didn't have any interest in learning how to work the forge. I saw myself working with animals or in the fields, but not working with steel.

The second day around midday, Molly brought us something to eat. As we ate, Jacob told me again, "Ida would love to see you…I haven't told her you're here, but I know she'll find out soon enough."

"I guess I should go and see her," I said. "Where is she staying?"

"At the old place… She's using the root cellar," he answered.

I asked Mr. Smiley if I could take a little time off. He consented when I explained that I wanted to check on Ida and he thought that might be a good idea. I took off my leather apron and headed towards the Marsh place, taking a shortcut through the woods it didn't take long to get there.

Walking across the Marsh's land, I didn't see much of the old place. It didn't resemble anything like it used to be. The ruins of the buildings left standing weren't worth using. I did see enough we could use to build a better place for Ida to live in.

When I came to the remains of the main house, I went around to the rear of the building ruins and found the root cellar. I smiled as I remembered hiding in it once. It had taken Ida half the afternoon to find me.

The storm cellar door was open. Knowing Ida was somewhere around the place, I called out, "Ida. …are you in there?"

I heard her scream out "Edgar! Edgar, you're alive!" She came running out of the cellar.

"Well hello…, hello…, hello… Haven't you grown up," I said as I ran to her. For the first time in more years than I cared to remember, I found myself happy. It seemed there was something to live for, after all.

As we got closer, I realized she wasn't the little girl I had left behind. I knew she had changed when I saw her in the wagon but I didn't get a close look at her that day. She had become a woman in spite of the war. I found feelings running through me I hadn't felt towards her before. Before I knew what was happening, she jumped into my arms and gave me a kiss. Releasing her, I managed to say, "Well, that's a first."

We stepped back, and she looked me over, probably thinking about how much I had changed since she last saw me. I was looking at the most beautiful woman I had ever met, and I was afraid that she wouldn't like what she saw in me. Then she smiled. Apparently, she wasn't too disappointed in what she saw. I returned her smile with one of my own.

My biggest fear was she would start asking me questions that I didn't want to answer. I wanted to be honest and open with her, but I knew I couldn't tell her everything. In fact, I couldn't tell her most of what had happened in the past few years. I didn't feel right telling her I knew about what her mother had become in Richmond. Though I understood, it was still hard to accept. I wondered when I would be able to talk about the war years knowing it had to come up sometime. I also wasn't proud of everything I had done during the war.

I did tell her that Mr. Smiley had put me to work. He knew I had no place to stay so he offered me the back room. I was reluctant to tell her, it took me a day and a half to come by to talk to her. It was on the way over my idea of not seeing her changed to wanting to be with her. Now that I had a job and a place to stay, I could give her some help in settling in on the old place. We found ourselves discussing the war and some things about it.

We sat down on a fallen log and talked about the war and about how conditions were now. She told me about the sharecroppers who were still around. Most of them had gone east or south, and one had gone up north. I got the feeling that the remaining ones were her inspiration to try to stay on and make a go of it.

Nothing in my memory of her as a little girl gave me confidence that she could make it in the old place. Like me, she hadn't ever done any hard work as a child. I reminded myself I was once the same way. During the war I had changed and probably so had she. I said, "We will see."

"I think I'll see if I might be of use up at the Hospital Tent," Ida suggested.

"I don't think that's a good idea" I responded. Having once been in one of those tents myself worried me. I didn't want her catching the fever from a patient, for that would mean I could lose her. After having feared she was dead once, I didn't want it to come true.

"We do what we have to in order to live" Ida said.

"I know, but there's got to be something else you can do" I said, afraid an argument was about to take place.

"You have a better idea?" she asked. "After all, I have to eat."

"I understand. Working for Smiley now isn't something I'm looking forward to either," I said agreeing with her. I continued, "Hopefully, once orders begin to come in, I'll be able to do something I enjoy. I'd like to get into more of the business side than the manufacturing side. It's the odd jobs that bore me."

"So it's settled then…I'll see what I can do to help them and, that way earn a meal or two. I doubt that it will last all that long, but it's something," she replied." She sounded as if she had won.

"I still don't like the idea, but I know it's of no use to argue," I replied as I gave up. Then I got an idea and I suggested, "Maybe there are enough children around a teacher is needed… I doubt anyone has the money to pay you but you can work for food."

"That's worth thinking about," she said.

In the end she did work in the hospital tent for a while. Then once she had talked to everyone and got them interested in sending their children to school she began teaching.

The conversation changed to old memories. We laughed when we remembered some of the happy times we had known as children, some of the silly things we had done. I wondered who had it worse, I with nothing left, or her with evidence of what once was. In the end, we had both lost, no matter what was left of the places.

"Oh, Edgar, I can't remember when I've laughed so much…It seems as if it's been a lifetime…Thanks," she told me with a warm smile.

"And thank you" I answered, wishing she would kiss me again. With the death, I had seen and the ones I had killed, it was good to laugh again. I felt justified in what I had done during the war, but I wasn't happy about it. My parents brought me up to respect life not to take it. Being in her presence was a pleasure I had nearly forgotten until then. Having Ida at my side made everything better somehow.

"I don't feel so alone now that you're here," Ida confessed with a tear in her eye.

"I know how you feel…we are the only ones left." I replied with a lump in my throat. "Yes, we are the only ones left," I thought to myself.

She looked at the ruins. "I guess there's no sense crying over something you can't change," she said.

"Are you planning to live in the root cellar long, or do you have other plans?" I asked. I found it hard to believe she would resort to living in that cold, clammy hole in the ground.

"I have straw down there for a bed and boxes of things Mother had stored down there to use for a chair and table. Someday I'd like to build a little house…Unfortunately I can't afford it right now," she answered looking as if she wished I would help her.

"Maybe Jacob and I can help you," I offered. Then I remembered Mr. Smiley would expect me to return to work, I added, "I had better get back."

"Thanks for coming. I've been worried, thinking you were killed in the war," she said. Smiling, she added "Come by anytime. And if you and Jacob could build me something, it would be nice."

"I'll talk to him…. Oh, by the way, Jacob said to have you come over for dinner this evening," I said. Her smile and the glint in her eye made it hard for me to leave. I knew she would make life bearable for me no matter how hard it got. As I looked away, I added, "I have a feeling Mr. Smiley is looking for me. He said he had a little job that he needed taken care of this afternoon."

With a questioning look, she asked, "Will I see you later?"

"I don't know… It depends on what he wants me to do" I shrugged. As we parted, I remembered Jacob had never said anything about her coming for supper. Now I had to make sure that was all right with them…

"You didn't need to fear…She's always welcome," Molly assured me.

"I don't know what got into me. We got to talking, and I found myself saying Jacob asked her to come for supper," I admitted.

Jacob laughed and said, "She has a standing invitation for supper."

"Still, it wasn't right for me to just up and invite her," I said.

"That's all right" he assured me with an understanding smile.

"You don't have to mention I've been here for the past day and a half," I told him, thinking that Molly wouldn't understand why I hadn't come to see her earlier.

Before Jacob could answer, Mr. Smiley came over to us and asked, "How's it going, Jacob?"

"Should have another dozen shoes done by the end of the day," Jacob answered.

From the way he looked, I felt something was amiss. "Is there something wrong?" I asked.

"Some men came by and told me they would put me out of business," he said as he walked off.

I ran and caught up with him and asked. "What do you mean; they'll put you out of business?"

"They said they will burn me out," he answered.

"Why?" I asked. What little he had told me, didn't make any sense. I didn't see any reason for someone to put him out of business. There wasn't enough business around for him, let alone someone new.

"I don't know," he answered.

"Where are these men?" I asked. "I want to talk to them. There has to be something that can convince them it's a waste of time."

"I think they're using the Willard place…I think they are from up north, maybe New York or somewhere up that way. They didn't sound like they're from the South. I got the feeling they're not from Fredericksburg," he told me.

"I'll see if I can find them," I said.

Sounding curious he asked, "What for?"

"To see what they have to say," I told him. Something bigger was going on with them than just trying to get into the horseshoe making business. I didn't like seeing good honest people pushed around, and it certainly sounded as if that's what was happening. I didn't know what I could do, but I would try to find some way to help him.

"Guess I can't stop you" he said, "What did you have in mind?"

"I don't know what I can do, but I'll at least talk to them," I said.

"Be careful…I don't think they like being told what they can or can't do," he warned.

"Everyone has their problems…They shouldn't get into something they can't handle." I replied. I then asked, "Have they offered you anything for the place?"

"Nothing," he answered.

"How dare they think they can get something for nothing? I know I have to have a little talk about their manners. You don't take things from someone without offering something in return," I replied.

"Just be careful, that's all I ask. I'd rather close the place down than see someone hurt. The war has caused enough losses," he told me.

"And just because we lost the war doesn't mean we have to give them everything either," I told him. I found it hard to remain calm. With all of us being broke, we were easy targets.

"I'm not trying to argue, but I don't want you to get hurt. This is the third time they've come to see me. I don't know what they will do the next time. They might try to burn me out on their next visit," he said as he put his hand on my shoulder.

"Not with me sleeping in the back room. If they try, they may find I will take offense to the idea," I told him with a grin.

"Do what you can. I haven't had too much luck with them," he said.

"Supper's on" Molly called.

"You had better get in there," Mr. Smiley said. He grinned and added, "She doesn't like to wait once she has put the food on the table, and she's one woman you don't want to make mad."

"I know…I wonder if Ida is here." I looked around, hoping to see her.

He asked, "Oh, she's coming for supper?"

"Yes, or at least she said she would," I told him as I waved. I went outside and looked down the road but didn't see her.

"Took you long enough…I remember when you were the first in line to eat" Ida said as I walked back inside Jacob and Molly's.

Startled a little I replied, "I have changed. Now I'm trying to get all the attention by coming in late."

"If your goal was to change you're doing a good job," Jacob offered.

"I don't need any help from you. I'm in enough trouble as it is," I told him.

"I've always liked a man that hangs himself," he returned with a smile.

"Thanks, I love you too." I said.

"We won't have any of that…He's my husband," Molly told me. Her comment brought laughter all around.

Ida came up to me and told me "Like I said earlier, I've missed you."

"You don't know how many times I thought about you… In fact my need to see you probably kept me alive," I offered. Then before I knew it, she wrapped her hand around my neck and gave me a kiss.

"You would never have seen them do that before the war" Jacob commented. He continued "and what have you been doing in the war?

"I know what I have done… Let's just say I never thought I would do what I did," I told him. I doubt anyone ever heard me brag and I wasn't about to start.

Ida asked, "Oh…Like what?"

"I don't think this is the time to discuss some subjects," I told her.

Ida asked, "Keeping secrets from us?"

"Maybe" I answered not wanting to go into detail.

"All I know is supper is getting cold," Molly told us.

We sat down to supper and had a good time talking. They tried to make me the center of attention but Ida and I pushed most of the conversation onto Jacob and Molly. I had the feeling Ida didn't want to talk about the past any more than I did. Her reactions confirmed I would be doing her a favor if I forgot what I knew. I still wanted to take her into my arms and tell her how sorry I was for her. Her mother had been the most wonderful person I had known as a child, other than my own mother.

The next day I went to visit Ida again

"Like I said earlier, I've missed you," she said

"You don't know how many times I thought about you… I answered.

She wanted to see my old place. It was a long walk, five miles away, but that gave us some more time to talk and get to know each other a little better. When we got to the opening in the fence to my place, she cried. She must have felt as close to it as I did to her place. She looked around at where the house had been and commented. "It's only been a few years, and now there's nothing left."

Later as we walked, we looked at what had once been a field of cotton. There were so many memories everywhere we went. I finally felt good taking her back to the root cellar. It was hard stirring up all of those memories.

The best part of the walk was just being with her. I had been to the old place a few years earlier as I was making my way back to my unit from up north. It had been very hard to see it then, and it was hard now, with Ida.

The part I did enjoy was the walk there and back, with Ida's hand in mine. She was no longer the playmate I used to visit. She was a grown woman in both mind and body, not the scrawny little tomboy she had been before the war.

As we left the place, she asked, "What are you thinking about?"

"I would love to have you in my arms on a cold winter night," I told her.

"We might have to try it this winter," she suggested with a squeeze of my hand and a smile.

Earlier that afternoon we had been sitting and talking. I had reached over and touched the top button of her collar. At first, she gave me a big smile. Then she took a deep breath and said in a stern voice "Now, Edgar…" But now as I talked about winter and having my arms around her, she was all smiles. As my father once told me, women are hard to figure out.

After I walked Ida home, I went back by the shop, then made my way to the Willard place. It was a small farm that had belonged to one of my classmate's parents. They only lived there a couple of years before they decided they couldn't make it and left. I had only been there two or three times, but I didn't think it was more than a few miles from Jacob's home.

Having worked all day and walked to Ida's twice, I didn't feel like walking anywhere. What kept me going was the fear something might happen to Smiley's shop. If someone were to burn it down, many people would suffer. Before taking off, I went to my sleeping quarters and got my pistol. I wasn't planning to shoot anyone, but I wasn't taking any chances.

As I headed out, I didn't expect to meet anyone. Knowing how the Army had stripped the land, I would have been surprised at running into even an animal such as a cow or goat. Night was coming on, and my only concern was tripping over something in the dark. I wanted to take a lantern but decided against it, for I didn't want to alert the guys that I was coming. I also didn't want Smiley to ask questions about where I was going or what I was doing.

The road toward the Willard place wasn't used much, but it was better than trying to cut through the fields that were overgrown with weeds. After about twenty to thirty minutes, the house was in sight. Even from a distance, I could see lights in the windows, indicating that probably someone was inside.

"Hoot… hoot… hoot," an owl cried, not far from me.

"Surprise, surprise, I'm not the only one out tonight," I told the owl softly.

Approaching the house, I moved slowly, keeping one eye on the window and the other on the road. From time to time, I could see someone inside moving past the window, but no one was paying attention to what was going on outside. That was reassuring, but I still worried about tripping or snapping a twig. Before getting up to the house, I wondered what my chances were of getting onto the porch. As old as the house was the boards had to be loose and noisy.

"Hoot, hoot." the owl called again, making me nervous.

Crouching down, I walked slowly towards the house. I kept an eye on the windows and luck was with me. From what I could see, it appeared that no one knew I was around. Feeling more confident, I slowly crept nearer to the house. I reached the porch and stepped carefully onto it. There was a slight creak but it didn't seem to draw any attention. I took another step, that didn't make any noise at all. I stood there for a second and took a deep breath. I knew I should go to the door and talk to them, but I wanted to see if I could learn something by eavesdropping. As I got closer to a window, I heard voices.

"Hoot, hoot," an owl cried out again startling me.

Under my breath I told it, "Shut up, fool." Then I tried to hear what the people inside were talking about.

"There's no big hurry," a man's voice said.

"I know… I just want to get everything together so we will be ready when the time comes." another man replied.

"I'm not too happy about doing this. There are other ways of getting him out," the first man said.

"He's nothing but a Rebel…" the second one answered.

"That's the only reason I'm going along with it. I just hope it's worth it" the first man continued.

"The contract with the railroad will make it worthwhile. They'll need a lot of parts, and we can make and sell them," the second man said.

"You don't have to remind me. I'm the one that talked to them, remember?"

Hearing what I had, I was getting mad. I had learned that there was a way for Smiley to expand his business. The problem now was to get these two men out of the picture so he would be able to do that. As I was about to knock, I heard someone coming to the door. I stepped quickly around the corner of the house to see what they were going to do.

"Let's get these rags and oil to the wagon," the first man said as he came out of the house.

"Not so loud. We don't know who might be around," the second said.

"Who would be out here that would hear us? It's dark, and there's no one around that I can see. Even during the day there's no one around," the first man answered.

"Me," I told them as I stepped around from my hiding place.

Startled, the second man asked, "Who are you?"

"What do you think you're doing here" the first man got out.

The first man was carrying a lamp. He stepped back right to the edge of the porch, where he lost his balance, dropped the lamp and fell down, knocking an oil container out of the other man's hand. The oil covered his clothing and the flame from the lamp ignited the oil. His clothing burst into flames.

"Help me!" he screamed.

He was beating at the flames as he lay on the ground. The rest of the oil was spilling out of its container, soaking him even more. The flames were shooting up a good four feet, making it hard for the second man to do anything. He also had spots of flames on his coat and was trying to put them out.

I was so angry at them that I didn't really care what happened to them, but out of instinct, I guess, I tried to give them a hand. I shouted to the man on the ground, "Roll across the ground and put it out."

He tried to roll as I ran over to him. Meanwhile the second man had put the flames on his coat out and turned to help his friend. He shouted, "Do something! Save him!"

"I'm not going to…," the first man screamed.

"Throw some dirt on him," I shouted back as I began throwing dirt on the flames. But it was too late. I knew he was dead. I rolled his body across the ground until the flames were out. Then I stood up and told the other man, "He's dead."

"Hoot… hoot," came from the owl.

"You killed him," the surviving man shouted at me as he knelt on the ground.

"I didn't kill him…It was an accident," I said. Then I saw a glint of metal and drew my pistol. "Put the pistol back or I'll kill you where you are… and trust me, I won't feel bad about it. He got what both of you deserve." I told him,

He got up slowly. I hadn't seen him put his pistol back into his coat, so I kept mine out in plain sight. He reached out as if to push himself up, but he slid forward. In his right hand was his pistol. As he raised it, I fired and watched him fall over on the ground. I hadn't meant to kill him, just wound him, but when I saw him fall, I didn't care whether I had killed him or not. I kicked his pistol to one side.

"You shot me," he cried out.

"Be glad you are alive enough to complain," I told him. Cautiously I picked up the pistol and put it in my pocket. I saw it was a nickel-plated Colt, 30 caliber pocket pistol it was quite a pretty piece. Looking back at the man, I decided to let him lie there and started to walk away.

The owl hooted again in the silence.

"You can't leave me like this," the man cried out from behind me.

"Think not...? Watch me," I shouted back.

"I'll die if I don't get help..." he cried again.

"Call out for one of your Yankee friends," I told him under my breath as I walked away. As I walked toward Smiley's shop, I couldn't stop thinking about the man who had just died in the flames. I had seen many men die during the war, with holes through their heart or limbs severed from their bodies. Each death was horrible to watch, but none had been like seeing the man behind me die in a ball of flames. I knew I couldn't leave the other man to die there by his friend, unattended. I turned around and started back to the house.

Reaching the house again, I looked over to where I had left him. As I walked up to him, I said, "I changed my mind."

"Hoot, hoot. The owl seemed to be answering me.

The man didn't move or answer. I gave him a slight shove and got no reaction. I realized then he was dead. I inspected the body and I saw where I had hit him. From all appearances, the man was lucky to have lived as long as he had. With a clear conscience, I decided to bury them.

As I walked away, I heard the owl hoot.

"Yes, I'll take care of them," I told the owl. I found a shovel in the barn and went to work; it took most of the night to bury them. Tired as I was, I didn't look forward to walking back, but thanks to the two scoundrels, I didn't have to worry about walking. While in the barn hunting for the shovel I found a carriage and a horse. After burying the two men, I put the shovel back, and with the last bit of strength I had left, I harnessed the horse to the carriage and drove it back to the shop. Back at the shop, I removed the harness from the horse and put him in the broken down corral behind Jacob's place.

When I got to bed, there wasn't much left of the night. I didn't bother to undress, just fell onto the bed and slept. It didn't seem long before I heard something in my sleep. At first, I thought it was a voice reminding me of something. I recalled that my visit during the night was one more thing I could tell Ida about. Then as I got awake, I realized someone was making a noise.

"Ping, Ping, Ping," rang out as Jacob struck a piece of molten metal.

"That's all right, Jacob… I didn't want to sleep anymore," I muttered as I crawled out of bed.

"Good morning…You don't look as if you're awake yet" Mr. Smiley said greeting me. Then as I yawned, he asked, "I saw a horse in the stable this morning and a carriage in the barn…are they yours?"

"A present for you from the two men, for bothering you," I managed to mutter with another yawn.

"That was nice of them." He looked at me, obviously curious. "I take it I shouldn't ask any more questions."

"They also said you might want to go see the railroad…people. They need more parts that they can't make for themselves," I answered.

"Really…? Maybe as slow as it is today I'll go up to Fredericksburg and see if I can talk to someone," he suggested.

"Jacob's getting tired of making horseshoes," I replied. Rubbing my eyes, I said, "I think I need some water."

"Go over and see the Missus she might have a few pancakes left," he offered.

"I think I'll do that…Thanks," I said as I tried to smile.

"Get going…Tell my wife I'll be home late tomorrow night," he said. I wondered whether I had the energy. But I asked, "Want me to harness the horse and wagon for you?"

"I can handle it," he answered as he headed for the corral.

The thought of coffee and pancakes made my stomach cry for food and it drove me to his place. His wife greeted me smiling and told me she was doing her cleaning. Then she saw how tired and sleepy I looked and told me to sit down. After a strong cup of coffee, she fixed me a couple of pancakes. With a few cakes in my stomach and a couple of cups of strong coffee, I went over to see Jacob.

I asked, "I don't have any deliveries to make this morning, do I?"

"Maybe later, but not now," he answered.

He wiped his forehead and asked, "What's up?"

"Nothing," I said. But then I added, "You know Ida needs a better place than that root cellar."

"She sure does" he replied. He picked up his hammer and began pounding on a piece of steel again.

"Ping, Ping, Ping," the hammer rang out driving me nuts.

"Stop for a minute" I pleaded.

"Got to hit it while it's hot," he reminded me.

"I need to talk to you." I said as I rubbed my eyes. Watching him put the hammer down I told him. "I told Ida we might build her a place."

"We can do that…. All we need are the materials, and that takes money. We don't have the tools to cut our own, and we don't have the money," he said.

"That is a problem, isn't it?" I replied. I pondered how long I would have to work for Mr. Smiley before I could afford to buy the materials.

"I've been meaning to pass a message on to you," he said.

I asked, "What message?"

"Before your parents were, killed…" he began. He wiped his forehead, came over and sat down beside me. "Your mother came by the morning she was killed."

"Why?" I asked. I couldn't see any reason why she had come to see him. I also wondered why he hadn't told me this earlier.

"The message she gave me didn't make any sense and I forgot about it until just now. She told me that she was worried something might happen. Then, if nothing happens, the message wouldn't matter." Wiping his forehead again, he added, "She said you should go to your tree."

I wasn't sure if I had heard him right. I asked, "My tree?"

"That's what she said," he said confirming what I thought I had heard.

"My tree…are you sure she didn't say anything else?" I asked. The only tree she could have been referring to was the one I had planted as a young boy. It is a weeping willow that had grown into a large tree over the years. I remembered Mother had always referred to it as "Edgar's tree." Why would she have wanted me to check on it?

"That was all she said. Then that afternoon we learned the Yankees had killed your parents," he answered.

With a lump in my throat, I replied, "I so wish I had been there to kill those Yankees. My tree…If you don't mind, I think I'll go up and check it out."

"No one will miss you," he said with a grin.

"Thanks," I replied as I threw a rag at him.

Once again, I found myself going for a long walk that I didn't feel strong enough for. But my mother had gone to the trouble of leaving the message for me, one of the last things she did on the day she died, so I had to go. "Another few miles and my legs will fall off" I said to myself as I headed out.

Soon a wagon came by and gave me a ride. I had the driver drop me off where the gate to our place hung from one hinge. As I got out of the wagon, chirping birds greeted me. I had the feeling their greeting was symbolic. I knew it wasn't a "welcome home," for there wasn't any home left. Even if I had the money, I wouldn't rebuild on the place. As far as I was concerned, the birds and animals could have it.

All of my childhood memories and memories of my parents washed over me once again as I looked down the drive. I almost turned and walked away to shut out the memories. It was hard to look out over the neglected land. I saw the fields, now almost bare, that once were full of cotton.

In my mind I could see workers out there, picking the cotton in the summer heat. I could see the house as it used to be, and the stables where I kept my horse. Looking around memories of Raymond and Pan Face came to mind. It was a time when the three of us together, were without a care in the world. Now everything was gone, and I had no idea what the future would bring.

As I thought of mother making that walk, I headed for my tree. It wasn't hard to find my tree, for it was in an open area by itself. It was swaying with the breeze, almost as if it was calling me to it. Standing under it, I didn't see anything different about it. It had grown a few feet but it looked the same as before. My eyes followed one branch down to the crotch, and I remembered telling Mother there was a pocket in the tree many years ago.

I reached into the pocket and felt around. My fingers touched something that felt like leather. I grabbed hold of it and pulled it out of the tree; it was one of Father's powder sacks that he used to carry on his belt when he went hunting. As I lifted it, I heard a jingle. It was full of gold coins. Around me I still could hear the birds chirping, matching the flutter in my heart.

I looked at the gold in my hand and I began to cry. I looked up and said, "Thank you, Mother."

A New Start for Us

I have the feeling the next series of entries will seem as if a different man made them. Having gotten back to my home country with my weapons the clothes on my back and my diary I'm looking forward to a new beginning:

After I found the gold in the tree, I went back to the shop. I didn't tell Jacob what I had found, but we did a lot of talking. The main subject of conversation was Ida's need for a house. Jacob knew more than I did about building one, so I let him tell me what we needed.

Ida decided that she could use one of the old slave homes and we could repair it and add on to it. I agreed with her that getting her a better place to live would be faster and cheaper that way. Jacob looked it over and decided the only thing we needed was a few boards and some shingles. Though the one Ida chose needed fixing up, it didn't take as much as building a new one. In the end I never told either of them where the money for those few supplies came from.

Mother had somehow managed to keep a hundred and twenty dollars in gold from father, and that's what she had left in the tree for me. It wasn't a fortune, but it gave me a sense of some security. A number of times I thought about taking the money and going out west, but the thought of Ida kept me from doing that. Since she needed a house, it was better to spend some of it on that. She would need something to make it comfortable. Some of what she would need was a bed and some other furniture. The rest of the gold I hid for the future.

I did spend forty some dollars on two horses and a wagon. Unfortunately, they cost a third of what Mother had left me. The price was a little high, but there wasn't anything else available. I figured that I would get my money's worth out of them over time. I hated to think I had spent that much, but if we were to get into farming, we needed our own rig. We had been borrowing Mr. Smiley's, and I didn't like borrowing what I needed. Since Ida was under the impression that I didn't have any money, it was a little hard explaining to her how I had been able to buy the horses and wagon. To solve that problem, I told her I was just keeping the horses and wagon for a farmer.

Other than Ida, needing a house our next problem was the time of year. It was too late to plant crops, so our jobs were the only thing that kept us alive. With our friends, Jacob and Molly's help, the four of us were making it. Thankfully, we didn't owe anyone and that made it easier.

Carpetbaggers irritated us by continuing to offer us money for Ida's place. Their offer of three hundred dollars was tempting. Though that was only a small percentage of what the place was worth, three hundred dollars would have kept us going for quite a while. Since we weren't married, I left the decision up to Ida. One other man had made an offer a little higher.

One night Ida said, "Those men haven't been by for a couple of weeks."

"What men?" Many people had been passing through over the past few months.

"Wilson and Williams," she answered.

I asked, "Those are the two carpetbaggers from Nashville (Fredericksburg)… or am I thinking of someone else?"

"Yes… that's the two," she answered.

"Someone ought to shoot them" I replied. "I think those two have been burning people out."

She stopped stirring the stew and asked, "Do you know that for sure?"

"No… It's just a feeling." I had heard about these two men. I had talked to some people heading west and their names had come up too often. I was to learn some suspected that they burned down houses of people who refused to sell to them.

I had thought about visiting them and learned they lived in Nashville (Fredericksburg). That was a little too far to run over for a friendly conversation. Yet if I got the chance, I would have a little chat with them. I didn't want it to go as far as it had with the men at the Willard Place, I just wanted to talk to them.

"I have to say they're not all that friendly. Their offer of three hundred dollars wasn't anything I would even consider," she told me as she turned back to the stew.

"At least the other man is offering you something you can do something with," I replied as I went over to get a better look at the stew. I added, "Looks good,"

"It had better be," she answered with a smile.

As we ate, we didn't talk any more about the three men. Our conversation was about what we had done that day and about Jacob and Molly.

Ida told me that Molly was disappointed that she had not been able to give Jacob a son. I laughed a little at the thought, and said that they couldn't afford any children at the time, anyway. Ida admitted I was right. Molly knew that too, but it hadn't changed her feelings.

The next morning Jacob and I had an interesting discussion. He started by asking me, "Have you heard about this new Klan, or whatever it might be?"

I asked, "What are you talking about?"

"It's some kind of group that wears hoods to hide their identity," he explained. Then as he pumped the bellows, he added, "They're trying to get rid of all of us Darkies."

"No I haven't… And let me tell you something. I don't ever, and I mean ever, want to hear you refer to yourself as a Darky. You are a man of color with two legs and two arms that works hard. You also have a wife and the two of you are my best friends," I shouted.

"Just using the terms they do," he said.

"I'm sorry, but it irritates me when I hear degrading terms like that. I was raised with people of color and I don't see any difference between any of us," I explained. Seeing his smile, I asked, "What are they doing, this Klan?"

"Burning down their homes…, shooting and hangings aren't uncommon," he said.

"No one is doing anything about it…? Where's the Army that's supposed to be protecting us?" I asked. I was wondering where I had been, for I hadn't heard of any of this going on.

"People have too many other problems to worry about us. The Northerners blame us for the war, and most Southerners believe it. With that kind of thinking they are willing to turn their heads…With no one pushing for the Army to protect us, they have more to worry about than our problems," Jacob offered as an explanation.

"Can't they think for themselves?" I asked "Everyone knows the truth… I can't believe people can be so stupid" I replied as I sat down.

Thinking about the army, I added, "The Army isn't doing anything to protect us. If they were, we wouldn't have these carpetbaggers running around stealing everything we have.

I have a feeling the Army is busy stealing what the carpetbaggers haven't and doesn't have time for anything else," was Jacob's remark.

"When times are rough, you blame whoever you can for your problems." Jacob said. You would be the last I would blame," I said. "And I agree with you about the Army. I haven't seen a single soldier since the end of the war," I added.

We let the conversation die, but I continued to think about it. With this new Klan and the Carpetbaggers, did I want to stay around here anymore? I began to think again of going west. Considering everything going on in the South, it was hard to find anything pleasant in our lives.

Mr. Smiley's shop had changed in a few short weeks. What I had heard from the two men who were bothering Mr. Smiley was correct.

The railroad had some big plans for extending their tracks from the east coast to the west coast, and they gave us a lot of business. We were so busy that Mr. Smiley was talking about hiring some help.

With all the work at the shop and Ida's teaching, we both kept busy. Occasionally, we did find time for walks and got to know each other. With some effort, Jacob and I finally got the house livable for Ida. She was so happy to get out of the root cellar she would have done anything for us. It made her even happier when she realized winter was right around the corner. It was nicer to visit her in the house than in the cellar and in the new place, she had a wood stove that kept us warm. Molly also appreciated it because I would be having supper with Ida. It gave her and Jacob some time to be alone.

One evening Ida said, "I'm going to enjoy it."

I asked, "Do you mean the house?" I asked.

"No. I meant us being able to celebrate our first Christmas together since the war," she explained.

"I had almost forgotten about the war..., and Christmas," I said. None of us had had the time to think about the war or much of anything except what we were doing that day.

We had talked a little about our plans for the coming summer. We intended to plant a crop of corn in the field not far from the house. With rest of the families in the area planting crops also, that meant the children were needed at home during planting season, so Ida wouldn't have to quit teaching.

"I know what you are saying about the war. I haven't thought about it for a while... My mind has been on celebrating Christmas here this year. We could invite Jacob and Molly over for supper," she said.

"We invite?" I was surprised she had included me in that manner. I too found myself thinking in terms of "we." More and more I began thinking of us as a couple. I kept thinking of the days when she would tell her parents we would marry each other. I still felt she was the most beautiful woman I had ever met. I then added, "Sounds good to me... They have helped us so much that we should pay them back by inviting them."

"I'm glad you agree," she said.

"Come to think of it, what would you like for Christmas?" I asked. I didn't know what I would buy her other than a new dress, not that I knew where to get one anyway.

"Neither of us can afford anything… I want us to agree not get each other anything… A big supper will cost us enough," she told me firmly. Then with a smile, she added, "Maybe some nicer weather than we are having tonight."

"Sorry, but I can't do anything about the weather" I told her. She was right; we couldn't afford anything. Just putting together, a big supper would cost a lot. I knew Molly would fix something too, but none of us could afford much. However, for Ida I would consider using some of the gold mother left me. I told her, "I agree, no presents."

"Thank you… Now get out of here so I can get some sleep," she ordered.

"Yes Ma'am," I answered as I got up. She came over and gave me a hug and a kiss. Then with a smile, she added, "Thank you."

I asked, "For what?"

"For being you," she answered.

As I opened the door, I saw it was raining hard. How great it would have been if I could have stayed with her instead of going out into the rain. Grinning as I, left I said, "Just hope I don't wash away. And I don't know why, but it's no problem being me when you're around" I added as I went out the door.

As her door shut, I felt a pang of pain. It was as if something had ended. I had that feeling more and more every time I left. I also realized I didn't want to leave her house.

That night I laid awake thinking I had to make her something for Christmas, even though she had said "no presents." I thought of a gift that might put an end to my loneliness. I knew the only one who could help was Jacob. The next morning I asked him to help and he agreed, though he probably thought I was crazy.

On Christmas afternoon Jacob, Molly and I made our way to Ida's place. I was carrying my present and the two of them were joshing me about it. I knew my idea was crazy but I thought it was cute. I also knew it would save me several tongue twisting words.

"You know there is something wrong with your head, don't you?" Jacob said, laughing.

"The same as is wrong with hers," I told him.

"They are a perfect pair," Molly reminded him

"May we never get that bad!" Jacob said.

"Be nice… It's Christmas," she scolded.

"I want you two to go in first," I told them. I wanted Ida's attention to be on them, not me. Then once I went in, I could surprise her with my gift.

Jacob knocked on the door as Molly and I stood to one side. When the door opened, he greeted Ida with "Merry Christmas."

"Merry Christmas," Molly and I said together.

"Come in out of the cold," Ida invited.

"Sounds like a good idea" Molly said with a smile.

"Merry Christmas, Edgar," Ida said greeting me. Without waiting, she reached up and gave me a kiss. She noticed the wrapped package and asked, "What's with the present?"

"This isn't a Christmas present…, just a gift," I explained to her.

She gave the package a curious look and asked, "What do you mean…? It's wrapped like a present."

"Yes, because it's special," I said as I handed it to her.

"He made it himself," Jacob told her.

She took the gift from me, turning it repeatedly. She seemed, to be trying to figure out what it was.

"Open it" I suggested.

"We want to see what it is" Jacob said, grinning.

I grabbed Ida and wrapped my arm around her. She smiled up at me as Jacob and Molly waited for her to open the package.

She opened it and saw it was a picture frame. She looked up again and said, "It's empty."

I explained to her "I would've put a picture of you and me in it, if I had one."

From the expression on her face, I knew she was willing to become my wife. The only thing we had to do was find a preacher. Fortunately, one had just moved into the old preacher's house for the winter. He hadn't decided whether he would stay past winter, but he would be here long enough.

"It looks as if we need to see the preacher tomorrow," Molly said as everyone laughed.

"About time they got, married… Edgar's shoes are wearing out, with him going back and forth the way he has been" Jacob said.

"I think it's about time to eat," she said with a big smile. Then coming over to me, she whispered, "I love you."

"I love you too," I told her with a kiss.

We had a wonderful supper and discussed the future. Molly and Jacob kept asking how many children we were planning to have. I kept pleading to let us get married first, and everyone began laughing.

"Don't worry… I'll see if the preacher will marry us on the first of the month," I announced.

Jacob looked puzzled when he asked, "You did say the first of the month?"

"Yes, I thought I would end this year single and start the New Year off married," I said. I got another round of laughter on that one.

"On that, I think it's time to go. Smiley has another order he needs to deliver last week," Jacob told us.

Molly sounded confused when she asked, "Last week?"

"He means it's a rush order," I explained.

"Trying to confuse me," she said as she gave her husband a slap on the arm.

"See, this is what you're in for when you get married," Jacob said warning me.

"I know" I told him and got a slap of my own.

"And don't forget it" Ida warned me.

"I think I'll join you," I told Jacob and Molly.

Ida pleaded "So soon?"

"We have to get an early start tomorrow…and it's almost eleven o'clock." I explained.

"All right…" See you tomorrow," she said.

"Good night." I kissed her good night.

We said our good-byes and went on our way.

The next morning, I got up and ran over to the preacher's place. He agreed with a big smile to marry us on the first day of January.

Our wedding wasn't anything big. Attending were the Smileys, Jacob, Molly, and the preacher and his wife. Mr. Smiley gave Ida away and Jacob was my best man.

Ida was in one of her mother's dresses, she was the most beautiful bride God had ever seen. She was so beautiful I forgot I was only wearing my old dirty work clothes. Even though there wasn't a party, there was one in my heart. Every sore thing that had happened over the past four years was forgotten right then. As I looked at Jacob and Molly, I knew they were happy for us. From their grins, I knew they felt for us as we did to each other. Though our families were gone, we had our own new little family.

Like Ida, I wished our parents could have been there for the wedding. At least, because she was wearing her mother's dress, her mother was there in a way. I believed our parents might have been looking down on us, anyway. With that feeling, I was the happiest man in the world. I had the prettiest, hardest working woman in the world as my wife. My only concern was the conditions we had to live in. I said a silent prayer that things would get better.

We went home right after the short ceremony.

Molly had wanted to throw a party, but Ida wouldn't have it. She insisted that parties reminded her too much of her parents. Rather than have her cry anymore we decided, we agreed to forgo any festivities. Besides, it was so cold no one wanted to be out late anyway.

Ida saw a look of concern on my face and asked, "What's wrong?"

"I just wish I could give you a better life than we have now," I said.

"What more could I ask for…? I have your love and the love of two good friends," she said. Then she took my head into her hands and gave me a kiss. As she pulled away, she told me "It'll get better… Have faith."

"I pray you are right," I replied as I let her go. Without thinking, I added "With these carpetbaggers running loose stealing everything they want…, I doubt it."

"You have to have faith this will all end. It may not be as it was before, but it will get better… Just wait and see," she said.

"I'm waiting but I don't like it," I said. Taking her into my arms I told her, "I want a place where we can feel safe to raise our children."

With a twinkle in her eye, she asked, "Who said we even wanted children?"

"You mean," I began to reply but she closed my mouth with a kiss.

Knowing that we need to begin planting crops in the middle of April even though it was some time away I knew, we had to start planning in January. Everyone thought I was crazy and worried about the work at the shop and school. Finally, they came around to my way of thinking and we began making plans. The main problem was where we would get the money for seed? As the four of us talked, no one had any ideas.

One night Ida suggested, "As we discussed a few weeks back, I could sell some of Mamma's belongings. I should be able to get enough money to get us started."

I asked, "What are you talking about?"

"I have mamma's dresses and jewelry I could sell," she explained.

"You won't get much for them," I said.

"Whatever I get is better than nothing… It doesn't look as if I'll have any use for them," she told me.

"It's up to you." I told her. I had still not told her about gold I had stashed away. I was reluctant to use gold right then, fearing I wouldn't get its full value. With the war over, the value of gold was at an all-time low, and I prayed it would go back up in a year or so. Knowing how she must be feeling about giving up her mother's belongings, I told her "It's not costing us anything to store it. You might be, surprised how soon you'll be wearing those things."

I then realized our old ways were gone and that she didn't want any part of memories of those days, so we dropped the subject. With me, she was forming new memories of our life together, and that was good.

As we got ready for bed that night, she asked me "Why don't you talk about the war?"

"What is there to say? I notice you don't have anything to say about your experiences either," I reminded her.

She didn't answer. She crawled into bed looking deep in thought. The look didn't offer any information, which was all right with me. I didn't feel like talking about what her mother had gone through. I wasn't proud of what I had done, either.

It was the same when I heard of the assassination of Abraham Lincoln, I felt sick thinking about it. I knew my trips north had played a part in it. When I got home, I asked her, "Have you heard the news?"

As she was doing her chores, she asked, "What news?"

"Lincoln was assassinated, a few days ago," I told her.

With a shocked expression, she sat down and she asked, "What? Someone killed him?"

"They're saying it was a Confederate plot. He was killed while he was at a theater with his wife by some actor named John Wilkes Booth," I told her.

As she shook her head she said, "That's terrible. I could understand someone doing it during the war, for it might have meant the war would have gone the other way. But now, why? What good is it going to do for anyone?" She asked.

"I agree." I didn't want to talk more about it further.

"Did they get this Booth fellow?" She asked. Before I could answer, she added, "It would be a shame if he got away… Was he a Southerner?"

"They say he was a <u>Confederate</u> sympathizer… According to what I've heard he was killed in a barn, in Virginia," I told her. I had met him once and learned he was from Maryland. His biggest complaint was that Lincoln had instituted martial law in Maryland. To get even he wanted to join the Confederate Army, but his mother wouldn't let him. The original plan didn't have him going anywhere near there. I worried about that for the longest time. We knew the Army would go after him, but he wasn't supposed to head for that part of the state. Everything in the plan took into consideration the Army would track him down and make it appear they had killed him in a battle. Then they would send him to Europe, along with a large sum of money from the South and from others sympathetic to the Cause, enough money to last him the rest of his life. I didn't tell Ida any of this. I just said, "I don't know any more. A farmer from up north came by the shop and gave us the news."

She asked, "Did he have any other news?"

"Just that the Klan seems to be getting bigger… It seems they are killing more colored people," I told her.

I didn't mention it to her, but he had told me something else that bothered me. The farmer reminded me about Lincoln, having instated the draft in '62. I had learned about that from other soldiers, but I didn't know he had given men an option: If a man didn't want to join, he could buy his way out for $300.00. When I first heard this, I thought briefly if I had been a northerner, that I would have taken that option. Then when I thought about it, I knew I would have joined anyway.

As she turned around, she asked, "What?"

I told her what Jacob had told me and what the farmer had added. I agreed with her that the country was going crazy.

I had also heard that things out west were booming. If we were to leave, our life couldn't be anything but better, but I knew that Ida wasn't ready to give up on our life here. I had loved her all my life and I couldn't risk losing her now. I didn't even bother to tell her what he had said about the west.

As I waited for supper, my mind was on things that were more important right then. We had decided to plant corn, and I wondered how we would be able to get the crop in. I had talked to Mr. Smiley, he wanted to take part in planting and raising the crop, and if his wife helped us we would have five people to get it planted and picked. If Molly weren't expecting a baby, much to her and Jacob's delight, we would have had six. Still between the work at the shop and Ida at school, I figured we should be able to plant enough for all of us. With all three families going together we were able to get together enough money to buy the seed. With what farmers were currently getting for their crops, I didn't expect that we would make much, but whatever we got would help.

As Ida set supper on the table, she asked, "What are you thinking about?"

"Getting the corn planted" I told her.

"We have a few weeks to worry about that just relax and have your supper," she said with a smile.

"All right… I'll try not to worry. Still, tomorrow I need to go after some seed corn," I reminded her.

"See… you'll be doing something to get us going" she replied.

"I guess you can look at it that way," I said. I didn't seem to have any time to relax. The more I did, the more there was to do. There were a lot of preparations to be made before we could begin planting. For one thing, we needed to find or make a couple of plows. With Jacob's talents at the forge, I knew he could make one. There was enough wood around to make the rest of the parts needed for one. Seeing the strain in her eyes, I decided it wasn't worth the effort of talking. I would talk to Jacob in the morning.

Over the next few weeks, I bought the seed for us to plant from a merchant in Fredericksburg. Meanwhile Mr. Smiley found two plows on vacant farms that had been left behind when the previous occupants left.

I was concerned about the rumors coming from Fredericksburg, to the effect that no one was likely to be interested in buying anything we had to sell. Mr. Smiley and Jacob reminded me that rumors are rumors and not to worry until the time came.

Other reports said the Klan was still getting larger, and that was unnerving. They said the Klan was getting so bad that people all around were alarmed. Though I didn't know the people, several of the local farmers had been found hanged. I heard that if I were to ride around our area, I would find a number of burned crosses. These crosses were Klan symbols indicating that what they had done was what God wanted done. Though I wasn't a church going person, I couldn't believe God approved of their actions.

A few days later, I was to find an example of what everyone was talking about. I had a delivery west of Ashland and found a farmhouse and outbuildings that had been burned to the ground. In front of the house was a burnt cross that suggested it was a Klan burning. Then I saw the body of a man hanging from a tree. He had been dead for several days, for his body was covered in flies. This was a new horror, it was the first time I had seen a hanged man. Though it was cool, it was a beautiful day. Here on such a day was the decaying body of a man who had done nothing to anyone. He breathed air just as I did, probably had dreams and worked his fingers to the bone. I didn't see where he was any different from anyone else I knew, except the color of his skin.

Since I could do nothing else for him, I cut him down. I looked around, trying to find a shovel that I could use to dig a grave for him. Finally, I found the remains of one in the burned out barn. Without the handle, it wasn't easy to dig with it. I finally got a shallow grave dug, and as I covered his body, I vowed, "Someone's going to pay for your death."

As a parting gesture, I pulled the cross out of the ground. All that remained was a hole in the ground. Looking at the cross in my hand, I decided to send a message to the Klan. I turned the cross upside down and drove it back into the hole. I hoped the Klan would see the cross and get the message that we didn't care for their deeds. What the upside down cross wouldn't say was that I would be looking for them.

As I rode off, I looked down at my horses and told them, "One of you will learn to carry me on a saddle." It almost seemed as if they understood.

When I got back, I put the wagon and horses away and as I was coming out of Mr. Smiley's barn, I met Jacob. He gave me a funny look as I walked up to him. I figured the saddle on my shoulder was the reason. I knew he wasn't worried that I had stolen it from Mr. Smiley. He had been there when Mr. Smiley told me to take it. With what he received for the horse and carriage he figured he could give me the saddle.

When I reached him he asked, "A little late I see… You have a problem?"

"Found a little chore I had to take care of," I told him not going into detail. I decided if he asked I would tell him, more as a warning than anything else.

With a confused look he asked, "A chore…? I wouldn't call delivering horseshoes a chore."

"I don't want to talk about it… Still I should probably tell you as a precaution," I answered. I told him the rumors about the Klan were accurate, and that it appeared they were getting closer to us. Then I told him what I had found and done. With his poker face, I couldn't get any idea what was going through his head. I finished with, "I don't want that to happen to you or Molly."

He asked, "What do you want me to do…? Take Molly and run?"

"I don't know. I'm just worried and mad," I replied. With neighbors living around him, he had a good chance he was safe.

As he pointed to it, he asked, "What's with the saddle?"

"I want to do some riding… I might find those so called messengers of God," I told him as I headed for home. I didn't know what to do, but I had to find an answer. The horses I bought I had meant to use only for pulling a plow or wagon. I didn't know whether anyone had ridden them or not. I didn't care, because I know I would be riding one of them.

When I got to the house, I found Ida on the porch. She asked, "What's with the saddle?"

"Thinking about doing some riding," I told her. I set the saddle on the porch and went inside. As she followed, I said, "I think we need a barn."

"All right" she answered. I thought she would have asked why I was late getting home, but she didn't. She went over to the fireplace and dished up supper. Then she said, "I could use a stove. I don't know whether the barn is more important, but a stove would be nice."

"I'll see what I can do," I promised.

As she set the food on the table, she told me, "I did something today."

As I tried to read the look on her face, I asked, "What did you do?"

"Well, you told me it was up to me…" she started to say as she sat down.

Impatiently I asked, "What are you talking about?" I asked impatiently.

"I sold mamma's prize belongings," she answered as she looked down.

I asked, "How much did you get for everything?"

"Forty-eight dollars" she answered.

"That's not too bad… It won't last long but it's better than nothing," I told her as I tried to smile. I knew how much it had hurt her to sell those things, but it was for the best.

She hesitated. "I… also sold the land."

"You sold it?" It was hard to believe. I didn't care what she got for the place, it still surprised me. I prayed it meant we could head west. I asked "How much?"

"Six… hundred" she answered. In explanation, she added, "It's more than the three hundred they first offered, and we still have forty acres."

"That's more than we need, I guess" I replied as I continued to eat. Wiping my mouth I reminded her "But you know everyone will be upset with you… us."

"They'll understand…. I'll tell them that those varmints gave me a decent price for the land," she said confidently. Then, smiling, she added, "Now we can buy our own set of horses and wagon."

"That's true," I said. Of course, I didn't tell her it would be nice not to continue with a lie. Now I was going to have to tell her the truth, that I had bought the farmer's horse and wagon. I remember my mother telling me once that a lie is something that keeps growing. I knew that one day I would have to tell her the truth. Just now, thinking about the Klan, I didn't feel like getting into it. Then as an afterthought, I asked, "Have you told anyone?"

"Just a few people who have come by the school are all. I didn't say what I got for it. I didn't think it was any of their business," she answered.

"I agree it's none of their business… That's part of the problem. Everyone knows what everybody else is doing before they even do it," I muttered to myself. Once again, I thought of how much better off we would be out of the area. I had heard of the riots that had taken place in Richmond over the last few weeks. From what I had heard over a hundred had lost their lives in the last one. I wanted to tell Ida about it but I knew it would upset her.

That was the end of our conversation on the subject that night. I had a feeling the subject would come up again. She finally asked me about my day, and I told her what I had found and what I had done. She asked me what I thought could be done and I said I didn't know. As with my experiences in the war, there were things she needed to know and others she didn't.

The next two weeks it rained almost every day and that brought my patrolling almost to a halt. When I got the chance, I rode a few miles in each direction. When making deliveries, I was able to stop and talk to a few people once in a while. The rain had slowed down the Klan's activities, apparently, for it was hard to keep fires going in a downpour. I still kept my eye open for any strangers who might come through, though the rumors said that most of the Klan members were local people.

One evening we went to Jacob and Molly's for supper and we left their place late that night. As we were heading home, I saw a red glow in the sky over some trees. I told Ida, "There's a fire over there. I had better check it out."

As she looked around, she asked, "Where?"

"To the north," I answered as I ran for my horse. Though the mare that I had trained to carry me wasn't as nice as my old one, she still did the job. I shouted back to Ida, "Go back to Jacob's place... I'll come and get you."

I thought I heard her ask why but I didn't hang around to answer, for I was afraid I wouldn't get to the fire in time. Most likely the Klan has started the fire, and if so, someone was about to lose his life. I wanted to get them before they hung anyone or they left.

Getting there took a little time and I worried with each hoof beat. Suddenly, as I came around a bend, I saw the flames from a building. I wasn't sure whether anyone was there or not. Unsure what was happening I rode at a full gallop to see if I could save anyone who might be there and still alive. And I wanted to make sure the ones who were responsible would pay.

Approaching the fire, I saw a group of hooded men waving lit torches, sticks, rakes, shovels and rifles in the air. I could also hear chanting. To my surprise, I didn't see anyone hanging from a rope, which gave me hope. When I saw how many there were, I drew my horse to a stop, for I couldn't charge in and expect to survive. Still I had to do something to break them up and maybe save whoever they were about to hang

Off to my right I saw a clump of trees. On further but closer to the fire was another. I decided to use the trees as cover and begin firing into the group. In doing that, I might hit a few and maybe drive them away. If I were lucky, I might have a chance to save whomever they were planning to abuse. I urged my horse forward and drew my pistol.

As I started my run, I ran through my mind what I was going to do. Between my pistol and rifle I had only seven shots, but that would be enough to at least scare them. Then I could ride out of sight, reload and make another attack. My ammunition, every ounce of powder and ball, had come from the war. That was fitting, because I was fighting a war of another kind. From the first clump of trees, I fired the first round of shots. When both weapons were empty, I rode off a short way.

"Someone's shooting at us," a voice in the mob screamed.

"We have one down here…," another screamed.

"Get him," someone cried out.

Another shouted over the noise, "Where is this shooter?"

"Another is dead over here," someone added.

"I didn't see him," another shouted back.

"Another is dead over here," someone said.

"I have two wounded over here" still another reported.

"Keep an eye on that Darky," someone added at the top of their lungs.

"You won't find me," I said under my breath. I felt good knowing I had hit five of the crazies. They were all screaming in confusion as I reloaded. I rushed to reload my pistol and rifle so I could make another run, for I didn't want them to think it was over. I wanted to keep them in a sense of panic. Though a panicked mob may be dangerous, it's also almost impossible to control.

After I reloaded, I made for the second clump of trees. I didn't empty both weapons on them I moved around, shooting from different angles, to make them think there were several shooters hiding in the brush. I prayed that if they thought there was a group, they would run rather than fight.

The flames gave the scene an eerie look. Before I was through with them, they were surely going to find it eerie.

Then I heard a flutter. I guessed it was an owl losing interest in the fire and the mob. I would have been willing to bet he was going after his supper. Watching him in the darkening sky, I told him, "Eat hearty."

"Get whoever it is… Then some of you get the wounded out of here" a Klan member shouted out to the mob.

Someone asked, "What, about the dead?"

"They got another," a man cried out.

"Let the dead lie where they are… and rot," the first voice answered.

"That makes six," I muttered to my horse. Hustling I made it back to the first clump of trees and emptied my pistol and fired my rifle into the group. As I fired, I was, reminded of the reports that Klan was burning black farmers' places to the ground. To make it worse, in most cases the farmer and his family lost their lives.

"Did anyone see where the shots came from?" Someone asked. From the pitch of his voice, I knew he was scared.

"To the right of that clump of trees" a Klan member shouted back. Someone fired a few rounds in that direction.

I answered with my last four rounds. Then I rode some distance from where I had been, and as I reloaded, I made my way behind the burning house. The flames were dying down, so I could see the entire mob gathered in front. I had to laugh because they were trying to find me back in the trees. If they had just turned around, they would have seen me. Then firing the pistol a couple of times, I rode back to safety.

"Let's get out of here," one of the Klan members screamed out to his friends.

"They've got another," another cried out. Before anyone could say any more, the same man announced, "I'm not staying here any longer… You can all get yourselves killed, but not me."

As I turned my horse around, all the shooting had ended. Then as the man announced his plans, I fired again. One of the men fell to what I figured was his death. I thought to myself, "That makes eight."

"I'm not waiting to get, killed," a man said to himself as he passed within a few feet of me.

As he passed, I raised my pistol and took aim at him. I tried to keep out of their sight as I fired a shot at him. He cried out as he fell to the ground, "I've been shot."

"Be thankful I wasn't aiming for your heart," I replied as I rode off. At least three of them were still alive and would remember this evening, and those who died couldn't harm anyone ever again.

A man shouted out "Who cried out?"

"I'm over here," the man shouted back to his comrade.

I had just killed several men and wasn't proud of it even though they deserved it. Seeing the man come to his friend's aid, I brought my horse to a stop. I took aim at him, but then I had second thoughts. Rather than shooting him, I fired a shot at his feet, and he turned and ran. As he ran, I fired another shot a few feet in front of him. I turned back to the sight of the burning house and saw most of the men had left.

But one man stood his ground with a rifle in his hand. As he was staring me down, I knew I was in for a fight and I was ready. Keeping my distance, I fired at him once and waited to see what his reaction would be. I had intentionally aimed at him but wanted to scare him more than anything else. As I watched, I saw him look down at his stomach. Blood was spurting out of that part of his body. He dropped his rifle as he slumped to the ground.

"I guess I missed," I said to, myself as I rode toward the burning house. As I got closer, I continued to watch the last man I had shot. Though I was sure he was dead, I didn't take any chances.

Then not far from his body I saw a colored man huddled down next to a coffin with his hands over his head. I figured he was waiting for his executioners to take his life. He was one colored man they wouldn't be killing that night.

I was seething with anger, but I also felt pity for the white people, supposedly my neighbors, who could do such a thing as what they had done to this man. I wondered why men couldn't treat each other as they would like to be treated. Why did they have to blame bad times on their neighbors and friends?

"I won't shoot you," I told the colored man as I dismounted. He looked up at me. Seeing fear in his eyes I told him "I came to rescue you…, not kill you."

"Oh thank you Master," he said as he slowly got up.

"I'm not your Master," I told him a little harshly. I went over and looked at the body of the last man to die. He was about Mr. Smiley's size. Having heard reports that members of the Klan were everyday people, I worried that it might be Mr. Smiley. I was relieved that I didn't recognize the man when I took his hood off. At least he was a stranger, not a neighbor. Forgetting about the colored man's presence, I said to the dead man "You should have gone with your friends."

"Sorry, sir" he said as he looked around. He then walked over and exclaimed, "That's Master Rogers!"

I was surprised that he knew the man. "Who is he? I don't think I've met him."

"He was my Master before the war." He smiles. "He won't be beating me anymore."

"I guess not" I replied. As a child, I had heard of masters beating their slaves. I had no idea whether my grandfather had done that, but my father never did. All of our slaves were part of the family, and Father would never have thought of beating one. If he had, he would certainly have heard about it from Mother!

I left the colored man to go about his business. I had a wife waiting for me back at Jacob's place. With that thought, I jabbed my heels into my horse's side and headed home. I knew I would tell everyone some story, but I wasn't sure what.

Over the next few weeks, we waited for the weather to clear. Mr. Smiley had more than enough work for us, so we weren't bored. Meanwhile I continued chasing carpetbaggers out of the area. I enjoyed cutting their harnesses or chasing off their horses. Some of them got the message and never returned. The problem was that once one carpetbagger left, he was replaced by two more. It seemed I had taken on more than I could handle.

The sun finally came out and we could get to the corn planting. Mr. Smiley, his wife, Jacob, Ida, and I worked for more than a week.

When we finished, we were very proud of ourselves. I was especially proud of myself because I had never done any farm work before. I had to smile when I thought about what Mother and Father would have said if they had seen me behind a plow.

Of course Molly wasn't of much help with the planting now that she was carrying the baby, but she helped by making sure we had enough to eat. Without her, Ida would have had to do the cooking and wouldn't have been able to help with the planting.

Ida knew more about corn planting than the rest of us put together. From what she told us, the biggest thing we had to do now was to wait and pray for rain, and keep the weeds pulled. Once we planted the corn, all there was to do was to continue with life as it had been.

I was happy having Ida at my side. There were times when I wondered why I married; but down deep, I knew why. As He had with Jacob and Molly, God meant for us to be husband and wife. The first thing in the morning when I looked at her I would say, "Thank you, Lord. Isn't she wonderful?"

Then July came and everyone began asking, "When do we start harvesting the crop."

"All I know is that I've been making sacks for us to use," Molly told us as she held one up.

"I don't know either… Mother and I left before our sharecroppers picked any of it," Ida said.

"I could tell you about cotton but not corn," I replied. All of us agreed it looked like a good crop, but were at a loss to know what to do with it. At least Ida had gotten us off, to a good start.

One day a man stopped by the shop. As he watched Jacob at the forge, he mentioned, "Looks like a good crop of corn down the road."

"Yes it does," I said.

"Those people should be picking some of it…I would think," he added.

"I hate to tell you we own that crop and we don't really know what to do with it," I confessed.

"I can tell from how they are hanging... The easiest way is to bite into an ear and see if it's sweet. If it is, then it's ready for picking." he told me. He went on to tell me what we needed to do.

I looked at him first wondering if he was serious. I didn't want to break a tooth knowing how hard the kernels were. I decided to try a bite after seeing the grin on his face. I bit into it and I found it had a sweet taste. I threw it to the ground thinking Elsie said cooking corn made it even sweeter. If that was the case, this was going to be sweet corn. I immediately ran into the house and gave Ida the news. I got everyone together that night and explained what we needed to do. I ended the conversation with, "I guess we won't be looking to sell the crop for a while."

"From what that man told me it would be rotten before we got it to market... So now we wait and pray we don't get any rain," I said.

Everything is coming together

As I begin writing I'm thinking back over the last few months. The two greatest things on our mind were the child Molly was about to give birth to and selling the crop. Thankfully Ida has been doing better than the price of corn:

Then over the next week, we harvested a portion of the crop we could use for ourselves. The remainder of the corn we tied the stalks together in a teepee configuration. With the last ear picked we were tired and dripping with sweat. Molly saved the day by bringing us a bucket of water. With her being as far along as she was, Jacob yelled at her for hauling something so heavy, afraid she would hurt herself or even lose the baby. Once we had our fill, we looked at the harvest and talked.

"The price of corn I hear is forty-seven cents a bushel in Fredericksburg," Mr. Smiley announced with excitement.

"With the crop we have. We should make enough to last us a year," Ida said with a big smile. As she sat down, she wiped the sweat from her brow.

"I doubt we will get a half dime a bushel," I told them. I propped myself against the wagon as I let them think it over. Taking out my handkerchief, I wiped my forehead. It was hotter than normal and the three of us had put in a hard day. Fortunately, the crop was in before the rains. Now we had to get it to market no matter what the price might be. At that particular time, I would have been happy just to break even.

With a worried look, Ida asked, "What are you saying?"

"He's right… Hopefully it won't be that bad but we probably won't get full value," Jacob said.

"I'm like Ida; I don't understand" Molly said.

"Right now, it's not worth worrying about… First we have to let it dry before we can sell it," I said.

"I think Edgar is still worried about the Northerner's views of us Southerners, other than the railroad, no one wants to give us a fair price," Mr. Smiley told her as he shook his head.

"They don't hesitate about charging full price for seed," Ida added to the conversation.

"I was lucky that McGrath even let me buy anything let alone get a deal," I said. I shuffled my feet and added, "From the rumor's I heard everyone in Fredericksburg is charging Southerners top price."

"We lost the war, so we have to pay," I added. Jacob and Mr. Smiley shook their heads in agreement.

Our conversation reminded me of a traveler who had come by the day before.

Jacob asked, "What are you thinking about Edgar?"

"Just something that a traveler told me the other day," I said.

He asked, "What was that?"

"He was telling me about a general I served under for a while," I said.

He went on to ask, "Who was that?"

"General Johnston… It seems he surrendered to Sherman twenty days after Lee surrendered to Grant…" I said. I had a flash of a memory of serving under General Joseph E. Johnston for a few days. There had been some talk about him not being aggressive enough but he did win the first battle of Bull Run. While serving under him I found his men liked him more than any other General was liked. I then added, "I have been wondering if he survived or not ever since the war ended."

"It seems it takes forever to learn what is or has happened," Jacob said.

"You know, this is the first time you've said anything about your part in the war," Ida said.

"As I have said it isn't something I'm proud of," I said.

"On the same subject there is something else that's bothered me for long time," Ida said.

I asked, "What's that?"

"Well I understand Mr. Davis not visiting…but I would think Mr. Lee or Grant would have visited the old place once since the war ended. If nothing else but in memory of our parents," she answered.

"They're busier now than they ever were," Mr. Smiley offered as weak excuse for them.

"I'm sorry, I shouldn't be thinking about the past but what we're going to do. The war is over and we now have this crop," I said.

"It just isn't fair… All the work we have put into this crop," Ida said as she got up. "Let's go in and get the men something to eat.

"I'd better leave now," Mr. Smiley said. Turning to go home, he added, "I'll see you in the morning Edgar… We might as well get an early start for Fredericksburg."

"I guess we'd better. I doubt the rain will hold off for too long," I said agreeing.

"The women don't seem too happy," Jacob said as we walked towards the house.

"You have to be realistic… They knew the truth before… I don't want to come home three or four weeks from now with pennies rather than dollars," I replied with a shrug.

"That's for sure," he said as he held the door open for me.

No one said much during supper. We all seemed to be in our own thoughts. I had the feeling I had let Ida down and I didn't know how. How the North treated us was also getting to me. Regardless of what color I was or where I came from, I should get the same respect. It never occurred to me we wouldn't get a fair price. At forty some cents a bushel, we would barely break even. Before the war, farmers were lucky to get seventeen cents, so the current price was high. If everyone else was getting forty cents a bushel, so should we. The trouble was that we had a few months before we could even take it in to sell.

Though it had only been a few months since we tied our crop together it was now harvested and ready for shipment.

Mr. Smiley and I met early the next morning and took the harvest to Fredericksburg. The trip was uneventful. We didn't do as poorly as I had expected, but we still only got a third of what everyone up north got. I tried for a better price but the man at the elevator told me if I didn't like it, I could try elsewhere. Mr. Smiley stepped in and said we would sell just to get rid of the crop. It was better than nothing but I certainly didn't like it.

Later that night at home, I told Ida what we had run into. I said, "We still came out twenty-three dollars ahead… That is, each of us did."

She shook her head and said, "That's not enough to make it worthwhile."

"I know." On the other hand, it was twice as much as I made in a month working for Mr. Smiley.

A few weeks later Molly gave birth to a baby boy. From the way, she had been moaning and groaning we were looking forward to the birth of their child. Jacob complained that each day seemed like a week. He couldn't have been happier when the day came. He rushed over to our place bragging that he had a son. Catching his breath, he told us they named him Little Joe.

"If I remember right, your father's name was Joe," I said.

"Yes, and he would be so proud if he were here," Jacob answered.

"Come to think of it, you never said what happened to him. You haven't said anything about where your family is," I said. I remembered Jacob working in the stables on the Marsh's place as his family worked the fields. I never knew his family, but Mr. Marsh always had a kind word about them.

"As soon as the war broke out, they headed north… I haven't heard anything from them," he told me. "I'd better get back to the house. Molly and Little Joe might need me."

"I understand," I said. He went to his place and I went home to tell Ida, for she would want to hear the news right away. She and Molly had been discussing the change a child could make.

"So the day has finally come… Daddy is proud of his new son," Mr. Smiley said, catching me as I was leaving. "Have you and Ida thought about starting a family?"

"I have no problem with the idea. I guess it's up to God" I replied. I was hoping he wouldn't delay me for I was eager to tell Ida about little Joe.

"Maybe you should go home and tell Ida about the new addition," he suggested.

"I was thinking of doing just that." I headed out the door.

After I got home and told Ida the news, she put on her shawl and we went over to Jacob's place. Strangely enough, she was so excited she didn't say anything. It was probably just because she was so excited about the new baby. But also, because it had rained the night before, she had to pay attention to where she was walking and keep herself from slipping in the mud.

When we got to Jacob's, I reminded her, "Molly probably doesn't feel like having visitors."

"We won't stay long… I just can't sit over at home and not see the baby," she said.

"I know. I wanted to see Little Joe myself" I replied as I opened the door.

We didn't stay long. He was asleep while we were there and so was Molly. Though I hadn't seen many babies, I thought Little Joe was cute. After looking at Jacob's little bundle of pride I had to say he looked like a strong little boy.

"Now it's our turn," Ida said as we walked home.

"I know," I said as I felt a raindrop. We had talked about having children someday, but it hadn't seemed important to her. I didn't know whether that was from fear of putting her children in the same position she was in. All I knew was that I wanted children because of my love for her. I also wanted to see them grow up and have children of their own.

As we talked, I was glad that I hadn't pushed our earlier feelings. Since there had been no minister around no one would have thought ill of us if we had lived together as man and wife. My fear was more about what Ida would have thought of me if she knew her own mother's past. I was glad I had taken the time to let her come to her own conclusions. I felt a smile on my face thinking that my parents were also proud of me.

It Was Getting To Be Too Much

I find myself writing in my diary as a different person. I am home, free of the war and married. Though there are problems, I'm still happy with my life:

Two years almost to the day of little Joe's birth, my first son was, born. For nine months, I fretted just as Jacob had, and he laughed at me about that. The worst moment was waiting for Molly to come out of the bedroom to tell me Ida was all right. I had bought Ida a stove, and Molly had me boiling water, mostly just to keep me busy.

Ida had been sick for the two weeks before the birth, and I had the awful fear that she might die in childbirth, which wasn't uncommon. When I found out that both she and the baby were fine, I went in to look at my son.

Though he looked more like his mother, he displayed an attitude that was similar to my own. Looking down at him, I wanted to pick him up, but he seemed so small I was afraid I might hurt him.

"Go ahead, he won't break" Ida told me. She sounded a little tired.

"You should let both of them sleep. They've had a hard time," Molly reminded me.

"Let me hold him for a minute," I said to Ida as I picked him up. To Ida I suggested, "How does Harold sound?"

She asked, "What?"

"Naming him after your father," I said as I came to her side. Lowering our son down so she could see him, I added, "He looks like he's from your side of the family."

She didn't answer. Instead, she bit her lip and turned her head. A tear ran down her cheek. I gave her a kiss and told her "Get some rest."

As I turned she nodded silently. I put little Harold back down and let the two of them sleep. I went out to the living area and found Jacob and Molly talking. He was trying his best to keep Little Joe under control but it was a losing battle.

Jacob told his son, "Get back here!"

"You can see the baby tomorrow," Molly said.

Picking him up, I assured him, "Tomorrow."

"Baby," he said as he pointed to the bedroom.

"Tomorrow and many more after that" I told him as I set him down. With his feet on the floor, I added, "Right now the baby has to sleep."

For the first two years of our marriage, we hadn't had any children. Then when Harold came along, it got our family going. Jacob laughed, saying it must have taken us two years to learn how to make babies. Then over the next five years, we had four more children, Mark, Luke, John, and Annabelle. The other three boys we named after books in the Bible. Our little girl we named after Ida's mother.

One of the drawbacks to having the number of children we did was the lack of room in the house. I kept adding more and more rooms to make space for them. As a result, the one room house was becoming a large home, complete with glass windows to be proud of, and I hoped Ida felt the same way. Having the children made all the work well worth it. Every time I looked at the place, I had to smile, thinking that old sharecroppers who had once used the place wouldn't recognize it. With enough rooms for kitchen, rooms for the children and us to sleep in, the house was getting larger.

In the original place the cooking had been done in a kitchen behind the house. Ida now had an inside kitchen, which she considered an improvement. The glass windows were also different from what they had known. However, it was still a lot smaller than the houses Ida and I had known before the war.

Our children were the center of our lives, and the best part. Our crops would come in and we couldn't get much for them. As with our first, we made money but nothing compared to what farmers up north could get.

One day, while reading a paper I got in Fredericksburg, I learned about a better place. The land the article talked about was not one specific area, but to the country west of the Mississippi River. The writer called the land "The West." I had read some articles saying that farmers were easily able to get good crops in California. It sounded wonderful; but from Ida's reaction when I mentioned it to her, I knew we weren't ready for the move.

Then a family came by the shop and I offered them a place to stay for the night. I hoped Ida would listen to what they had to say and get ideas of her own.

When I took them to our place, Ida and Harold were in the yard. I had no idea where the rest of the children were. I gave them a wave and got a big grin back from both of them. I greeted them with "Hon… Harold, I have a few guests for dinner and the night… I hope you don't mind."

"I thought so…I can see a couple and their wagon coming behind you," she answered with a hug and a kiss.

When the wagon stopped, the couple came over to us. I introduced Ida, "This is Mr. and Mrs. Wilcox. This is my wife, Ida…The Wilcox's are on their way north."

"This is great… I don't get to see too many people anymore. It's a pleasure to meet the two of you," Ida offered. Then with a short pause to look at me, she asked them, "Care for some water? I could put a pot of coffee on if you would like?"

"I like your place. Our place wasn't as large as yours is," Mrs. Wilcox said as she touched some of the furniture admiringly. "We tried to get our lives back together like you have, but we didn't make it."

As the two women talked, I motioned for Mr. Wilcox to follow me. As we walked, I told him "As you can guess the crops aren't worth anything up north."

He shook his head and said, "Yes, I know… I tried beans and I couldn't get any money for them. I even went farther north and got less than I did in Fredericksburg."

I understood what he had gone through. I was curious as to what he was planning on doing. I asked, "Then why are you going north?"

"Well…, we're going first to Kentucky to get my brother. Then we're heading to Indian country. I heard the government has opened some land there and I thought it might be better than staying here," he answered.

"I've been thinking about taking my family west…From what I have read, in California no one cares who you are. My only problem is convincing my wife. This is where she grew up and she hates the thought of leaving it," I told him.

"A nice piece of land," he commented as he looked around.

"It was larger before the war…Her folks didn't make it through the war and she sold everything but forty acres," I said. I found myself thinking of Ida's mother for the first time since Annabelle was born. The last memory of her mother still bothered me.

"I know how it is. We've lost several good families in the area," he said. Looking back at the house, he added, "I don't think the war was worth fighting. I know we lost and are still losing more than I hoped to gain."

"We might as well join the women," I said. Seeing the clear sky, I added, "At least it looks like you have picked a good time to leave."

"I just wish we weren't as old as we are," he replied, laughing.

"…Is it worth it? Edgar has been talking about going west for some time now. I expect someday soon we'll be heading that way ourselves," Ida was saying as we entered.

"I like your place… If it wasn't for the low prices for crops and all the bad memories, I'd have stayed where we were," Mr. Wilcox said. "Our place was about this size. After the war, we made a room in the barn."

Harold had been listening to his mother, he began to get excited. He asked her. "Are we going somewhere, Mama?"

"Not right now, Honey," she answered.

"You have such quiet children," Mrs. Wilcox commented.

"Oh, they are until they get to know you. Until then they're a little shy at times," Ida answered with her motherly smile.

"Harold's her little boy," I remarked. In reality, she didn't show any special attention to him. Though he appeared interested in what I was doing, he followed her more than he did me. I didn't feel bad about it. After all, he saw more of her than me.

Unprepared for company, Ida hadn't made anything fancy. Supper still satisfied everyone and our company did spend the night. To our surprise over the next three weeks, we had four more families spend a night or more. I became concerned when one family had a sick little girl and we kept them for a week. Ida and I both worried that our children would end, up getting sick. We were lucky when they went on our way and everyone in our family remained healthy.

It almost seemed as if the Wilcox family had opened the gates to a stream of migrating people. I knew that wasn't the case, though, because families had started moving since the war ended. Everyone who stopped had a story similar to the Wilcox's, so apparently our problems were no different from anyone else's. I found myself asking Ida after each one left, "Why don't we join them?"

"It'll get better," she would assure me every time I brought up the subject. I would remind her it had been six years and since nothing had improved in that time, it would be a long time before anything would change for the better. As I told her, I prayed it would be better for our grandchildren. She never argued, but I knew she didn't go along with my way of thinking. I prayed many times that she would lose some of her ties to the memory of her parents.

Although I sometimes doubted her love for me, my love for her continued to grow. I understood how her life had been so secure until the war. Then because of the war, everything had fallen apart. At times, I thought she missed the old place more than her parents. Her change in attitude I felt was the result of her and her mother's experience in Richmond. The only thing Ida had told me is that they existed on almost nothing but not how. One night she finally told me, her mother had died in her arms. From the look in her eyes, I knew there was more to the story. I wondered if that was what her mother had let herself become. I believed her mother did what she did to keep Ida alive. I wondered if Ida had come to the same conclusion and felt guilty for it. Was trying to save the old place her way of paying her mother back?

I too had lost my parents, home and friends. The difference was there was no shame about what I had lost, just anger. My only guilt came from what I had done and all the men I had killed, even though the killing seemed justified. My guilt was one reason I wanted to go west, away from everything that reminded me of the war. I prayed that once I was there, I wouldn't have to face memories of what I had lost.

I didn't know what I could do to help Ida handle her guilt. I just wished I could do something that would ease her pain.

One morning I got up before anyone else. I looked around our home and realized how sparse it was in comparison with how comfortable my parents' home and Ida's had been. Although we were now living better than most of the workers, it wasn't the same as it had been when we were kids. With this realization, I began to think. I took my idea and headed for the shop before Ida got up.

As he came into the shop, Jacob asked, "Couldn't sleep?"

"Not very well, I've been giving Ida some thought lately," I told him. Then as I turned to the stove, I said, "I have some coffee on."

"I thought Mr. Smiley told you not to make coffee," he said.

"My coffee isn't that bad," I said. I grabbed a cup and poured him some.

He took a sip. "Not if you're talking about paint remover." Then, smiling, he added, "It's been worse."

"Thanks," I said as I saluted and I raised my cup.

Sounding concerned, he asked, "What's the problem with Ida?"

"Well…you know the comfort she was raised in," I began to explain.

"I remember… Those were the days. I didn't go inside the house often, but I used to dream of living in a fancy place like theirs," Jacob replied as he drank his coffee.

"At least it's waking you up" I said as I raised my cup.

"And curling my teeth, you were saying about Ida" he pushed me on. Grinning about having given me a bad time, he added, "Something tells me you have a plan in mind."

"Well… you know how excited she got when I bought her the stove," I reminded him. Then letting him think about it I added, "I would like to do a little better."

"What do you have in mind? The stove almost made you a God" he joked.

"Since I came in this morning I began wondering how much stuff people leave behind when they go west. I might find something she would appreciate," I told him.

"I would think there's a lot they've left behind," he answered.

"What's going on this morning?" Then seeing the coffeepot on the stove, he shook his head. Then with a smile, he asked Jacob, "You or Edgar makes it?"

"Edgar," Jacob answered nodding in my direction.

"In remembrance of my father and his rotten coffee, I'll have a cup," Mr. Smiley said as he picked up a cup. He shook his head again, grabbed the pot and filled the cup. As he raised the cup to his lips, he said, "I guess this is as good a time to die as any other."

"It isn't that bad… We're both standing," I told him.

Jacob and I filled him in on my idea of a way to get some more furniture for Ida. With a smile, Mr. Smiley told me, "Take the day off."

"Mind if I borrow your rig...? I don't want Ida to know what I'm doing" I asked. If I took our own wagon and horse, Ida would ask questions. Even if she didn't, she would know I was up to something. This way, she'd have no idea what I was up to.

"Go ahead... I don't have any use for them today. If you find anything worthwhile, you don't need let me know," he answered.

"Same here, brother" Jacob added, smiling.

I knew what the smile was all about, for Molly was like Ida and would appreciate having some new items for the house. He too had dreams of living in comfort. If I could find something they could use, Molly would be pleased and his life and hers would be happier. With the houses so far apart, I was in for a long ride. Thankfully, the war had gotten me used to long rides, so I headed out.

It was late that evening when I finally got home. As I pulled into the yard, Ida came out to greet me.

"I was wondering what happened to..." she stopped when she saw what was on the wagon.

"Mr. Smiley let me use the wagon and team," I told her as I got off the wagon. "I went around to the other houses and found a few things you might be able to use. You might need a few more, but at least this is a start."

"Oh this is wonderful," she said, as she looked all of it over. Then she began identifying everything on it. She asked, "I can't believe it there's a washstand, bureau, and even a sofa. Where did you get that wonderful sofa?"

"The old Williams place," I answered.

Our son Mark came out and looked at what was in the wagon. He then asked, "What are you doing?"

"I brought home some furniture for your mother," I told him.

He asked, "Why?"

"To make our home nicer," I told him.

Ida asked, "Can we take it all in?"

Mark asked, "Can I help?"

"I don't think you're big enough yet" Ida told him.

He didn't like this answer. "I'm big... I'm almost as big as Little Joe," he told his mother.

"That may be true, but we will have to see," I told him.

Annabelle came out of the house. "Mamma, John took my piece of bread… Hi Father…" Mark said greeting me.

Then she announced, "We've had our supper already," Annabelle told me.

"I know I'm a little late tonight," I said.

"I'll get you another piece when we get these things inside," Ida told her. Then she told the two, "Now stay out of your father's way."

"I'll get you this time," Mark yelled at his sister. With that, the two ran back into the house.

"Everything is so beautiful" Ida exclaimed as I began taking each item off the wagon.

"That's true," I said agreeing with her. As I handed a washstand down to her, I commented, "It's getting cool early this year."

"I kept the stove hot, so you can have a hot supper," she told me.

"Good" I replied gratefully. After getting all the furniture inside and arranging it, I finally got some supper.

Over the next few days, I made a few more trips for furniture. Jacob and Mr. Smiley joined me one day, pleased that our wives were pleased. After the last load, I caught Ida twirling around in the middle of our main living area. She had the biggest smile I had seen since the birth of Harold. I asked her "What's happening."

"Just thinking about Mother," she answered as she stopped twirling.

I asked, "What about her?"

"How she might feel living here. It isn't like the old place but it does look homey," she answered smiling. Then she gave me a kiss and said "Thanks."

"You're welcome…but I'm not really sure what for" I replied.

Harold came out of the children's room asking, "Are you working today?"

"Yes. Harold" I answered.

He asked, "Can I go with you?"

It was the first time he had asked to go with me, and I was pleased. So he did want to be with me, after all. He seemed genuinely interested in what Jacob and I did all day. I even took him on a delivery and he delighted everyone he met.

It pleased me to see Ida smiling more in our newly furnished home. She now referred to the place more and more as "our home" and not "the house."

Though the place had been a personal frustration, it wasn't the worst. The worst had been not being able to do anything about it. When Ida had sold the largest section of her place, the Campbell's, the new owners, built a new house and barn. The following summer they planted their crop around our property. The first day of construction, I met Mr. Campbell. I got the impression that he thought he was better than Jacob and me. From that point on we had very little to do with him.

Still through the years, we bumped into each other and remained civil. One day Mr. Campbell needed some work done, and he came over to the shop to see Mr. Smiley about it. In conversation, he mentioned how much he had gotten for his crop. Mr. Smiley, Jacob and I got tired of hearing about him getting three times as much for his crop as we had for ours, just because he was a Northerner. I knew it was something that bothered Ida. In spite of this apparent injustice, she still dreamed that we would make a success of our place.

One summer Mr. Smiley asked me, "How much do you think Campbell got for his crop?"

"I don't even want to think about it," I answered.

"Me, neither" Jacob added as he shook his head.

"For one cent I would move west" I told them. Hearing myself say those words I had said, I realized how often I had said them. I kept thinking if it weren't for the children, I might grab Ida and leave.

Ida and I had a good marriage, and because of that it was easier to handle our frustrations. Although we didn't talk that much, we also didn't fight. We did what we had to do to exist, and collapsed exhausted each night in bed. Any free time we gave to the children. Like Ida, I tried to give our children as much attention as my parents had given me, if not more. Then as time went by, I found we were talking more and more each night.

I got home one night and I found a stack of money on the table. I was stunned to see the stack of bills alongside a steel box. The first thought that came to mind was we could go west with that money. Then feeling hands tugging at my pants, I told the children "I want the five of you to go outside… Your mother and I need to have a talk."

Once the children left the house, I called out to Ida "I have a question or two for you."

"Yes, Hon," she answered as she came out of our room.

She saw me holding the steel box and looking inside it. Setting it down I asked, "Where did this come from? No one around here has this much money that you could have even stolen it from."

"It came from Mama," she answered smiling. Allowing me time to grasp what she had told me. She then added, "I didn't know it was in one of those boxes in the root cellar. I never looked in it until last year."

"And you didn't tell me about it," I commented.

"I didn't think we needed it, so I kept it under our bed," she said.

"If I had known I was sleeping on so much… I see the dates on the bills are 1860 and older," I commented as I looked over the bills. I didn't know how many were in my hands but I knew it was a good sum.

"And they're all Union bills," she said. It was during the war; Mama must not have thought they were worth anything. Still, not liking to throw money away, she kept it safe in the cellar."

"I just don't understand why you didn't you tell me about finding it," I said as I set the box back on the table.

"I knew we would need it more going west than here," she answered.

"But we…" I started to say, but she interrupted me.

"Hearing all your talk of going west, I knew we would someday," she said, still smiling.

"We owe your mother more and more every time I turn around," I replied as I sat down. I silently went over our options in my mind. I couldn't believe we might be moving west at last. I looked up and saw Ida smiling at me. She looked relieved.

"I owe you so much…" she began to say.

I asked, "How's that?"

"For allowing me to fulfill an impossible dream," she answered as she also took a seat. She then added, "I wanted to bring the place back to what Mama loved. I knew we could never do it, but I wanted to try. As I thought about you and the children the other night, I saw how hopeless it was. I realized what was most important in my life was you and the children. I knew it was time to make our own life... Mama would be happier if I was true to my family and not to a lost dream."

"I love you," I told her as I went over and gave her a kiss.

From the doorway Harold asked, "Can we come in?"

"Yes, Honey." She took him into her arms and said, "Father and I have plans to make... We'll be moving soon."

Harold asked, "Where are we going?"

"Your father and I have to discuss that. All I know is that he wants to go west," she explained.

Harold looked at both of us and asked, "Is little Joe coming with us?"

As Ida and he waited expectantly, I answered, "We will have to see."

"Now go back outside," Ida told him.

As he walked away, I said, "He asked an interesting question."

"I know," she answered.

"I know Jacob's ready to make a move. I don't know about Molly, but something tells me they would go if we do," I said.

"Molly has wanted to leave as long as you have," she told me.

"Then what are we waiting for…? Your father made all the shovels, picks and pans for California, so now let's see if we can find out what's there," I announced wanted to jump up and down with excitement.

"Why wait…? Let's walk up to their place and see what they have to say about it," she suggested.

"They can't afford to," I reminded her.

"It's up to you… but I think there's enough there for both families," she said as she looked at the stack of bills.

"I'm for it. They have been better than good friends."

"Come on, children. Jacob and Molly are expecting us," Ida called as I shut the door.

Once we got to their place, Jacob and I stayed outside to talk. First, I told him what I found when I arrived home. I did that to ease his mind about the expense of buying him a new start.

After a while, the women came out. Molly went over to her husband and asked, "Well…What have the two of you decided?"

"I think you know the answer," he said as he gave her a hug. "I've had enough of this kind of life."

"The two of you have been good friends…If it hadn't been for you, we probably would have left a long, time ago," Molly said.

Over the next few weeks, we tried to decide what we would need to make the trip west and discovered that we had hardly any idea of what that would be. With winter coming on, we let the subject die for a while. Our discussions sometimes turned into arguments, so it was better to give it all a rest. Then to our rescue came Mr. Madison, who was planning on taking a wagon train west come summer.

From him we learned we needed to buy bigger wagons called Conestoga Wagons. To pull those wagons we needed four to six oxen and maybe an extra for safety. Then for the wagon, we would need buckets of grease to hang from the axles to grease the wheels. He also advised that we oil the wagon cover liberally to make it waterproof. He told us that people took or tried to take almost everything imaginable. He stressed that we needed to take enough food for four months. He said the water we needed to take would probably weigh 350 pounds. It seemed like a lot, but when he explained what kind of country we would be traveling through, we understood.

We would need rifles, axes, saws, planers, shovels, and plows. Clearly, we would need clothing and other personal items, and furniture. He told us most people brought their Bible, but the book we would need most was one giving recipes for home remedies and cures, and aids for starting a new life alone. Having lived as we had, I found the idea a little funny. If Richmond had been where we were born, and lived, I would have laughed.

After talking to him, I spread the news that he was putting together a wagon train. I found four more families that wanted to go west, and told them it was safer to go as a group than alone. Having given them the notice I had, they had time to gather what they needed for the trip.

One day Jacob asked me, "What do you think…? Are we ready, or have we forgotten anything?"

"As much as Ida has packed, there isn't much left to forget," I told him.

"Molly's just as bad. She told me that for all the work we have done to get where we are, she hated to leave anything behind. As for me, as long as Little Joe and Molly are with me, I'll be happy," he said.

"Father," Little Joe announced as he came out of their house.

"Yes, Son, what is it?"

"Good evening, Little Joe" I greeted him.

"Good evening, Mr. Buchanan…Mother said if you are planning on eating tonight, you had better get inside," Little Joe told his father.

"I'll be right in," Jacob told his son. Turning back to me, he added, "I guess tomorrow we begin loading the tools from the shop."

"This ought to be fun," I said with a laugh. I had been right about Smiley's business going under. I wasn't sure if it was Tredegar Ironworks or not, but someone was responsible. Once Tredegar got the cannon business Smiley previously had, everyone wanted to use them and considering the difference in size between the two operations, it was easy to see that we couldn't hold our own. Before I left I added, "Smiley seems as excited in the move to Fredericksburg, as we are going west."

"Yes, I think he's more excited than we are… Up there he'll be close to Washington and might get more business," Jacob replied.

"I guess I had better let you go and get home myself. If I don't, I might find myself without supper," I told him as I turned for home. I wasn't looking forward to the walk. It had warmed up, but it was drizzling. The two-mile walk meant I would get a little wet. I prayed Ida had the fire going in the stove so I would be able to dry off.

"Good night, Edgar… See you in the morning," he said as he went back inside. In the dusk, I could still see for a long ways. I found a little lump in my throat thinking about moving. Most of my life I had lived here and I knew I would miss it. But I said to myself, "Now I have a new life, and it's time to leave."

As I walked up our road, I looked at the house closely. I imagined the Campbell family moving into it, or renting it to another family. We didn't need it though, so why get upset? I wondered what Ida thought about it. I went up to the house and wondered how long she would take to bring it up.

"Hello, Father," John greeted me at the door.

I looked around for Ida, as I asked him, "Good evening, John… How was your day? Do you have anything to tell me?"

"You're all wet, Father," Annabelle said as she came up to hug my leg.

"Yes, I am," I said, still waiting for John's answer.

"Nothing," John said.

I asked, "That doesn't sound much like fun…Where is your mother?"

"She's lying down" he told me.

"She isn't feeling good?" I asked.

"I'm getting up" I heard Ida announce.

I asked, "Are you, all right?"

"I'm fine…The children were getting to me," she said. Giving me a kiss, she added, "I kept some supper warm for you… My, you look as if you're soaked to the bone. Why don't you change into something dry first and then have some supper?"

Playfully, I asked, "Want to help me?"

"Edgar…The children" she answered with a smile.

"I don't think I need their help…I would rather you did some of it yourself," I suggested.

"Get in there and change," she told me again with her cute smile.

She didn't let me get far before she asked, "What route will we be taking?"

"From here to Nashville, to Independence Missouri, up to Fort Laramie, then to Fort Boise. From there we'll be going due west into Oregon," I said.

She asked, "How long will it take?"

"Just to Fort Boise…, four to five months… If we don't have too many problems," I said.

She kept pushing by asking, "And the rest of the trip?"

"Two to four months… and that depends if we can get there before winter sets in. If we don't, we may have to stay in Boise until spring," I said.

"I hope it's going to be worth it," she said.

"It will be," I assured her.

The next week we spent getting Mr. Smiley's shop packed and loaded ready for shipping to Fredericksburg. It surprised me that Ida wasn't upset about Smiley moving her father's factory. She even wished Mr. Smiley luck in his new location. Once he was on his way, we began finishing what we needed to do. Since Jacob and I had been to Fredericksburg a couple of times we had gotten all the supplies we needed.

As we got our things together Ida said, "You know I'm going to miss the children."

I asked, "What do you mean. We're taking them with us."

"No, silly… The children in school," she said correcting me.

"I know," I said not knowing what else to say. The few months she took off after our children were born were bad enough.

When Mr. Madison came by to pick us up, we found we had a few problems. Though the other families were ready, Molly and Little Joe were sick. With everyone needing to walk beside the wagons, we knew Molly wouldn't be able to make it. So we told him to go on without us. Once they were feeling well enough, we would catch up with them. Then Annabelle got sick, delaying us even longer. Two of the other families planning to join us also had problems. Thinking we had lost our chance of going west with the wagon train, I told them what Mr. Madison told me. He said he was making a few stops to pick up other wagons. As long as we went straight to Independence, Missouri, we could meet him there. He didn't think he would be there for seven to nine weeks. I prayed he was right and we would get there in time.

A week later, everyone was well enough to make the trip. Under the circumstances, we decided to take off for Nashville in the morning. To make it easier we stayed at Jacob and Molly's place the night before. In the middle of the night, I woke up and Ida wasn't beside me. Thinking she was taking care of one of the children, I rolled over and went back to sleep. Suddenly I woke up and saw flames shooting up outside the window. Looking out I saw it was our place on fire. I muttered, "Must be the Klan."

I jumped onto my horse bareback and rode as fast as I could to try to put the fire out. When I got there, I didn't have any idea how to put it out, and there wasn't anything I could do. I sighed and thought of all the work we had put into the place, then I turned and went back to Jacob's. As I entered the house, I saw Ida by the window.

"I couldn't do anything," I said as I wrapped my arms around her. She didn't say anything at first, just stood watching the fire with me.

"No one else will benefit from our labor now," she said. She added, "Now they have full value of what they paid for. I hope we didn't leave a candle burning."

"We took them all with us when we left...I went back and checked" I told her. With that, we went to bed and got a little more sleep. Walking beside the wagon would be tiring and we needed all the rest we could get.

"Edgar, Ida. It's time," I heard Jacob say as I tried to open my eyes.

"I guess so," I muttered.

Ida rolled off my arm and asked, "What...? Is it time to get up?"

"You'd better get the children up and fed... We have a long walk ahead of us," I answered.

Jacob asked, "Did you hear something in the middle of the night? Something woke me up, but I went back to sleep."

"Our place burned down... Sorry, but when I left I must have wakened you. When I got there it was too late for me to do anything" I answered.

He looked as if he didn't understand me, he asked, "It burned down?"

When Molly joined us she asked, "What burned down?"

"Our place," Ida answered her as she sat up.

Molly asked, "How?"

"I don't know... All I know is that when I got there it was too late. It seemed as if there was something fueling it," I told her. I got up, feeling every joint in my body ache. It had been some years since I had slept on a floor.

"I guess it doesn't matter, since we're not planning on moving back there again," I said as I buttoned my shirt.

"That's true," Jacob added, heading toward the front door. He opened it and said, "I think I'll hitch up the oxen."

"Wait a bit and I'll join you," I said as I looked for my shoes.

"Want some coffee first?" Ida asked knowing I didn't do anything without my first cup.

"I'll get a cup before we leave," I assured her.

"Don't forget to fix a few eggs with it," Jacob told Molly and Ida with a wink. Seeing their reaction, he suggested, "You can hitch up the oxen if you want."

"I know when we're beat let them play with the oxen. We'll get the children going and get something to eat," Molly conceded.

"I think we got the better deal," I told Jacob softly.

"I heard that," Ida shouted out as we left.

"She thinks she's funny," I commented.

"She is," Jacob replied as we got to the corral. With a laugh he added, "You just don't appreciate her humor."

"There's so much to appreciate about her… Or at least that's what she tells me. I don't have time to worry about her humor," I told him.

"Sounds like a bit of bragging to me" he said as he got hold of an ox.

"Possibly a little" I said with a laugh.

It didn't take long for us to get on the road. The other families joining us were also ready. As their leader, Ida and I took first position as we made our way to Nashville.

"It's a beautiful day for a walk," Ida said as she grabbed my hand and gave it a squeeze. Before I could respond, she added, "I hope your dream comes true."

"With you at my side and the children, it has come true…and it can only get better," I replied as I looked into her eyes. Thinking of California, my feet began to hurt realizing the distance we would cover. To get there wasn't just a matter of weeks but months.

Getting to Nashville was only the first step. Once there I prayed we could find a guide that could get us to Independence, Missouri. If we got out of there in time, we could still catch up with Mr. Madison and the wagon train. If we didn't, I wasn't sure what we would do. Not knowing that part of the country, I didn't look forward to living there for six months. It would be a waste if that were to happen. I did my best to keep my fears to myself and continued as if there wasn't anything to worry about.

We had been traveling for a while, for the first time on the trip Ida asked, "When do you think we'll get to Nashville?"

"In the morning I suppose," I answered. Carefully I kept my eye on the oxen. I had made this trip several times but not in this fashion. I was used to making it in three and a half weeks not five like we were doing it in. I knew it would be hard, but we might find it exciting. My only fear was from hearing of the deaths suffered by so many in making the trip. The idea of losing Ida or one of my children was frightening.

Before we settled down for the night, Ida said, "I burned the house down."

Her statement caught me by surprise. I asked, "What?"

"I said I burned the house down," she repeated.

I shouted out, "You what?"

I realized how loud my outburst was and I looked around. In a softer voice I asked, "Why would you do that?"

"I didn't want those people to gain any more from all of our hard work," she said as she fluffed a blanket for us.

"Well, I'll be dogged." I replied not knowing what else to say. Well, now I had learned what her feelings were about leaving the house. I had to chuckle since I had been thinking that it might be the Klan or as she suggested a lit candle left behind.

With only a few problems the next morning, we made it to Nashville. Having some knowledge of the city I headed toward the biggest stables in town. It didn't take long and I saw the sign:

NASHVILLE STABLES

I brought the oxen to a stop and told Ida to stay in the wagon with the children. Having known the owner, Mr. Dennison, for a while, I asked one of his hands if he was there. When he came out to talk to me, I found he couldn't help us. As I went through our options, I motioned for Ida to join me. When she came to my side, I told her "He can't help us."

She asked, "What now?"

"I'm not sure," I answered as I looked around. Then I caught sight of Mr. Williams, a member of our little wagon team coming toward us.

Mr. Williams walked up to us with other members of the wagon train following him. Every one of them had a concerned expression on their faces. He asked, "What's happening, Edgar?"

"Trying to find someone that can guide us to Kearny," I said.

Mr. Williams asked, "Why don't you take us there…? You got us this far."

"More by luck than knowledge or skill," I told him. Then holding my hand up to quiet them, I told them "It might take a day or two, so I have asked the man at the stable if we can keep the oxen there. He said it would be all right and he won't charge us."

"Bless him," one of the women said.

"I agree. Anything we can save is good," Ida said for the group.

"Anyway, let's get them out of their yokes and boarded. Once that's done I'll see about finding a wagon master," I told them. As the women took care of the children, I went about my business.

I had seen Ida talking to a man so I asked, "Who was that?"

"Paul Gallagher…It seems he's a shop owner. He said if we need any help, just come over to his shop," she answered.

I looked around thinking I might spot him. I asked, "Where's his shop?"

She pointed to the shop he had shown her as she called to the children, "All right, everyone…Let's get something to eat."

I went back to the wagon with her and grabbed a piece of dried meat and a piece of bread. As I stood there, I saw a man on a horse wearing a Confederate Kepi cap ride by. In passing, he tipped his cap to us and continued on his way.

After I finished eating I told Ida "I think I had better talk to a few more people. Mr. Dennison wasn't able to help us maybe this other man can."

"Here's hoping you find someone," she answered as she cleaned up the children's mess. Waving to the children, I walked over to the shop to talk Paul Gallagher. He didn't seem optimistic, but promised to do what he could. Not being able to do anything, I went back to join the group.

Then Paul called to me, "Mr. Buchanan…I might have your problem solved for you, after all." He gave a nod to the man next to him

"Good morning, I'm Edgar Buchanan…, but Edgar will do" I greeted the man. Sizing him up, I got the idea right away that he knew his business. My greatest fear was that he was so young. I knew we needed someone, so if Paul Gallagher thought he was good enough, we would have to trust his judgment. It seemed we didn't have a choice, since there weren't any wagon masters available. With so many people going west all of them were guiding wagon trains already.

"Matt Duncan… It's good to meet you, Edgar…" the man replied. "Most call me Matt. I doubt if I have used my last name more than once this year."

"I know how it is," I said.

"I'll let the two of you talk over the details…Good luck, Matt, and you too, Mr. Buchanan," Paul said as he went back to his shop.

"As I was telling your friend there…" I began to say but Ida interrupted us. Taking her hand, I introduced her to him, "My wife, Ida… and this gentleman is Matt."

"A pleasure to meet you, Matt," Ida said, smiling.

"Same here… A pleasure to meet you," Matt said.

It was interesting to see Matt's reaction to meeting my wife. This was one of those few times I had been able to witness a stranger's reaction to her. It seemed he found her as attractive as I did. Seeing his reaction made me feel proud to have her for a wife. However, now I wondered how he would treat her on the trail. That was a genuine concern.

"As I was just about to tell Matt, we need to be in Independence, Missouri to meet the wagon train four weeks from now…, but nothing had gone as we planned. If there is any way we can catch up with them, we would like to try. There are few wagon trains leaving now. As you know, most people are going from town to town by wagon or by rail.

We can't afford to take the train, so we need the company of as many wagons as we can get together," I explained to both of them. The man began to laugh at me making me mad.

"I know it isn't funny but getting you there in four weeks is impossible… If everything went without a hitch we would be lucky to get there in five or six weeks," Matt told us. He let it sink in before he explained, "Just losing a wheel or the weather could hold us up two or three days."

Ida asked, "What are we going to do?"

"Let's see what he thinks is best," I suggested.

We went on and talked about many things. I learned he had lived not too far from us back home. He had also fought in the war and lost his family. He acted as if it was a painful memory and he didn't go into it. He did tell us about driving delivery wagons into Texas, Fort Dodge, Kansas and Kearny, Nebraska. After I asked him a few other questions, I agreed he was the man we were looking for.

We parted with the understanding that we would leave the following morning. He made it clear he didn't want to make the trip to the coast. Kearny was all right but no farther. He seemed confident we would be able to catch up with Mr. Madison's westbound train. I went back and told the group we had our guide or wagon master.

I explained to them that Mr. Duncan was sure the train wouldn't leave Kearney for a week or so after they got there. He said he knew of a trail that should shave off a couple of days. He said if we were lucky we could make it in eight or nine weeks. I also reminded everyone that we didn't have anything to lose and they agreed.

After talking it over with the group Ida said, "I don't see where we have a choice."

"You've always been partial to a man with a strong back," I replied as I looked around at our wagons.

She asked, "I married you, didn't I?"

As I turned back to her I asked, "You're saying I don't have a strong back?"

"Oh, you have a strong back… and a few other good qualities," she answered as she gave me a kiss.

"I love you, too," I told her as I let go of her. Giving her hand a squeeze, I knew we were on the road going west together. She was not just following me.

Kearny Is Now Behind Us

I was thinking, "Writing in my diary is something I don't have much time to do. I don't know how but I have to find the time.

So much has happened that I don't want any of it forgotten. If something happens to me, I want my children to know about our experiences, and how I feel about them and their mother.

So, I begin to write:

We had been traveling longer than I wanted to think about. To make it worse we had just started and I knew I didn't dare think about what was ahead of us. As I thought about my quest I heard Ida speaking to me.

"It looks like the children have been drinking more than usual over the past few days," Ida told me one night. "They're even fighting over each other's water."

"It is dry out here… I've been drinking a lot myself," I said. As we talked, I tried to find my diary. When I gave up, I asked her, "Have you seen my diary?"

"I think so. But shouldn't you sleep? You can write in it later," she suggested.

"I know I should be sleeping, but I want to get down everything I can…This move is a major step in our family's life," I said.

"I'll see if I can find the diary for you" she replied.

"Thanks," I answered feeling more tired than I had for a long time. If my memory served me correctly, I haven't felt this way since I was in the hospital before the war's end. She found my diary, handed it to me, and went to the end of the wagon to check on the children.

I heard her tell them, "We have to leave early tomorrow morning; I want all of you to go to sleep."

"Yes, Mama," Harold answered.

"I'm not tired," Luke said.

"Go to sleep anyway," she answered.

She was gone for what seemed like a long time. When she returned, I asked "What's going on? You didn't come back right away."

"Luke has another fever," she answered.

I recognized the concern in her voice. I got up from the bedroll not knowing what to do. I asked, "Think, he's all right?"

"I don't know. I wish we had a doctor on the train," she said. "I doubt that it's anything serious..., but as a mother I worry when I don't know for sure."

I told her I would ask around but I didn't remember anyone saying there was a doctor with us. I remembered Mr. Madison had suggested we buy a book on remedies for various illnesses, which we had done. I didn't know what to think about Luke's fever after reading part of the book, but it looked as if it would be a good idea to have a doctor look at him. I didn't want to scare her, so I didn't tell her how I felt. I also checked and confirmed there weren't any doctors on the wagon train. He said we would have to wait until our next stop, Fort Laramie or we could make our way back to Fort Kearny. Everyone with us decided to go on to Fort Laramie.

As we moved on, we found Mr. Madison to be a private individual. As we slept around the fire at night, our conversations turned to him, and the more we talked, the more we found we didn't know much about him. But one thing was certain: Moving my family to California had been only a dream until he came along. From what we learned from him, none of us could think about doing anything else. His presentation sold us on letting him guide us there.

Like everyone else, we walked alongside the wagon. That included the children who were old enough, while the younger ones sat inside so they wouldn't hold us up. For a few days, Luke had been feeling poorly and he remained in the wagon bundled up. One day I noticed Ida wasn't by my side. I didn't think too much about it because she was always checking on the children. When we stopped at midday, I went looking for her.

Seeing her through the back of the wagon I asked, "I was wondering what happened to you. Is he all right?"

When she didn't answer, I jumped into the wagon. I saw she was crying and I asked, "What happened?"

Between sobs, she said, "I heard him coughing and crying so I came over to check on him. He was shaking so hard the wagon was moving more than usual. I wrapped him in my blanket to keep him warm. He was so still it scared me…"

She stopped mid sentence and stroked his head.

When I looked at him, I knew my worst fears had come true. My little boy was dead and I couldn't find words to express my feelings. Wishing I could do something for him, I told Ida, "I'll take him."

"I wanted to come and get you," she finally managed to say. She let me take him as she wiped the tears from her eyes. Meanwhile she stroked Annabelle's head adding, "But I felt he might be more comfortable if I wrapped him up in the blankets. I held him in my arms…"

"I understand," I said. I felt more helpless than I had ever felt before, in my life. This was beyond my control, and it was almost unbearable.

She stopped sobbing for a moment and said, "He died in my arms."

I was in shock as I cradled my dead son. I began doubting myself as I heard people outside the wagon saying, "What if we hadn't started this trip? Would he still be alive?" I was in a daze. I didn't know who was saying what or what I said in return. I also heard our other children talking to their mother. I didn't understand what they were saying, either. The thought that my son was dead and it might be my fault was torture. I knew I had to quit thinking about it but I couldn't.

I heard Annabelle say, "Mama, I don't feel so good.

Ida cried out, "No, God, not another one... not Annabelle too."

It wasn't that I didn't care about Annabelle but Luke was in my hands. My main concern was to take care of him, though now that meant burying him. I went to the wagon to get a shovel. Seeing my distress holding him and getting the shovel, Jacob came to help me. As I dug the last shovel of dirt out of the grave, I saw Ida coming towards me.

As I placed him in the ground a member of the group asked, "Would you like me to say a few words?"

"Thank you," I said. As Ida joined me the rest of the group joined us.

"Lord... As you know one of your own has come home to join you. We..." the man began to say.

I wasn't listening as much as trying to comfort Ida. I was also a little dizzy standing there with the sun beating down on me.

"I don't want to leave him," she cried with her arms around me.

I told her softly, "He's God's to take care of now."

I let her cry on my shoulder for a while and everyone respected our need for privacy. At one side, Jacob and Molly were crying with us.

Molly took hold of Ida as Jacob and I finished burying my son. With each shovel full of dirt memories of him came to mind. It seemed as if it took forever but we finally finished. I found it hard to take because I couldn't think of any words to express my feelings other than I loved him and he would be missed.

When it seemed the right time, I took Ida back to the wagon. I knew the other wagons had to go on without us.

I didn't like the idea but I understood their concern about the possible plague or whatever that had struck my family. I also knew they felt bad for us but they had a deadline to keep. I needed to ask Mr. Madison if he wanted us to go on our own or if we could continue with them. As we walked back to the rest of the group, I saw Molly coming toward us.

"I'll take care of her," Molly offered.

"Thank you," I answered letting Ida go off with her. In parting, I reminded her, "Annabelle may need you."

I went to talk with Mr. Madison. He in turn had spoken with the rest of the party and they agreed to let us continue with them. Once we got to Fort Laramie, we would see a doctor and get his advice.

I was feeling ill now, too. My legs felt heavy and as if they were burning up. My thoughts turned to Annabelle as we went back to the wagon.

Jacob and Molly were already at the wagon. The children wanted to go with them, but Ida didn't think it was a good idea. I agreed with her not wanting Little Joe or either of his parents to catch whatever illness Luke and Annabelle had.

"I had better get ready to take off again," Jacob was saying as I arrived.

"I guess I had better do the same," I said as I followed him.

"We are so sorry about Luke." He sounded choked up.

I didn't have to look at him to know he was crying. I managed to say, "Thanks. Now if we can just get there without losing any more."

That first night without Luke, Ida and I slept in each other's arms. I don't know who fell asleep first but both of us did some crying. As we drifted off, we both muttered, "We won't forget him."

The only problem we had with the wagons was that Jacob's wagon lost a wheel. It didn't hold us up along with it being a simple repair. Unlike most of the others in our group, we carried an extra wheel for just such an emergency.

So it didn't take long to make the repair. Mr. Madison offered to help, but I refused his offer and Jacob and I took care of the problem.

"Maybe we can get it fixed at Fort Boise." Mr. Madison said as he left us to our work.

"Good," I believe I replied but I was too busy to care.

It took us over another week to make our way to Fort Laramie. When we got there, Annabelle was burning with fever. Ida stayed with her and the other three children. To our surprise, there weren't any doctors at Fort Laramie. But, we did get some information. Mr. Madison learned that the best thing we could have done for Luke was to give him quinine. It wouldn't have helped to know that earlier, since we didn't have any quinine available. He tried unsuccessfully to get some for us in case Annabelle was to get worse but there wasn't any available. Not finding any quinine, he learned that the next best thing was to force her to drink plenty of water, which Ida did. That seemed to be our only hope of curing her.

Around midday, we heard a shot ring out. Mr. Madison rode at full gallop to check it out. Coming back by, he told us, "Don't worry, it's not Indians. Mr. Wilson just shot a big elk."

Ida and I remembered seeing the elk and thinking he was a beautiful animal, but now our thoughts turned to fresh meat. We couldn't wait for supper.

Mr. Madison added, "We've been doing well for the past few weeks, so we might as well stop for the night. I could use some fresh meat for a change."

"It sure will beat the salt pork and dried beef we've been eating for months," I said as we joined the rest in circling the wagons.

"I'm not one to argue," Ida said with a smile.

"I'll fix some beans," a woman shouted, sounding as excited as we were at the prospect of a really good supper.

"I'll help," another one replied.

"I'll make some corn bread," I heard Molly add.

"Right now, I don't care what you fix... I'll eat it," a man around the fire announced.

Still tired, hot and grieving the loss of our son, I nevertheless enjoyed supper. It helped us watching Annabelle eat a little with us. She had been, feeling poorly for a few days but now she was much better. Then her condition changed and she felt bad for a few days. We prayed there would be a doctor at Fort Boise who might be able to help her.

I knew I needed a doctor too. I had mentioned to the wagon master that I was feeling bad, but I hadn't told Ida.

As we ate, we talked about our plans. Ida and I were looking forward to seeing Oregon City. After that, we weren't sure what we would do, but I was thinking of going south. In answer to everyone's questions, I replied, "Don't know yet. I want to get this trip over with first."

After supper Annabelle got sick again. Ida left me with the other children at the fire. My little girl's health concerned me more than what the other families were talking about, even though I probably wouldn't have been able to contribute much.

Ida finally came back and said Annabelle was better. She had cleaned up Annabelle's mess and wanted something else to eat, but at this point, unfortunately, nothing was left of the elk but bones.

"You've been saying you needed to lose some weight," I said as I kissed her.

"That was before we started on this trip," she reminded me.

Molly walked up and asked, "Everything all right…? I saw you leave a few minutes ago."

"Annabelle lost her supper, but she's all right," Ida assured her.

"Good," Molly replied.

A little later I lay down but I wasn't sleepy although I was feeling ill. Ida said she would check on the children and I fell asleep before she got back.

The next morning Ida asked me, "Are you feeling all right?"

"I'm fine," I answered as I struggled to get everything ready for the day's journey.

That day's traveling wasn't easy on the oxen or us. With each step, we gained altitude and the air got thinner. The only ones that were enjoying the trip were the children. They loved looking over the edge of the mountain and watching the wildlife. I had to laugh thinking of Mr. Madison's warning. He was right on the button when he said we wouldn't make too many miles that day. At times, I wondered if he knew where we were going. From what I could see, no one had traveled the trail for a long time, and probably few ever had. When Ida asked me about the trail, I had to agree with her that we could be off a mile or so. I told her we had the mountains to go by and there was only one pass. As long as we headed toward the pass, we had nothing to worry us.

While I kept the wagon moving, Ida saw Annabelle. I would have loved to stop and helped her take care of my daughter. I figured getting to Fort Boise was more important than stopping. I left Ida to take care of her as we continued. When Ida stuck her head out the front of the wagon I asked, "She's not doing so well?"

"No," Ida answered, sounding tired and worried.

That night Mr. Madison gave us some good news. He told us we had passed through the roughest part of the climb. He added the following days would be an easy trip to Fort Boise. His parting remark was "keep your hands on the brake."

Once over the summit the next day Ida and I took turns working the brake. This chore made it feel like it was the longest part of the trip. I tried to make it easier for her by staying at the brake longer than she did. But feeling as ill as I was, that wasn't easy for me. When I was on top and it was her turn, I shouted down to her, "Back up here, your highness."

"Yes, sir, I think I did a good job," she grinned as she waited for me to take the whip from her.

"Not bad for a beginner," I joked. She hadn't done a bad job of controlling the oxen. Besides now, I didn't need her up there anymore to do any braking, so she could take care of Annabelle. As I got off the wagon, my head was spinning. I didn't get more than two steps before falling.

I barely heard Harold ask, "Is something wrong with Father?"

In my consciousness, I heard Ida and Mr. Madison talking. He was saying, "We had better get him into the wagon."

"Make room for Father," Ida told the children. I felt her touch and heard her say, "He's burning up."

"I'll be all right shortly," I mumbled between coughs.

I couldn't hear well but I did hear Molly tell me, "We love the two of you."

My next memory was of Mr. Madison shouting out, "Let's get those animals moving." Then alongside the wagon, he added, "It's another ninety miles to Fort Boise."

I barely heard Ida answer him, "I know."

I could hear Harold ask, "How's Father doing?"

"I don't know, Honey," Ida answered.

Mr. Madison rode up to the wagon and stopped. He asked Ida, "How's he doing?"

"I was thinking about checking on him," she answered.

Mr. Madison said, "Edgar told me five days ago he thought he had the fever. He said for me not to tell you, because your daughter was worried enough. He wanted to make sure you got out west and that was his main concern."

While Ida has been driving the wagon I have been writing in my diary. In hearing Mr. Madison, I know everyone's concerned… so am I. I wish they would worry more about my little girl. I don't know how much longer I can hold out. I pray I hold out long enough until Ida gets to me. I know I'm about to die, and I want to tell her I love her. I just wish that Matt Duncan fellow was here to take care of her but I guess Jacob and Molly will have to do…I can hear…

Author's note: The men of the wagon train buried Edgar and Jacob made a marker for his grave:

Here lies
My best friend
Edgar Buchanan
1873

Though I don't have anything to go by it seems Annabelle, his daughter died within hours of her father. The men buried her next to her father. After what I assume a short prayer was said I noted she looked into the heavens and said, "I hope you know I loved you, Edgar, and always will. Now it's up to you and Mama to take care of Annabelle."

Later she was to go back to say goodbye to Edgar and her daughter. She found the headstone had been changed:

Here lies
My best friend
Edgar Buchanan
1873
And his daughter
Annabelle

He also got his wish for his family and they eventually moved to California. They didn't make the final move until Ida renewed her acquaintance with Matt Duncan and they were married.

There was also one page in the diary not written by Edgar that surprised me:

Edgar my love,

Maybe in adding this to your diary you'll get it. I have done you a disservice by not telling you that I have known your secret. When mother died she told me that you had seen her. I can't thank you enough for not reminding me what my mother had turned herself into.

I will always love you,

Ida